OUR LIFE

D Gourlay

CONTENTS

And then my soul saw you, and it kind of went, "Oh, there you are. I've been looking for you."

—UNKNOWN

COPYRIGHT

DEDICATION

To every single person out there, who has ever wanted to do something, but their doubts and fears got in the way.
Don't be afraid. Jump in with both feet. You are capable of so much more than you can ever imagine.

A big thank you again to all my friends and family, for supporting me, no matter how much I annoy them.
Special thanks to Tracy Blasby and Sarah Bell for proof reading.

PROLOGUE

What the fuck? Where am I?

Wait-

I sit bolt upright and the searing pain coming from my face and skull turns my stomach. I'm trying to make out where I am, but my eyes can't focus on anything. The more I try to focus my eyes, the less I am able to see. Something warm is dripping down my face, my nose is throbbing and I have no fucking idea what's going on. My eyes close and I try to remember, well, anything.

In the distance I can hear something. A siren. No, lots of sirens.

Shit.

Suddenly an image flashes in my mind.

Rachel, lying unconscious at my feet.

Me wrapping tape around her wrists and ankles.

Her escaping.

Us fighting.

My hand travels to the top of my head, and I feel that my hair is a sticky mess. As my fingers move around, I fleetingly feel a huge gash under my matted hair, before an agonising pain travels through my entire head.

The sirens are getting louder and I know I need to get the fuck out of here. I manage to pull myself up, but the pain is so intense it's a struggle to even move.

Pull yourself the fuck together. If you don't get out of here now, you will end up in prison, and that cunt will get to live happily ever after with your daughter and some rich bastard who you need to end.

My feet are dragging across the ground, but at least they are moving. I fish the keys for the van from my pocket and pull myself into the driver's seat.

Fuck, how the hell did this go so wrong?

All I can hear is sirens, seemingly coming from every direction. I start the engine, and fight back the urge to vomit. The world is spinning and going black, but I've got to move.

"Kevin, what the fuck have you done. Why are you calling me?" The voice of my best friend echoes around the van, but gone is the friendly, jovial tone I'm so used to hearing.

"Mike, I've fucked up. I need your help."

"My help? Are you shitting me? You fucking killed her! You killed her you piece of shit! Nobody is ever going to help you out of anything again."

"But- No, Mike- Everything's fucked. I'm fucked! I need"-

"I couldn't give a shit what you need anymore, you've got that money, take it and fuck off. Don't you ever contact me again, or next time I'm called in about you at work, I'll tell them everything."

The line goes dead, and my stomach drops at the realisation I've gone too far. I've got nobody left to help me. For the first time in a long time, I feel fear. Genuine fear, and the temptation to just drive this van off the nearest cliff is overwhelming.

No! You can't give up. Not without making sure the rest of her life is going to be as miserable as yours will be...

CHAPTER ONE

Rachel

My eyes open and panic shoots through me.

"Shit!"

I sit up abruptly, and Tad stirs next to me.

"What's the matter?" He murmurs still half asleep.

"Tad my alarm didn't go off, it's gone six! Ami is going to be wondering where I am!"

He rolls over and rubs his eyes like he isn't quite with it yet. In all fairness, we did have a pretty late one last night.

I didn't manage to sneak away from my parents until gone eleven. I was so tired on my way here I had planned on just going straight to bed with him, to sleep. But then I saw him, and my body had other ideas. I think we only got to sleep at about two.

I jump out of his warm cosy bed as fast as my legs allow and start searching the bedroom floor for my clothes.

"Tad! Help me!" I throw his t-shirt at him and run downstairs to try to find my clothes.

I have only managed to find my bra and jeans, which I am trying to pull up while searching the sofa for my shirt. I finally see it, hanging from a picture frame, and I briefly stop and smile at the memory of how it got there.

"Missing something?" Tad's voice shouts down to me. I jog over to the stairs and he is stood at the top with my knickers in his hand.

I had better not die on the way back to Mum and Dad's wearing no bloody knickers.

He is grinning at me as he walks down the stairs. I snatch them from him and put them in my pocket. He starts to laugh at me.

"You know this really wouldn't be an issue if you just told your parents about us." He smirks.

"I just think it's a bit soon that's all. I don't want to be dealing with questions and judgements at the moment." I say as I am slipping on my shoes and jacket.

"Hmmm."

"Don't *hmm* me! I will tell them!"

He is standing on the bottom step and I walk up to him. He pulls me in close and kisses me on the top of my head.

"See you tonight?" He mumbles into my hair.

"Of course."

I look up into those incredibly blue eyes and can't help but absolutely beam. This wonderful man is mine, how on earth did I get this lucky?

"I love you Rach."

I kiss him lightly on the lips.

"I love you too."

I open the door as quietly as I can when I get back to my parents'. Not that it matters as Mum, Dad and Ami are all sitting in the kitchen having breakfast, and they can all see me sneaking back into the house.

They all glare at me accusingly.

"Mummy! Where were you? We were all really worried!" Ami shouts. She folds her arms at me and I can't help but giggle at her.

"It's not funny Mummy. Nanny wanted to call the police."

Oh shit.

"Oh I'm sorry baby. I went out last night to see a friend and must have fallen asleep. I promise it won't happen again." I walk over and give Ami a huge cuddle, and she wraps her arms tightly around me.

She has been very protective of me recently. I tried to hide as much from her as possible about what happened with Kevin. But the bloody press are like vultures, and the second they get even the slightest sniff of a story they just won't let it lie. I had to tell her what Kevin had done. Not only to that poor woman, but also to me.

Seeing her sob in my arms absolutely broke my heart. She had got it into her head that it was somehow her fault; that I only stayed and put up with Kevin because of her. After lots of cuddles and two days holed up watching films, she seemed loads better. I still see her staring off into space every now and then but it's only been a couple of weeks, and this is an awful lot to take in for her. Her school have been absolutely amazing, she sees a councilor twice a week, and none of the kids have said anything to her. The head teacher had a word with her class before she came back to school, and amazingly it seems to have worked.

I catch my Mum and Dad giving me a look out the corner of my eye. That very same look they used to give me when I stayed out too late as a kid.

"Mum I'm so sorry. I didn't mean to worry you. I just went to see my friend but fell asleep and hadn't taken my phone with me."

Mum just stares at me stony faced.

"A friend hey? And which *friend* might this be?" Christ she really isn't happy!

"Uh Sarah." I blurt out. I don't know a Sarah.

"Sarah who?" Mum's eyes narrow as she sees straight through my lie.

"Mary, for God sake leave the poor girl alone!" Dad interrupts. "She isn't fifteen anymore you know." He stands and gives Mum a peck on the cheek before going to make me some coffee.

I take a seat at the table and Mum just glares at me.

"You got your swimming stuff ready for school today baby?" I turn to talk to Ami. I need to change the subject before Mum gets the chance to start again.

"Um I'm not sure. I think so. I'll go check."

No don't go!

Well that backfired.

Ami skips off up the stairs as Dad puts a steaming mug of coffee in front of me. I wrap my cold hands around the mug and inhale that beautiful smell. I take a sip and as I lower my mug I see Mum, still glaring at me.

"Mum! Keep staring at me like that and you're going to freeze my coffee!"

"You're hiding something from us Rachel, and I don't like it. Not one bit."

"I'm not hiding anything Mum." I lie. Badly.

"Rachel, we aren't stupid." Dad chimes in from behind me. "We know that you haven't been sleeping here."

Oh bugger.

"Uh"-

"Mum?" Ami calls out as she is running down the stairs.

I quickly stand and walk over to her and pray that maybe my parents could temporarily develop short term memory loss so we can forget that they know I don't sleep here.

"Mum I need a pound coin for the locker."

"I have one baby." I reach in to my pocket and as I pull out the coin, out falls my red lace thong that I wore to Tad's last night and didn't manage to put back on this morning.

I think it is pretty safe to assume that my cheeks and that thong are currently exactly the same colour.

I snatch them up off the floor and turn to see my mum stood looking at me, eyebrows raised, arms folded.

Might be time I come clean with them after all.

I've just got back from dropping Ami at school and am making us all coffees.

Mum and Dad are sitting at the table waiting for me to talk.

I put the mugs of coffee on the table and sit down.

"So, what do you guys have planned for today then?"

The looks on their faces make it apparent that they are not even a little bit amused.

"Ok, look, just please don't make a big deal out of this. I met someone. And he is amazing, and I can't seem to sleep without him after everything that happened. So yes, I've been sneaking out once everyone is asleep every night since you guys got back from holiday."

Mum and Dad both shoot each other a look. They look confused.

"Well when did you meet this man?" Mum asks.

"Uh, he is the guy who Kevin accused me of sleeping with, the night of the fundraiser, three weeks ago. The night he... You know..."

"So you had been having an affair?"

"No, Mum! You know me better than that!"

"Well I'm confused. How long have you known him?"

"I only met him that day."

"Right, Leo, go and find something to do a minute please. Me and Rachel need a girly talk?"

A girly talk? Well this can't be good!

Dad stands whilst muttering to himself about being dictated to in his own home and walks into the front room. We hear the TV come to life and Mum turns to me.

"Rachel, start from the beginning and tell me everything."

I take a long breath in.

"Ok. Well me and Tad- that's his name by the way, bumped into each other on the morning of the fundraiser. Just two total strangers in a coffee shop. Then it turned out he was the person who organised the fundraiser, and he was sat next to me all night. He was the one who pulled Kevin off of me and stopped him from doing God only knows what. Anyway, we had this connection. After everything kicked off with Kevin and I realised what he had done I went to Tad's and we have been pretty much together since then."

"Wow, ok. And you didn't tell us because...?" Hurt has replaced her anger, and I feel a pang of guilt. Mum always thought we shared everything, when in reality I was hiding so much from her about my life. I think that was the hardest thing for her to take when all of this came out. And now she thinks that I am hiding even more from her.

"I don't know Mum. It all happened so fast and it seemed so crazy. There was so much going on in my life, in our lives. I just didn't want to complicate things any more. I'm sorry."

"You don't have to hide anything from me Rachel, ok? I'll always help you, or just listen, but please promise not to keep me in the dark anymore?"

"I promise."

Her face softens and she smiles at me.

"So, tell me, what is he like?" She asks and my face immediately breaks into one of those sickeningly in love smiles.

"Oh Mum. He is just incredible." I swoon. "He is gorgeous, and kind, so kind Mum. Brown hair, incredible blue eyes. He is just..." I trail off as there aren't any words.

"Oh my!" She interrupts.

"What?"

"You're in love with him?" I smile and nod at my concerned looking Mum. "But you hardly know him!"

"Trust me, I've battled with this too. I've never been one of those people who thought love at first sight was a real thing. But- I just can't explain it. What I do know is that I don't sleep unless he is next to me, all he has to do is hug me and immediately I am calmer, and he would do, and has done everything in his power to look after me, and Ami. And I love him."

"Well if you are happy darling then so am I. Just promise to be careful ok?"

I stand up and wrap my arms around her shoulders from behind.

"Love you Mum."

"Love you too darling. Now when is this Tad coming over for dinner?"

CHAPTER TWO

Tad

I haven't heard a word that Suze has just said to me down the phone. I think she mentioned something about a castle... Maybe? I can't concentrate at all. Rachel has just walked into my office looking sexy as fuck. We are going out on a double date tonight with Celine and Danny to a new restaurant that has just opened up. Rach is wearing a sexy little black dress that shows off her curves and cleavage. Oh that cleavage, it's inviting me in, teasing me. I'm debating telling her to cancel dinner and I will just eat her instead. But I know she is really looking forward to going out.

"Suze, can we pick this back up again tomorrow?"

"Have you even been listening to me?"

"Yeah, yeah of course. Look don't worry. I'll call you in the morning."

"Thaddeus"- I can hear her protesting as I press the end call button. I'm sure I will pay for that tomorrow, but Rachel is far more important right now.

"Rach you look stunning."

Her cheeks go a rosy pink colour as she blushes at my compliment.

"I wasn't sure about the dress, but Celine said it looked nice. I think it shows a bit too much off to be honest."

"Well I don't think it shows enough!"

I pull her in for a hug and it takes a stern internal talking to myself to get my cock to behave. I give her a long peck on the lips, but pull away before I can't stop myself.

"So what was it you needed to tell me?"

"Well you will be happy to know that I told my parents about us."

"You did? What made you change your mind about telling them?"

"Well they said that they knew I hadn't been sleeping there, and then I managed to throw my knickers on the floor in front of them from out of my pocket... So I didn't have much choice!"

I can't help but laugh out loudly!

"Trust you Rach!" I kiss her softly on the cheek as the memory of those little red panties creeps into my mind. "What did they say?"

"Well Mum was upset at me keeping something else from her. And worried as it's all so new. But I think she saw my face light up when I spoke about you, and that seemed to fix everything. Think I'm off the hook, and she seems happy." She looks at me and smiles. I can't help but lean in and kiss her. I will never get tired of feeling these soft, beautiful lips against my own. Her tongue ever so gently pushes through my lips and a sudden rush of heat flows through my entire body, settling in my trousers. The effect this woman has on me without even trying is just insane.

I run my fingers down her back towards her perfect backside and I feel her grip tighten in my hair. Her breathing quickens, as does her kiss. She pushes herself into me and the pressure on my cock is almost unbearable. I just want to throw her down over my desk and fuck her into next week.

My hand runs down her leg to the hem of her dress, and I slowly move my hand under and back up her leg. Fuck! She is wearing stockings, and a suspender belt. Holy shit. I moan into her mouth as I finger the tops of her lace stockings, and I can feel her smile.

Suddenly she pulls away, smiling at me.

"Hey! Come back here!"

"The cab will be here in a minute babe, we should get ready to go."

"Fuck the cab Rach." I walk straight towards her and pull her roughly back into my arms. I try to go back to kissing her but she turns her head to the side, still smiling at me, then pulls away.

"Oh God Rach! You can't leave me like this!" I sound like I am begging. Fuck it, I am begging! What does this woman do to me?

She slowly walks up to me and runs her finger along my cheek to my lip.

"Remember this later when you're spanking me."

She leans in and nips my bottom lip, then turns and almost runs out of my office before I can catch her.

I groan loudly as I try to readjust myself. I am not going to be able to think of anything else but fucking her into oblivion now. I am *so* going to get my own back on her as soon as we are home.

Stop thinking about it!

I really need to try to calm myself down. God this is hell!

I hear the doorbell go.

"Tad, cab's here."

Deep breath. Calm down. And torture her all night.

We are both sitting in the back of the cab. Rach, has the leg closest to me crossed over the other. Her dress has ridden up and I can see the top of her stocking peeking out at me. I am still rock hard and I genuinely don't think that's going to go anywhere until I get to fuck her.

I am holding her hand but I slowly let it go, and move mine onto her leg. She turns to look at me, her lips curving into a playful smile, silently daring me.

I start to gently stroke the naked flesh just above her stocking. Her skin erupts in goosebumps under my touch. Painfully slowly, I move my hand towards her sweet pussy. She shoots me a cautious look and nods towards the driver. I smile back at her.

Fuck the driver.

My hand keeps moving until I can feel her smooth pussy against my fingers.

Holy shit, no underwear.

I must look shocked as she starts to giggle.

Her giggles soon stop as I pull her leg down with my other hand and my finger moves up to her clit. I gently brush over it, barely even touching it, but it's enough. Her breath catches and her tongue is running along her bottom lip. I move my finger gently, round in circles, and her breathing becomes heavy. It's lucky the driver has the radio on or it would be very obvious what was going on. She is biting the corner of her lip and has closed her eyes, as if trying to concentrate on not being loud. Or not coming. I apply slightly more pressure and her hand shoots up and grabs my wrist, but she doesn't pull it away, instead she pushes it harder into her. I start moving my finger faster, her breathing is loud and she practically throws her head back. I think she has completely forgotten where we are. Her finger nails are digging into my wrist as she grips me tighter and tighter. I can see the muscles in her leg tense as she is about to come. And then I pull my hand away and turn to face the front of the car.

I don't need to look at her to know how she is feeling. Probably just how I felt before we left the house!

I risk a look over. Her cheeks are flushed pink and her breathing is ragged. She is staring at me with fiery eyes. I lean in and whisper softly into her ear.

"Don't start something that you can't win." I pull back and she is half grinning at me. I kiss her softly on the lips and pull away again.

Rachel

F uck. I'm in trouble.

We pull up at the restaurant. It's opening night, and it's ridiculously busy outside. Tad gets out of the cab and then walks around to open the door for me.

I really, *really* didn't think through this whole not wearing any underwear business. I am absolutely soaking wet, and I'm trying to keep my legs pressed tightly together to make sure nobody else realises I am commando and totally excited beyond words. Tad is chuckling to himself as he grabs my hand and we walk past a line of people queuing to get into the restaurant.

We walk in through the glass doors and we are greeted by a very pretty blonde, with a short bob, and an even shorter dress. She catches sight of Tad and her eyes sparkle as she smiles sexily at him.

Cheek of her, I'm standing right here!

Tad seems totally oblivious to her staring and walks towards her.

"Reservation for Turner."

The blonde starts nibbling on the end of her pen while tapping the keyboard on her computer.

"Mr. Turner, the other members of your party are already seated, please follow me."

We walk through the restaurant. It is beautiful. It is a seafood restaurant, and the interior has been made to look like the inside of an old ship. Wooden floors and paneled walls. Little port holes along the walls that have stunning paintings of the sea inside of them. The tables are very modern, and slightly out of place though with the interior. White table cloths, a little tree for a centerpiece, and elegant glasses and silverware. All the tables have different chairs around them. Some have wooden dining chairs, and some have big leather arm chairs. It all seems a little mismatched, but somehow works.

Our table is right at the back of the restaurant, behind a wooden screen that separates us and another table from the rest of the guests. Just at the side of the table is a huge opening in the wall, so we can see into the kitchen. Already all of the chefs are busy running around. There is shouting, and sounds of cooking, and a general buzz of excitement. I've never seen a real kitchen in action before.

"Rachel! You look fucking stunning!" Celine shoots up out of her chair, walks over and wraps her arms around me for a big hug. "I told you that dress was awesome didn't I?"

"Thanks Cel." I blush as I hug her back.

Danny gives me a friendly hug and shakes Tad's hand. I go to sit down but before I have the chance Tad sweeps in and pulls the chair out from under the table for me. He looks over at me and smiles the most gorgeous smile in the world. I feel all warm and fuzzy inside. That's my smile. Reserved strictly for when he is looking at me. I beam back at him as I sit down. He pushes my chair slightly under me, and as I look up I can see Celine staring at me, smiling softly.

There is already a bottle of wine on the table, which Dan starts pouring into our glasses.

"Tad you look very dashing too, don't want you feeling left out." Celine says.

"Well thank you Celine, it's difficult to be noticed when you are around someone as beautiful as this one." He gently strokes me on my cheek and I look down to try to cover my embarrassment. And my huge smile!

I see Celine swat at Dan's arm in front of me.

"How come you don't say nice things like that to me anymore?"

"Hey, there's a ring on your finger, I've already got you. I don't need to try anymore." He winks at her and they lean in for a kiss.

Tad's hand finds my leg under the table and he gives it a gentle squeeze. I look over at him and his eyes are lit up with such passion and desperation that it takes a lot for me to not jump on him right here in the restaurant.

"So we have some news." Celine quickly reminds me where I am and I give my head a little shake to try to get some blood back to my brain as I feel like it is all currently residing in between my legs.

"News? Oh my God are you"–

"No! I am not pregnant!" She laughs and waves her wine glass at me. "We have set a date for the wedding, and booked everything today!" The grin on her face almost spreads from ear to ear.

"Oh that's amazing! I'm so happy for you guys! When is it?"

"Christmas Eve Eve!"

"Wow, that's soon?"

"Well the hotel we were looking at called me yesterday and said that they'd had a cancellation. Very last minute. Everything had already been booked, cake, flowers, room, registrar, food, you name it sorted. Even the suits have been reserved. All we need to do is get the guys sized up for their suits and I need to find a dress. The planner at the hotel gave us the contacts for everything and we got it all booked and confirmed this afternoon. At a bargain price too!"

"But you don't get to do any of your own planning or choose anything yourselves?"

I had hardly any say in my wedding, Kevin and his parents took over almost everything and I hated it. I'd never really been one of those kids who walked around the playground at school, with their friends lifting their skirts pretending to be a blushing bride. But even still, I was getting married, it would have been nice if I could have had some say.

"I just see it as no stress, everything is sorted. I just get to turn up on the day and marry my soulmate." Celine leans into Dan next to her, and he kisses her gently on the top of her head. These two are so cute together.

Every time I have any doubts about Tad and I, and how it can't be possible to feel for him what I do, I just think of these two. Utterly perfect for one another and not afraid of anything at all.

Tad raises his glass next to me.

"To the happy couple." We all clink our glasses to his and take a sip.

"So, you will be my maid of honour right?" Tears prick at my eyes and I struggle to get any words out.

"Of course I will!" I manage to blurt out. I lean across the table and grab Celine's hand. "Are you sure you can cope with taking me dress shopping though?" I laugh at her.

Celine hates shopping with a passion. She goes into a shop and buys the very first thing she sees and then leaves. But when we go shopping together I make her go in every single shop, add items to a mental shortlist, try things on, before eventually going back to buy things. It has nearly broken our friendship on many an occasion!

"Yeah, there won't be any of your nonsense when we go out! The first dress that fits is the one!"

"We will see!" I laugh at her.

CHAPTER THREE

We have all finished eating and Tad has disappeared off to make a phone call. The food was to die for, and watching it all being cooked just next to us, seeing all the energy and excitement in that kitchen was amazing.

"You two look so cute together you know?" Celine says with a huge grin on her face.

"Oh shut up!" I laugh at her.

"No, really you do! Honestly he can barely take his eyes off you, at this rate it wouldn't surprise me if you guys end up married before me!"

"Uh, I think you are forgetting one slight detail there Cel, you know, that I'm still married to a murderer who is currently on the run."

"Oh, shit. Forgot about him for a moment. Any more updates?"

"Not since the CCTV footage of him at the ferry terminal in Calais. Robins is still trying to get the information about what passport he used, as it definitely wasn't his own."

"I thought it was supposed to be impossible to use a fake passport these days after making all the changes to them?"

"Me too. But apparently it still happens. Robins is convinced that he is still abroad, as his photo is everywhere now."

"You don't sound convinced?" Celine grabs my hand and gives it a gentle squeeze.

Of course I'm not convinced! We have been here before. Kevin was supposed to be in France and then he ends up in Mum and Dad's kitchen, injecting me with a ton of Ketamine and dragging me hundreds of miles away to do God only knows what with me. When the police got back to me the next day and said that he had escaped I was inconsolable. I'm now followed around daily by two of Tad's guards, but even they aren't enough to make me feel much better.

"Definitely not convinced. But there isn't much I can do at the moment. That man controlled me for years, I am not going to let him do it now."

"Good for you babe, a toast I think?" She lifts her glass and taps it on my own.

Just then Tad walks back over to the table. He looks seriously sexy. Dressed in dark jeans and a smart shirt with the top buttons undone. His hair is slightly messy on the top and he has just a touch of stubble on his beautiful face. He smiles at me as he is walking towards the table, and my stomach flips. I will never get tired of this feeling.

He sits down next to me and shuffles his chair closer to mine. His hand goes back to the same spot on my leg it has occupied most of the night.

"Everything ok?" He asks as he kisses me gently on the cheek.

"Yes babe." I smile back at him.

I turn back to Celine, to see her staring at us, all gooey eyed and can't help but laugh at her.

"What's the plan now then?" Dan asks.

"I fancy a drink!" Celine says very enthusiastically!

"You've already got through a bottle and a half of wine Cel!" I laugh.

"So there is plenty of room for at least another bottle, plus a few shots" She winks at me. "There's a nice bar down the road what do you think?"

"Sounds good to me babe." Dan stands. "I'll just grab the bill off of someone."

"Uh no need," Tad says, "I sorted it already."

"Oh, thanks mate. Drinks are on us then?" Dan says as Celine swoons at Tad a bit more from the other side of the table.

Tad stands and gently pulls my chair out, then holds a hand out to help me up.

As we leave the restaurant the cool breeze hits me and my head starts to spin a little. Celine opens her bag and takes out a pack of B&H Silver that only ever comes out when we have had too much to drink. She takes one out, lights it and takes a drag and then offers it to me. I am usually more than willing, but Kevin had such a thing about me smoking. The first time he caught me smoking he took the cigarette out of my hand and put in out on my arm. Didn't seem to matter to him that I was a grown woman, plus he smoked. But I just wasn't allowed to. I know Tad isn't Kevin. He is totally anti Kevin, but I haven't even asked how he would feel if I smoked. I know it's ridiculous, and he probably wouldn't say a thing, but I just can't shake the fear that arsehole instilled in me. I shake my head at Celine and she looks at me puzzled. I nod towards Tad and she rolls her eyes at me.

"Tad," She calls out to him. "You don't mind if Rach smokes on occasion when drunk do you?"

Fuck sake Cel.

Tad looks baffled and half laughs.

"No, why would I mind?"

"See." She says as she hands me the lit cigarette.

I sigh loudly at her as I grab it and take a long drag. Celine wraps her arm around my shoulder and leans in close.

"He isn't Kevin babe. He is nothing like Kevin. Don't let that fucker stop you from being you."

I rest my head on her shoulder as we walk. I really do love this woman. I may not have much in my life right now, but I have Ami, wonderful parents, an incredible best friend, and the most amazing man in the world. Even though I have so much to be stressed about, even though my life has more drama right now than an episode of Eastenders, I am so incredibly happy. I have everything I need and so much more.

The *bar* that Celine has taken us to isn't a bar at all, it is a club. It is dark, sticky, loud and sweaty. I am gripping tightly on to her hand as she pushes through the crowds, and pulling Tad along behind me. We eventually get to the bar and Celine pokes her tongue out at me.

"Funny bar Cel!" I shout at her.

"Ah shush you! I knew you wouldn't come if I said it was a club, but it's great in here!"

I feel Tad push up behind me and he wraps his hands around my waist. I turn around to look at him and even in the darkness I can see his deep blue eyes staring straight into mine. I lean in and kiss him softly on the lips. At least that's what I think I am doing. Until we actually touch, and I can't stop myself. My hands trail up his back into his hair, and my greedy mouth opens to make way for his hungry tongue. His hands are in my hair and on my arse and I just want to be alone with him so much. One drink and then I am taking this man back to his so he can fuck the life out of me.

I pull away suddenly and see his eyes are blazing. I think the thing I love most about Tad is his incredible kindness; but then when he is turned on, when he wants me, when we fuck, he is a different man. He takes on this whole different persona. He becomes fierce, and powerful. I would imagine a little scary if you were a stranger looking in, but I know he is still my Tad with a beautiful soul. But he is there, right now. Staring deep into me, wanting to punish me for turning him on like this and not being able to do anything about it.

Celine brings me sharply back down to earth by thrusting a bottle of wine into my hand. She grabs the other and pulls me through the crowd to a little flight of stairs that is blocked off by some red rope and some pretty scary looking bouncers. She leans in close to one of them and shouts something in his ear, he smiles and unclips the rope to let us in. We walk up the stairs to find four booths. They have tacky looking red leather chairs surrounding great big tables, but at least there are only a couple of other people up here.

"How did you get in here?" I shout at her as we all sit down around a table.

"I know the bouncer. He used to date someone Dan works with."

"And?" There is obviously more to this.

"Well, let's just say there is a very *very* embarrassing tattoo somewhere on his body that all of his big butch bouncer friends would rip him to pieces for if they found out!" She laughs and starts pouring out glasses of wine.

I turn to look at Tad and he is just staring me at.

"What?" I ask him.

"You are just so fucking perfect." He pulls me in close to him. "And I can't wait to have you screaming my name later."

My insides clench at his words. If Celine and Dan weren't here right now I don't think much would stop me from jumping on him right here.

"So Rach," Celine shouts across at me. "You staying with your parents for much longer, or moving in with Tad?" She winks at me and I wish the table was smaller so I could kick her under it.

"I'm staying with them until I can sort some money out to rent somewhere for me and Ami." I shoot her a look to tell her to drop it, and I think she notices.

"Are you looking for a job?" Dan shouts.

"I haven't been, but I suppose I will need to be earning money to be able afford rent and food and stuff!"

I can see Tad shifting on his seat like he wants to say something but I ignore him. He mentioned to me the other week that I could move in, but it's just not that simple. If it was just me, then I would have jumped at the chance. But I have Ami. And she is more important to me. I can't just move her out of her family home after her Dad murders someone, straight into the house of a man I haven't even known a month. He even offered to rent a place for me, but I need to try to stand on my own two feet for once. I went straight from living at home to being a stay at home mum with Kevin. I've never been independent, and think I need to learn how to adult!

"I actually know of an opening Rach, and can almost guarantee you the job if you want it?" Dan says over the table.

"Really? That would amazing! Doing what?"

"My uncle owns a luxury estate agents in Chichester, selling all the really expensive houses in the area. He needs a receptionist. Nothing major, no experience needed, just a friendly face and the ability to make coffee."

"Coffee I can do!"

"I'll get him to call you if you want?"

"Dan that would be amazing, thank you so much!"

"Not a problem! Now if you don't mind I am going to whisk my beautiful fiancée on to the dancefloor for a boogie!"

"Dan you're so cringe!" Celine laughs as she walks away from the table.

I turn to look at Tad and he has a weird look on his face.

"What?" I ask.

"Nothing babe." He grabs hold of my hand under the table.

"No, not nothing, what's with the face?"

"I just wish you'd let me sort somewhere for you to live so you didn't have to work."

"What's wrong with me working?"

"Nothing, I guess I just don't want to have to share you any more than I already do."

I shuffle closer to him and rest my head on his shoulder.

"It's reception work. Monday to Friday nine to five I bet, you work anyway, and we don't really spend the days together. So it won't be any different."

"And you definitely won't consider just moving in with me?" I look at him and he is grinning at me. I playfully slap him on his arm and go back to resting my head on him.

Tad

This woman is just so infuriating. There is no need at all for her to work. I understand that it just isn't possible to live together right now because of Ami, but I could rent them both a place close to me so we don't have to start scheduling each other in.

I'm feeling so frustrated, not just about this but the way she left me before we came out. All I can picture in my head is her over my knee later getting spanked. My cock has been in a semi state of arousal all night, and every time she even looks at me it springs right to life.

I pull my hand out of hers and rest it on her leg. I feel her head move slightly as if she is checking nobody is watching us. There are a few people seated at a table behind us, but there is no way they would be able to see anything. I gently push her dress up so that my fingers are touching the smooth satin stocking she is wearing. She pulls her head back and looks at me. As she slowly moves her lips towards mine, she grabs hold of my hand and slides it all the way up her leg to her sweet pussy. I gently run my fingers up and down her soft flesh, she closes her eyes and parts her lips slightly.

Slowly I push my thumb through her soft folds to find her clit. She bites down on her bottom lip and takes a slow breath in, as if preparing herself for what is coming.

Oh baby you have no idea...

I barely even have to move my thumb and she seems to already be right back on the edge. I could just make her come, or I could draw this out until we get home and leave her absolutely begging later. I much prefer the latter. I lift my thumb away and instead push my finger inside of her. She is so fucking wet. I'm going to leave her drenched. I lean in and start to kiss her as I am gently fucking her with my finger. I want to slip another in, I want to make her scream my name and feel her tight pussy clenching around my fingers as I make her come. But the thought of her panting, begging, right on the edge is enough to make me keep my pace. Painfully slow.

Her kiss starts to speed up, and she starts trying to move her hips with me. I use my other hand to hold her steady and then I gently push another finger into her. She bites my lip hard as she tries to stop herself moaning. Her breathing is fast and ragged. Her cheeks are red. I can feel her start to pulse around my fingers. So I quickly pull them out.

She quickly opens her eyes and looks a mixture of aroused, confused, and angry. Her eyes are wide and her pupils are dilated to the point her eyes look black.

"Tad, please!" She begs and my cock threatens to burst right through my trousers.

I just smile at her and lean in to kiss her. She turns her head to the side in protest so I trail kisses from her chin all the way to her ear.

"I want you to beg me to let you come." Her whole body shudders as I whisper in her ear.

"I am begging! Please let me come, Sir!"

Oh fuck! She knows how to push me.

"Later beautiful, we have company." I can see Celine and Dan waking back over to the table with more drinks.

Rachel shuffles around on her seat and tries to compose herself as she turns around.

"We got shots"- Celine starts, but she stops abruptly as she looks at Rachel's face. A smile creeps over her face. "Uh, we weren't interrupting anything were we?"

"No." Rachel squeaks. She clears her throat. "No, we were just chatting."

Celine raises and eyebrow and chuckles to herself. Rachel's cheeks turn even redder, if that is even possible, and I can't help but laugh to myself.

"I think I have had a bit too much to drink, I'm just going to go and splash some water on my face. I'll be back in a second." Rachel starts shuffling away from me.

"I'll come with you babe." Celine shouts over.

As they walk down the stairs I look over at Tommo who basically follows us everywhere now. I signal for him to follow them to the toilets.

21

Rachel

Celine is gripping my hand so tightly she is cutting off the circulation to my fingers. The club is absolutely heaving downstairs. Trying to push through the sea of people is almost impossible as we just seem to end up deeper and deeper in the crowd. I know that Tad will have sent Tommo to follow us but I can't see him anywhere. I can feel myself start to panic a little. I have never been great with crowds, but I am suddenly extremely aware of how close people are to me, and how many people are able to touch me. The floor is sticky, and it feels like there is broken glass all over it.

We are stuck right in the middle of hundreds of people and there doesn't seem to be any way out. Even if we could move I have lost all my bearings and can't see over anyone so have no idea where I need to be going.

Suddenly I feel a hand grab me on the shoulder, I spin around so fast I almost pull Celine on to the floor.

"Do you need any help?" It's a man who I don't know. Although he looks familiar, but I can't quite place him. He is smiling at me and he has an instantly likeable, kind face.

"My friend and I are trying to find the toilets!" I shout at him.

"Here, come this way." He pushes a couple out of the way and stands next to me. He rests his hand gently on my shoulder and with the other he starts shoving people out of the way. I pull on Celine's arm and she follows behind me.

Apparently all it needed was a big strong guy to come along and literally push everyone out of the way! The crowd starts to thin and eventually I see a door in front with a toilet sign on it.

I can't help but be very aware that this strangers hand is still on my shoulder even though it doesn't need to be anymore. I turn to thank him and see him staring at me intently.

"Uh, thank you very much." I say slightly awkwardly.

"It's no problem. Can I buy you a drink?"

"Oh, I'm here with my boyfriend, sorry."

"Pity. Well it was lovely rescuing you. See you around?"

"Uh, yeah, ok."

I walk through the doors and the relief on my ears to be away from the blaring music is immediate.

"Did you just get hit on?" Celine laughs at me.

"Oh shut up!" I laugh back.

We head into the toilets and I immediately go to the sinks so I can splash some cold water on my face.

"So?" Celine asks when she joins me at the sinks.

"So...?"

"What was really going on up there?"

I feel my face flush red and see Celine grin at me.

"You dirty sods! Can't even leave you two alone for five minutes!" She chuckles.

"It's my fault. I wound him right up before we came out so now he is torturing me."

"Wound him up?"

"Yeah, came onto him, got him all riled up and ready to go, then just walked out to get in the cab."

"Well, then you deserve everything you have coming!"

"I know." I grin at her and suddenly have the urge to go home right now.

The next second the door to the toilet flies open, hitting the wall with a loud thud and Tad is standing there, looking out of breath and furious.

"Tad!" I walk up to him. "What's wrong?!"

"Where the fuck did you go?"

I pull him out of the toilets and we stand by a fire exit.

"The crowd was massive, me and Celine got pulled into it and couldn't get out. I couldn't see Tommo anywhere either."

He pulls me into his arms and holds me tightly.

"Fuck sake Rachel. Tommo came running back up saying he had lost you, and then from the top of the stairs I saw you walking off with some bloke."

I push him back a little. What the hell does he think I was doing? Does he think I was going to cheat on him?

"What did you think I was doing exactly?"

"Fuck! Rachel, not like that. I just thought maybe he had got to you again."

My mind flashes back to that night when I got back to Tad's. That night when we saw each other after thinking we never would again. The way he looked at me. The way he held me. I immediately soften and lean back on to his firm chest.

I see Celine waiting for us with Dan by the door leading back into the packed club.

"Come on, let's go." Tad says as he kisses me on the top of the head. "You still need a spanking." He playfully swats my backside as I walk away from him.

Celine rolls her eyes at us and laughs.

CHAPTER FOUR

Tad

Rachel has half jumped on me before I have even managed to close my front door. Her hands are tugging desperately at my belt as she is kissing me in a frenzy. Seeing her like this, so desperate for me is more of a turn on that anything else.

"Rach." I mumble through her lips. "Baby, I have a surprise."

"Oh it can wait."

I manage to pull back.

"No it really can't. Come with me."

She huffs at me and I can hear her muttering something under her breath.

Just you wait!

I take her to the door under my stairs that leads to the basement. I open the door and stand aside to let Rachel go down first.

She flips a light switch, revealing my surprise. I have had a lot of work done down here over the last couple of days. There is still work to be done but it will do for now.

The floor has been carpeted, there is a white wooden four poster bed in the middle of the room and a big chest of drawers next to it. At the end of the bed, sits a huge wooden trunk and I am so excited to see her face when she opens it. She looks at me, puzzled.

"Uh, it's lovely. But I do feel like this could have waited!"

"Rach, open the trunk."

She looks at it, then back at me, and walks over to it. She lifts the latch and opens the lid.

"Woah!" Her eyes widen and her face erupts into a huge grin. "What is all of this?!"

Inside the trunk are whips, ropes, handcuffs, a multitude of toys, and all sorts of other things for us to play with together.

"I figured that eventually when, well if, you and Ami ever moved in, we'd need to be a bit more careful about things and make sure there would be nothing left about for her to find. I figured this could be our little space, just for us. Plus, it is pretty much soundproof down here."

She slowly walks towards me.

"I feel like we should test out that theory."

"Oh we will." I gently kiss her on the lips. "Tell me if it gets too much ok?" I whisper to her.

"Tad, I trust you completely, just trust me that I will tell you. Don't feel you have to say that."

I can't believe how lucky I got finding her.

"Take off your dress."

Without her eyes leaving mine she reaches around to her back, pulls down her zip and her dress falls to the floor. She steps out of it and kicks it behind her. Fuck she looks incredible. She is wearing a black bra, suspender belt and stockings, and that is it.

I walk over to the trunk and I pull out a flogger. The dark red leather tassels hang from a twisted black handle. The earthy smell of new leather fills the room.

"Lay on your back on the bed."

She walks over to the bed and does as she is told.

I slowly trail the tassels over her stomach and she wriggles underneath me.

"Did I say you could move Rachel?"

"No, sorry Sir."

I continue stroking the flogger up and down her beautiful body.

"Open your legs."

She does so without question.

I fucking love this about her. She is so strong and independent, yet with me, like this, I completely own her. She is mine and I know that she will do whatever I need her to. Knowing how much she trusts me after all she has been through in her life is an incredible feeling.

I gently trail the flogger from her stomach all the way down to her glistening pussy. He breathing gets heavier her hands are starting to grip at the bed. The tassels stroke her pussy and the inside of her legs and she can't help but move.

"Sorry Sir!" She cries out before I have the chance to say anything.

I pull back the flogger and without any warning I flick it quickly at the inside of her thighs.

She grits her teeth and sucks in a big breath. I gently stroke the tassels in the same spot that I just hit.

"Aahh!" She pants as she quickly clamps her legs together.

"Oh Rachel. What am I going to do with you?"

I throw the flogger down on the floor and open her legs again. Immediately I push two fingers inside of her.

"Ah fuck." She whimpers.

I start to fuck her fiercely with my fingers. Her hands are gripping the bed sheets tightly as she is desperately trying not to move, or come.

"Ah, fuck. Tad- Sir, please can I come?"

I quickly pull my fingers out and she shoots her head off of the bed.

"Please Sir!"

I lean over her and push my fingers into her mouth. She closes her eyes and gently sucks my fingers. I'm going to have to fuck her soon before I lose my mind.

I pull her up and sit on the bed with my legs over the side.

"No coming yet. You still need to be punished for earlier. Get over my knees."

Her face absolutely lights up with excitement.

She shifts over towards me and lays across my legs, her beautiful arse in the air, just waiting for me.

"Do you know why you are being punished?"

"Yes Sir."

"And why is that?"

"For being a tease."

I smile to myself.

I grab her hand in one of mine and with the other I start to gently stroke her soft, pink arse. Her breathing quickens and I can feel my cock rubbing against her stomach through my jeans. I definitely should have taken these off.

I pull my hand back and bring it back sharply down on her cheek. She throws her head up as my hand connects with her arse. The sound cracks through the silence of the room, the only other sound is Rachel's ragged breathing.

I pull back and slap her again on the other cheek. Her whole body jolts. I gently stroke the spots where I have just spanked and feel her shuffling around under me as she lets out a small moan.

I alternate between spanking and stroking her, until her cheeks are a beautiful shade of pink and I can feel the heat coming off of them.

"Rachel?" She turns to look at me. Her eyes once more look almost black from where her pupils are so big, her cheeks are flushed and she is panting. "Would you like me to make you come now?"

"Oh God yes Sir! Please!"

I fiercely throw her off of my lap and onto her back on the bed.

I jump down onto my knees, grab her legs and pull her towards me. Her legs wrap around my shoulders, pulling my face towards her beautiful pussy.

My greedy tongue pushes straight through her folds to find her clit, and she begins to whimper, desperate to come. My tongue flicks frantically, in between nibbling and sucking. Her legs start to squeeze tightly around my shoulders, and she is crying out with every breath.

"Oh Fuck Tad!" She almost screams as her entire body starts to writhe on the bed. Her hands are pulling at my hair and she is grinding her pussy hard into my face with every wave of her orgasm. Her body stills and the only sound coming from her now is her uneven, heavy breathing. I get up and sit next to her on the bed. Her eyes are closed, and her cheeks and chest are burning red.

"How you doing there?" I laugh at her as I start kissing all over her chest.

"Have I told you how much I love you?"

She rolls towards me and gently kisses me as her hands start to fumble with the button on my jeans. I lift my hips and pull them down and she immediately pushes me on to my back and straddles me. My heart starts thundering in my chest as she grabs my length and hovers just above me. She slowly lowers herself and I can feel every inch of her as I fill her up. A loud moan escapes her lips as she throws her head back. When she looks back at me her eyes are filled with fire. She lifts off of me and then slams back down, the feeling is incredible. She carries on, speeding up. I grab her hips and hold them down so I can thrust up with her. My pace quickens as my orgasm starts creeping across my body. Suddenly I feel the earth stop for a split second as I start to fill her up. She starts to grind slowly, and my legs feel like they are about to cramp where I have stretched them out so far. The last of my come spurts into her and she leans forward to kiss my chest.

I gently kiss the top of her head and she climbs off of me.

"Where do you think you are going?" I perch myself up on my arms so I can get a better look at her glorious body. My come has started spilling out of her, and is leaving a trail down her leg, marking her as completely mine.

"Well I was going to clean up and then go to bed, it's late." She smiles at me as she grabs a towel hanging from the drawers next to the bed.

"I don't think so Rachel. Get back here, now. And pick something out of the trunk on your way over." I wink at her and she smiles sexily at me as she starts to walk back to the bed.

"I think you have a problem Mr. Turner."

"Oh really, and what would that problem be Miss. Bennett?"

"You are a sex addict." She laughs at me.

"No, I'm a Rachel addict."

CHAPTER FIVE

Rachel

I can't move. My hands are tied up and my feet are stuck tight. It's dark. So dark. But I can hear loud, heavy breathing next to my ear. I can smell alcohol, and stale cigarette smoke.

I am laying on my back. I try to sit up but I am tied down completely. I can't catch my breath. I am terrified.

"Kevin?" I whisper.

I feel harsh stubble next to my face, and cold rough lips trailing down to my neck.

"I'm here." His voice answers through the dark.

"Why are you here? How- Why am I tied up?" I start to cry.

"Isn't this how you like it Rachel?"

"No, no! Please, not like this. Not with you!"

Suddenly it is light and the haggard face of my husband is right in front of me.

"Who with then? Him?" He stands back and points behind him, where my beautiful Tad is laying lifeless in the corner of the room.

"Tad? TAD!!" I scream and desperately try to fight against my restraints. "NO! TAD!!"

"Sshhh, it's ok. I can wear his face if you want?" That laugh. That crazed maniacal laugh. I sob and scream and weep.

He climbs on top of me and starts trying to hug me.

"Ssshh Rach, baby I'm here."

"GET AWAY FROM ME! TAD HELP ME!"

My hands are free and I swing in front of me and connect with something.

"Rachel! It's me!"

"Rachel, please wake up! It's me, it's Tad, I'm here."

Fuck.

He is bleeding. His nose is bleeding.

Why is his nose bleeding?

Where am I?

I stop fighting and look around. I am still in Tad's basement, on the bed.

"Fuck! I punched you!" Panic sets in as I realise what I have done. I must have been having a nightmare and then I hit Tad. Tears fill my eyes as the guilt creeps over me. "Fuck, Tad! I am so sorry."

"Hey, it's ok, besides it was more of a slap anyway."

I jump off the bed and sprint up the stairs into the kitchen. I grab a tea towel and throw some frozen peas inside of it.

"Rachel?"

Tad is standing behind me looking angry.

"Tad I am so sorry. I feel awful." I give him the towel with the peas and he puts it down on the counter and grabs my arms.

"Rachel"-

"No, Tad, your face! I'm so sorry!" I go to pick up the peas and he pulls my arm down.

"Look at me!" He snaps. I look at him and realise he isn't angry, he looks concerned.

He pulls me into his arms and holds me tightly. The sudden relief that he is here and he is ok, well not dead, is overwhelming. I start to cry.

"Rachel, I'm okay baby!" He strokes my hair softly.

"I am so sorry Tad. I was having a nightmare."

"I know, and I'm sorry."

"Why are you sorry? I punched you!" I look up at him and turn to get the peas for his nose.

"Slapped." He corrects me and laughs as he puts the peas on his nose. "I had to go and check my e-mails, you looked so peaceful, I didn't want to wake you. I ended up being a bit longer than I thought. Then I heard you screaming."

"I am twenty seven years old Tad. I should be able to sleep alone without having nightmares and attacking people in my sleep."

"You've been through so much Rach. Your only concern seems to be with how Ami is dealing with it, and while that's what you need to do as her Mum, it's really important you are dealing with this yourself. And you clearly aren't. Maybe you should revisit the idea of speaking to someone? Just to get it all off of your chest?"

I roll my eyes at him and sigh. As much as I hate the idea of telling some stranger all my problems and inner most secrets, I can't go on like this. It's not fair to anyone, least of all Tad.

"I'll call my doctor on Monday." I say as I rest my head back on his chest.

"No need Rach, I already have someone you can speak to. I'll give you her number and you can call her whenever. I told her to expect your call."

Why am I not in the least bit surprised?

"Who is she?"

"She is private counsellor who specialises in PTSD."

"How do you know her?"

He shuffles uncomfortably and scratches his head.

"It's late babe, let's get some sleep and you can call her tomorrow."

He is already leading me upstairs by the time I realise how exhausted I am. But I make a mental note to ask him about this counsellor tomorrow.

As we walk to Tad's room, I notice that the door to the spare room is open, and a strong smell of fresh paint seems to be coming from it.

"Have you been decorating?"

"Um," he shifts around uncomfortably again, like he is hiding something. "It's nothing. I'll show you tomorrow."

"Tad? What is it?" I am already walking towards the door before I give him a chance to answer.

I walk through the door to beautiful pastel pink, blue and green walls, a pink, wooden cabin bed with stairs at one end and a slide at the other. It's decorated with unicorn bedding and pillows. Next to the bed is brand new furniture, a dressing table, with a beautiful mirror and pink stool, and a chest of drawers with fairies painted on it. The cream carpet has been covered by the softest looking pink glittery rug.

He's decorated a room for Amelia.

My heart swells.

"Before you say anything, this isn't because I want you both to move in. I just thought eventually maybe she could stay over, just as a trial or something. And it will be nice for her to have her own space."

I am actually speechless. I feel the sting of tears in my eyes as I once again just can't believe how utterly amazing this man is.

All those years Kevin spent telling me I would never be able to find anyone else. Nobody would want me because I had a child. I was *damaged goods.* And yet here is this man, this wonderful, kind, sexy man, who is not only looking after me, but looking out for my daughter who doesn't even know about him yet!

I've been quiet for a while. I should probably say something.

"Let's go to bed." I smile and take his hand.

"What? That's it? No yelling at me?!" Tad asks jokingly.

"No. No yelling. I love you, and Ami will love that room."

His cheeks blush ever so slightly as he smiles at me.

My phone starts shouting at me at some ridiculous time in the morning and it's at that precise moment I decide that today is the day I tell Ami about Tad.

I don't mind the early wake ups so much in the week as Tad is usually up for work. But being up before six on a Saturday morning is just a crime. I roll over and swoon a little at the gorgeous man laying next to me. He had an important meeting in the week and had to shave for it. I didn't realise how much I loved that stubble until it was gone. I can't help but reach out and stroke it, I am so pleased it has grown back already.

"Hmm morning beautiful." He murmurs with a croaky voice. Fuck he sounds as good as he looks. He turns to look at me and I can see his nose and just under his left eye are looking slightly purple and swollen. The guilt I feel in the pit of my stomach is more than enough for me to definitely phone that counsellor this morning. I move my hand up and run my thumb over his nose.

"Oh your beautiful face!"

"Maybe I will look all rugged and handsome now." He smiles at me.

"This isn't funny Tad, I feel awful."

"Well don't." He sits in bed and the cover falls down revealing his bare chest. "It barely hurts at all, and really I should have known better than to try to grab you when you were clearly having a nightmare. Come here!" He pulls me into his arms and we sit in silence for a while.

"Shit! Tad!" I spring out of his arms and check the time. "I'm going to be so late, I forgot I didn't drive here yesterday!"

"Wait." Tad says as he reaches over and grabs his phone. He taps away at the screen and puts the phone to his ear.

"Tommo? Rachel needed to be home five minutes ago and has no car- Cheers." He puts his phone down.

"Quick go, he is probably in the car already."

"Oh Tad I love you. I will call you in a bit ok?"

"Ok, I love you too."

I run to my bag by the door and grab a pair of jeans and top. I am still buttoning up the jeans when I get to the front door. Tommo is waiting with the door open for me. I grab my shoes from next to the door and run out past him.

"Morning Tommo, I'm so sorry if I woke you!"

"Not a problem Rachel, just doing my job." He says as he opens the back door of the black Audi sitting on the drive way.

"So has it always been your job to make sure Tad's girlfriends get home safely in the mornings?" I joke as he gets in the front of the car.

"Oh, no, I didn't mean"-

"I knew what you meant, I was only joking!"

I think I see a hint of smile in the rear view mirror, but then again I'm not entirely sure Tommo knows how to smile!

I manage to sneak through the door with a couple of minutes to spare. I make my way to the kitchen and switch on my beloved coffee machine.

I used to love this kitchen. It reminded me of all the times me and Mum would spend entire weekends baking, or all the incredible meals I would watch her cook for us. But now every time I step foot in here all I hear is that laugh. It spreads through me and I feel utterly terrified. I can see the needle all over again. I can feel it plunging into my neck, feeling reality slip away and thinking to myself I would never ever see my baby girl again.

That bastard had every detail planned. A few days after he took me, a man was found in a little village in France called Allonne, not far from Paris, wearing a very distinctive coat. It turned out he was homeless. Kevin paid him £5,000 in cash to wear the coat, get the ferry across to France, and use his credit card in a few shops. All he had to do was make sure his face was covered and he was wearing the coat.

So much for him being stupid. And now he is out there. Somewhere. Plotting God only knows what. Tad has hired extra men to keep watch on Ami and I constantly. He didn't tell me at first, for whatever reason. But it became slightly obvious when there were huge guys in suits following me everywhere, sitting in cars outside of the house and Ami's school every day.

"Morning princess."

I jump out of my skin and the mug I was holding falls and smashes on the floor.

"Holy fucking shit Dad, you scared the fuck out of me!" I half scream at him.

"Oh God, I'm so sorry Rachel."

"No, I'm sorry Daddy." I walk to the other side of the kitchen to get a dustpan and brush to clean up the mess. As I'm sweeping up the broken bits of ceramic, my brain once again takes me back to that night. The stupid piece of smashed mug I was trying to use as a weapon. The coffee mug that smashed on the floor after I threw it at Kevin...

"Here, let me do that." Dad kneels next to me on the floor and takes the brush from me. I stand back and make us both coffees while he cleans up the mess.

"I'm a mess Dad." I say as he takes his coffee from me.

"You've been through a tremendous ordeal. If you weren't a mess I would be really worried." He smiles kindly and strokes my hand.

"I punched Tad in the face this morning."

"You what? What did he do" –

"Oh no! Nothing like that Dad. I was having a nightmare, I thought he was Kevin, and I punched him. In the nose. And gave him a nosebleed."

I take a long sip of coffee and feel myself relax ever so slightly.

"Oh Rachel."

"I'm going to speak to someone. Try to see if I can sort myself out a bit."

"That's a good idea. I can come to the Doctors with you if you'd like?"

"Thanks Daddy, but Tad has already given me the number of someone he knows."

He rolls his eyes at me.

"Tad this, Tad that, when do we get to meet him hey?"

"Who is Tad?" Ami says as she comes bounding into the kitchen.

Balls.

"Morning baby, how did you sleep?"

"Really good thanks Mummy. Who's Tad?"

"Uh, Tad is my friend."

"A boy friend?"

"Yes, a friend who is a boy..."

Ami takes a bowl out of the cupboard and starts to make herself breakfast.

"Tad is a funny name. Where are the Coco Pops?"

I walk to the cupboard and get the cereal for her.

"Tad is short or Thaddeus."

"Oooh wow, that's a cool name!"

"Actually I have some news! Aunty Celine and Uncle Dan have set a date for their wedding! It's just before Christmas, and they want you to be a bridesmaid!"

"Yay! That's brilliant! Do I get to wear a nice dress?" She absolutely beams.

"Of course you do baby!" I grab her the milk from the fridge. "And uh, I'm going to be bringing Tad along, as he is a- uh, special friend..."

"Mum! I am not five! I know he is your boyfriend!" She huffs at me.

I see Dad start to laugh out of the corner of my eye.

"Oh, um, sorry baby. I just wasn't sure how you would react..."

"Do you love him?"

Sometimes I hate how grown up this girl is. I don't need to be having this conversation with her, let alone with my Dad sitting right next to me.

"Um," I can feel my cheeks start to turn red. "Yes I do baby."

Ami smiles at me.

"Cool."

Cool? Cool?!

Oh this kid!

"That's it? Cool?"

"Mummy, you used to be so sad. But now you are happy. At least when you aren't thinking about Daddy..."

I take her in my arms and squeeze as hard as I can without cutting off her oxygen.

"Hello, you have reached the voicemail of Dr. Elizabeth Ross. I am afraid I am unable to answer the phone right now, but please leave your name and number and I will return your call as soon as I can."

"Oh, um, hello. My name is Rachel Bennett. Uh, I was given your number. If you could give me a call back."

I leave my number and hang up. I can't let that arsehole ruin any more of my life than he already has. I can't live in a constant state of panic that he may do something.

My phone starts ringing in my hands.

That was fast.

I look at the screen and see Tad's name light up. I instantly smile as I answer.

"Hey you."

"Hey beautiful. Did you make it home in time?"

"I did. But that shouldn't be too much of a problem anymore."

"Oh really?"

"I told Ami about you."

"You did? What did she say?"

"She said, and I quote, *cool.*"

I hear him laugh on the other end of the phone.

"Cool huh?! Well in that case I have a proposal for you."

"Go on...?"

"Well it's bonfire night tomorrow, and I was going to see if you wanted to come to a display with me. But maybe me, you and Ami could go?"

That is a big step. I wasn't planning on introducing them to each other until Celine's wedding...

"Um I don't know... It's just a lot for her in a short space of time. I'll think about it and let you know, is that ok?"

"Of course it is, no pressure- Shit, I've got another call and I need to take it. I'll speak to you later ok?"

"Yeah ok, love you."

"You too."

God I don't know what to do. I want things to move forward. I want Ami to meet Tad. I want them to get on and one day not too far in the future I would love for us to both live with him. But it's all so soon.

There's a gentle knock on my door.

"Rachel, I've made you coffee."

"Come in Mum, I was just on the phone."

Mum walks in to my room with a big mug of steaming coffee and a packet of biscuits.

"I thought I'd bring you up the nice chocolate ones before your Dad scoffs them all."

"Thanks Mum." I laugh as I take the biscuits from her.

"You ok? You look a million miles away love?" She asks as she sits next to me on my bed.

"Tad has invited me and Ami to a fireworks display tomorrow."

"Ah." She understands my dilemma without me having to say anything. I take a sip of my coffee. "I think you should both go."

"Really?" That surprises me.

"Rachel, you have been so- different recently. And I don't mean because of everything that has happened. You have seemed, happy. Even after all you have been through. I can't even put into words how incredibly guilty I feel that I didn't notice just how unhappy you were before. Looking back now it was so obvious. The little things. The way your whole demeanor changed when Kevin was around. The way he would belittle you in front of us, but in such a way that he made it like he was only joking. Even when he used to rattle his keys when you were all at our house and then suddenly you would be leaving. It all makes so much sense now. I am so sorry Rachel." Her eyes start to fill with tears and her voice breaks as she tries to keep herself together. I grab her hand in my own.

"Mum"-

"No Rachel, I'm your Mum! I should have noticed! Your Dad could see it. I thought he was just being over protective, you've always been his little princess. But looking back..." She closes her eyes, trying to hold back the tears. I put my coffee on the floor and pull her into my arms.

"Mum, please, *please* don't feel guilty. I did my very best to hide from everyone. I just wanted to pretend I had the perfect life. I am so sorry that I kept it all from you."

We sit in silence, hugging on my bed for a long time. She composes herself and lets me go.

"You have been so happy recently. That smile that lights up your beautiful face when your phone starts buzzing is brand new. After everything you have been through, I can't see you jumping into something with someone who doesn't really make you happy. You say you love this Tad?"

"I really do Mum." I beam.

"There is that smile again." She smiles as she cups my face in that special way that Mums do to their daughters. "Ask Ami. I bet she wants to meet him."

"I will. Thanks Mum."

"Drink your coffee before it gets cold love. I'm making stew for dinner."

CHAPTER SIX

Tad

I have so many contracts I need to be reading through, so much work that needs to be done, but I just can't concentrate on anything. I have to stay in London next week and I am absolutely dreading it. When I finally got back to Suze after Rachel interrupted our conversation, I realised what she was talking about when she was panicking about castles. Ted fucking Castle.

The guy started out with nothing but an idea, a brilliant idea in all honesty. Connect people from all over the world on his website, to enable them to create new inventions, new businesses. Meet people who are interested in the same things as you, discuss ideas, that sort of thing.

He charged a membership fee, and then sneakily added into the terms and conditions that he got a cut from any products or companies that become successful as a direct result of his website. Then he was onto a winner. He ended up making his first million with having to do barely any work. A film production company was his first major winner, and from then people came running to him. Money just started appearing in his pockets without him needing to do a thing. Of course, that's where all the trouble started.

He developed a bit of a God complex. Thought he was bigger, and more important than everyone else. He was then caught on camera snorting a line of cocaine off of a prostitute's backside. He then tracked down the photographer and beat seven shades of shit out of him. He ended up not only losing the majority of his members, but all of his advertisers pulled out. He lost everything.

Now it was plainly obvious to me what a good idea this guy had, and that was one of the reasons I pounced on him. Told him to sell to me, that way I could buy him out for a decent price rather than the company collapsing into nothing and someone else swooping in and taking all of his clients. He agreed to sell almost immediately. He needed money for all of his legal fees, plus as far as I could work out he was trying to pay off the photographer to get the charges dropped.

This was well over a year ago now. Since then, I've re-vamped the company. I hired someone to be the new face of the website, had my publicists working overtime to get members back and advertisers back on side, and the company is successful once again. I've decided to keep hold of his one for now. Seems like too much of a money maker to sell so soon.

At first I thought Suze was trying to tell me that he wanted to buy the company back from me. But no. Turns out the son of a bitch is trying to say I extorted the company from him. No idea how he thinks this is going to play out, I'm not an idiot. I have lawyers at all meetings when it comes to signing contracts and such.

He wants to meet with Scott and I next week. So I need to spend all of Monday with my legal team, checking we have no issues our side and I am meeting with the fucker on Tuesday. Then the Serenity takeover starts so I have to stay in London even longer.

It's going to be one hell of a stressful week. And yet all I can worry about is how I am going to cope without Rachel. And more importantly, how she is going to cope without me. I left her for less than an hour in bed, and it ended with her terrified, screaming, and slapping me in the face!

Dr. Ross really is amazing and I hope that she will be able to help her. I can't bear to think of Rachel, alone and scared.

I am so pleased she has told Ami about us. And I know, it's way too soon for me to be meeting her, but fuck it. I love this woman with every single part of me and I hate that we can't be together all the time. I completely understand, and I know I can't rush things. But I hope Ami likes me.

Shit. What if she doesn't? What if she hates me? What if she thinks I'm trying to taker her Mum away? My stomach starts to knot as I work myself up.

Why wouldn't she like you? Stop being a dick.

Still, it wouldn't hurt to help the situation out a little... I open up a new web browser page and quickly do a search on Amazon...

Rachel

'm sitting in my favourite place. Well, one of my favourite places now I suppose. I'm in Costa with Ami, having a latte while she sips a hot chocolate, piled high with whipped cream, marshmallows and a chocolate flake. I laugh at her as she lowers her cup, revealing a cream covered top lip.

"Uh hun, you've got just a little something"- I circle her lips with my finger to point to the mess- "well it's everywhere!" We both laugh as she wipes her face with a napkin. Oh those napkins. Every time I see them I now remember Tad wiping up his spilled coffee and me having to resist the urge to pounce on him. I remember that morning so clearly. I remember trying desperately hard to stare at my phone, as if I hadn't seen him, but of course I noticed him the second he walked through the doors. I kept repeating to myself *drink up and leave. Drink up and leave. Do not speak to him. Don't even look at him.*

It was like I knew. I knew the second I looked in those eyes I would completely lose myself. And I did. I turned and looked straight in his impossibly blue eyes and I fell. That was the exact moment. Seeing his cheeks blushing a slight shade of pink, the expression on his face as he was staring into my eyes. I've never ever known a feeling like it, I just felt like nothing else in the world mattered at that moment, or ever would. Like every little detail of my life suddenly made sense. My soul kind of went *"Oh, I've been looking for you."*

"Are you listening Mum?" Ami asks and I realise I have been miles away and not heard a word she has said.

"Sorry baby I was lost in thought. What were you saying?" A smile slowly creeps over Ami's face and she laughs at me. "What?" I ask smiling back at her.

"You look really pretty when you smile like that Mummy."

"Like what?"

"That smile when you're thinking of your *boyfriend!*" She giggles at me and I feel my cheeks flush bright red. Nothing at all gets past this kid! "Do I get to meet him soon?"

"Uh- Well actually he wants to meet you."

"He does?" Her little face lights up and it warms my heart.

"Yeah baby, he asked if we both wanted to watch the fireworks with him tomorrow."

"Oh yeah! That sounds awesome!"

She is so excited but my stomach is in bits.

"So you want to go then?" I ask.

"Well, yeah!" Seeing how excited she is relaxes me a little.

"Ok then, I'll tell him we will go."

"Yes!" She does a little mini fist pump and then takes a sip of her hot chocolate, once again covering her lips in cream. We both burst into hysterical laughter!

I am going to put on so much weight living here. Mum made stew and dumplings for dinner, and then apple crumble and custard for pudding. I really miss cooking, but she won't have me cook while I am here. My phone buzzes from the other end of the sofa and Ami gets to it first.

"Oooh it's from Tad!" She teases. Honestly I wonder who the parent is sometimes!

"Give that to me, you!" I laugh as she passes me my phone.

I miss you. What time can you sneak out? I need my Rachel fix. Love you x

When I look up everyone is staring at me.

"What?!" I blush.

"Go over and see him!" Mum says.

"No its ok, I'll pop over once I've got Ami to bed."

"Mum, I'm nearly ten you know." Ami says matter of factly. "I think I can go to bed by myself."

"Oh, ok. Mum is that"–

"Of course it is! Go, say hi to Tad for me. And ask him round for dinner!"

I roll my eyes at her.

"Thanks Mum, and maybe!" I stand and give her a kiss on the cheek.

"Bed no later than ten you, okay?" I say to Ami.

"Yes Mum. Love you."

"Love you too baby." I wrap my arms around her and kiss her soft hair.

I feel like such a kid when I'm on my way to Tad's. It's like all my Christmases and Birthdays are coming at once. My stomach flips as I ring his doorbell. A few seconds pass and Tad opens the door. His face lights up when he sees me.

"Rach! I wasn't expecting you till later!"

I push him backwards and shut the door behind me.

"I couldn't wait." My voice cracks a little as I try to contain my excitement.

"Oh..." He says as he pulls me in close to him. The atmosphere has shifted in a split second. It feels as though electricity is sparking from both of us.

I can hear Tad's breathing start to speed up. My heart starts to race as a warmth spreads through my entire body.

Ever so slowly Tad trails his hand up from my hip, the skin under my clothes erupts into goosebumps as his hand travels higher, up my side, over my shoulder and finally gently strokes a strand of hair behind my ear. I can't help but lean my head into his hand. My eyes close as his thumb gently strokes my bottom lip. His touch sends a shiver all the way through me and a soft moan slips out of my lips. He leans in and gently presses his lips to my own. The world just falls away when he kisses me. Life and all its problems slip away, leaving just me and the love of my life.

Without warning his hands are under my behind, lifting me into him. I wrap my legs around him as my tongue searches deeper into his mouth. It's greeted by a low groan as I rub up against the growing bulge in his trousers.

"Fuck me Tad." I whisper into his mouth.

"Oh Rach!" He moans back. He lifts me into his front room and drops me onto the sofa. I'm panting with anticipation as he unbuckles his belt and his hard cock springs from its confines. I am so excited I feel like I am having to focus on breathing to make sure I don't forget!

Before I know what I am doing I have sat up and taken his whole length in my mouth. He hisses and wraps his fingers in my hair. Mercilessly I suck his beautiful cock, hard and fast, savouring every inch of it. I can hear Tad desperately trying to keep his cool, but the occasional jerks from his hips and the groans slipping through his lips are enough to tell me he is trying to hold himself together. Knowing what I am doing to him, how I make him feel is amazing, and results in me getting wetter by the second.

Suddenly Tad pulls out of my mouth, leaving me breathless and waiting. He quickly slips his fingers under the waistband of my leggings and knickers and pulls them down in one swift movement. Before I have a chance to steady myself, he has pushed me back and his tongue is frantically searching for my clit. Then he finds it and, oh-Fuck! Immediately I'm there. I'm floating. I have to grab hard onto the cushions to steady myself. His arms have pinned down my legs so I can't move my hips with him. He flicks and sucks and licks and-

"Oh fuck Tad!" I whimper as I start to feel myself come undone.

My back arches, pushing my sex harder into Tad's mouth. I melt back into the sofa and try to catch my breath, but before I have any time to recover Tad thrusts deeply into me. I cry out. He is slamming into me with everything he has. His eyes are burning into mine, and I can't look away, or move. I'm bound just by his look.

"Don't come Rachel." His voice is stern, and yet all it does is spur me on. I can feel myself starting to pulse around him.

Breathe. Just breathe.

Desperately I try to control my breathing, and I can see his lips curve at one corner as he tries to conceal a smile. Harder and harder, rougher and faster he plunges into me.

"Tad, I can't"- I cry through gritted teeth. He doesn't play fair. How am I supposed to try to control myself when he is intent on making sure I disobey him? I can feel my orgasm building, I know I'm not supposed to come, and I start off trying to keep it at bay, but I know what's coming. I know how amazing it is going to be. And then I come. And I keep coming. I let the waves rush through me and I don't care about anything else.

Somewhere in the distance I hear Tad groan and still for a second as he comes deep inside of me. I feel the weight of him on top of my chest and he slowly pushes in and out of me.

My fingers wrap around his soft hair as he rests his head on my chest.

"You don't play fair!" I say whimper as I try to catch my breath.

"How's that?" He says as he turns his head to look at me.

"You can't tell me I'm not allowed to come and then fuck me like that!"

"I can when it means I know I get to spank you later." He grins at me.

Fuck, that smile.

CHAPTER SEVEN

Tad

Rachel is sleeping softly next to me on the bed in our little escape. I have well and truly worn her out and I can't help but smile at the thought. As much as I don't want to disturb her, I also don't want a repeat of last night. I know she feels more comfortable in my bed. I stand over her and gently slide my arms underneath her so I can carry her upstairs. She jumps as I lift her.

"Sshh baby, just grab on, I'm taking you bed."

Her body instantly relaxes. She wraps her arms around my neck and rests her head on my chest. Her beautiful scent wafts up my nose as I take a breath in and I can't stop myself from nuzzling into her hair and breathing her in.

Somehow I manage to get her up two flights of stairs without waking her.

The inner kid in me high fives myself thinking I must have *really* worn her out. I gently put her down in bed and cover her over.

I watch her sleep for a little while. Her chest rises and falls softly, and every so often she smiles. I hope she is dreaming about me.

I quickly go downstairs to check my phone to see a load of missed calls, all from Scott.

I quickly call him back.

"Yo Tad!" He sounds smashed.

"Hey, you called, lots. I thought it was urgent."

"It is urgent man."

"What's up?"

"I need my wingman back!"

"That is not urgent." I half laugh.

"It is dude, ever since you've been shacked up you don't come out with me anymore. There is nobody to help me out with the chickas!"

"You don't need help with the *chickas*," I laugh, "you need help in general!"

"We are going for a night out next week, no excuses."

"Yeah, yeah. Now if you don't mind I have an extremely hot, naked woman in my bed I need to check on."

"You wanker. Hope your cock falls off."

"Ha! Night!"

"Yeah whatever..." The line goes dead and I laugh at what a total idiot that guy is.

I grab two bottles of water from my fridge and make my way back up to bed.

Rach is sleeping soundly when I get back. I climb into bed beside her and turn to lay down facing her. Beautiful chestnut brown hair is tumbling down the side of her face and I reach out to gently stroke it behind her ears. As my fingers touch her soft cheek, she smiles and sighs softly. I never thought I would ever be this happy. Never thought it would be possible. My own parents put me off the idea of settling down as a child, and my own experience with women as I got older only served as proof that relationships just weren't for me. They seemed suffocating, and like you had to change who you were, just to make one other person happy.

I decided that I would be better off on my own. Rarely, I had an itch that I wouldn't be able to scratch myself. And that is exactly how I got into trouble a few years back. I got totally taken advantage of, and if it hadn't been for Suze wading in and giving me a reality check, fuck knows where I'd be now.

First and last time I made that mistake.

Rach stirs in her sleep and rolls so she is facing me. Fuck. The way I love this woman is crazy. I haven't had to change a thing, she loves me for exactly who I am, and I feel exactly the same way about her.

I lay next to her and gently slide my arm under her head so I can pull her in close to me. She fits perfectly. Right in the little space that was always meant for her.

I can hear my phone buzzing on the bed side table. It's still really dark out. I turn to grab my phone and see it's Tommo calling. At 4.45am this must be important. I sneak out of bed into the hallway, and pull the door shut, so I don't disturb Rachel.

"Tommo?"

"Boss, I'm sorry to call at this time, but I know you said you wanted to know any new info immediately."

"That I did. What's happened?"

"We think he's been seen near Leicester."

My stomach drops.

"What- Where? How?!"

"We got a message off a Facebook post saying he was seen in a bed and breakfast, in the middle of nowhere, paying in cash last night."

I scratch my head and curse inwardly.

Fucking Robins.

He assured us there was no way of Kevin getting out of France without him knowing. I swear the police are fucking useless.

"We're on it Boss, I've sent some guys to the B&B to check out the CCTV, and I've left Robins a voicemail."

"Thanks Tommo. Who is watching her parents tonight?"

"Freddie and George are there now. I'm gonna make my way to yours now to be extra safe."

"Ok, cheers for the update. I want to be told of any news as soon as you know."

"Of course boss."

How the fuck is he doing this?

How is he just flitting back and forth between countries with nobody noticing even though Interpol have sent his photo as a red flagged suspect to every fucking country out there?

At least my men are on the ball enough to have noticed before he turns up.

Although at least if he did turn up I could fucking kill him...

There is no chance of me getting back to sleep now, coffee and catch up on some work it is then.

I tip toe back to bed and move my pillow under Rachel, as if I am still next to her. The last thing I want is for her to panic and have another nightmare.

It is amazing how much work you can get done at stupid o'clock in the morning, fueled by copious amounts of coffee. Suze will be proud. I have gone through every last contract detail from that fucker Castle and he doesn't have a leg to stand on. I've drafted correspondence to him and his legal team, and sent it all to Scott to sign. I am not letting this wanker try to bring me down just because I have managed to rescue the company that he so carelessly almost destroyed.

A ping on my computer tells me I have an e-mail and I go to check them.

There, sitting in my inbox is a message that makes me feel physically sick.

I quickly minimise the window and push myself back from my desk as tears burn in my eyes.

Fuck.

Just delete the e-mail.

I take a deep breath and open the page back up.

"It's almost time! Check into your room now to save time when you arrive at Caesars Palace."

My mouse hovers over the delete icon and I can't help myself. I just cry. I can feel the hot tears rolling down my face and splashing onto my desk in front of me. The more I try to compose myself, the more ugly tears escape. I have never once cried over the loss of my brother, but this is just too much.

There will be no Caesars Palace, or Las Vegas. There will be no birthday celebrations. Because there is no more Seb.

I push my keyboard out of the way and rest my head in my hands on my desk.

I don't have much of a chance to think about him anymore, which has been good in a way, but, fuck.

I can hear shuffling coming from the stairs. I quickly compose myself and delete the e-mail. I cannot let Rachel see me like this. I have to be strong for her. She has enough on her plate, and possibly even more so now that Kevin might be back. Although I see no point in worrying her what so ever until I know for a fact she needs to know.

I hear the door squeak slightly as she pushes it open and feel the warmth from her arms as she wraps them around my neck. The warmth spreads right the way through me and I feel better almost instantly.

"Why are you up so early?" She questions, her voice husky and sleepy sounding.

"Just couldn't sleep babe, thought I'd try to get some work out of the way so we wouldn't be interrupted today."

Her hand finds my face and she turns my face towards hers.

"You sound funny? And your eyes are red. What's wrong?" She looks terrified. She strokes my face and spins my chair so she can climb on my lap.

"Nothing is wrong!" I try to laugh. "The only thing wrong right now is that you are sitting here with all of your clothes on."

"Don't try to change the subject. I know something is the matter." Her eyes are searching my own for answers that I am just not comfortable giving her right now.

"Honestly, I am fine. It's just a bit dusty in here. Will have to make sure the cleaner is in here more often!"

A puzzled look replaces the concerned one.

"You have a cleaner?"

"Well, yeah? You don't think this place cleans itself do you?"

"No, I just thought you cleaned? I have never seen anyone here except your security."

"She has a key and comes whenever she has time. A lot of the time she is here ridiculously early in the morning. And she is very good at staying hidden. I'm not usually here this much so I have never really noticed just how quiet she is! Honestly, if the house wasn't sparkling I wouldn't think she even turned up!"

She leans her head into my chest and winds her fingers around my own.

"So where were you, when you weren't here?" She asks quietly.

"I have a penthouse in London. It's easier for work to be in the city."

"Ooh a penthouse hey? What's it like?"

"It's- well I won't lie, it's a bit extravagant." That is possibly a slight understatement. "I did have a tiny place, just somewhere to keep some clothes and rest my head. But I started spending more and more time in London, and occasionally I would invite potential clients to mine for an *informal chat.* Suze thought my place just wasn't appropriate so I gave her a budget, which she ignored, and she bought me this huge penthouse with a retractable roof over an indoor pool and barbeque..."

Rachel's head shoots off my chest to look at me.

"You have a posh penthouse, in London, with its own pool and a retractable roof, and you haven't taken me there yet why...?"

"Well I was going to see if you wanted to stay for a couple of days this week, but you've gone and got yourself a job haven't you."

"Oh... Forgot about that..."

"As soon as you have found out what days you are working, let me know. When you have some time, I will send a car for you." I kiss her on the head and breathe in her gorgeous soft, sweet, Rachel smell.

"So I thought you were supposed to be Susan's boss?" She giggles softly.

"Yeah, I thought so too." I laugh back at her.

CHAPTER EIGHT

Rachel

My stomach is in knots. I'm on the way back to Mum and Dad's to pick Ami up. Tad suggested we go for a late lunch first, and then Ami could decide if she still wanted to go to the fireworks together.

So much is riding on this I feel physically sick. What if Ami just doesn't like him? What if she doesn't want me to see him anymore? After everything she has been through, this is such a huge step.

I walk in the door and see Dad and Ami sitting at the dining table. Dad's reading the paper, and Ami is engrossed in some homework. Her head shoots up as she hears the door and her face lights up when she sees me.

"Mum!" She squeals as she rushes over to give me a hug.

"Hey baby, you ready to go?"

"Yeah! I'll just get my coat and shoes on."

"Ok." I say meekly while chewing my bottom lip.

Dad's eyes appear from over the top of his newspaper as my voice wobbles and lets on just how nervous I am.

"Everything okay there princess?"

"Uh, yeah." I lie.

Dad folds his newspaper and takes off his glasses.

"What's wrong?"

"Just a bit nervous, that's all."

"What do you have to be nervous about?"

"I don't know. This just all seems so soon... And I am so worried she won't like him." I whisper, to make sure Ami doesn't hear.

"Why wouldn't she Rachel? You like him, don't you?"

"Well of course I do." I can feel my cheeks blushing.

"Well there you go then."

"It's not quite that simple though is it Dad. I don't want her to feel like Tad is trying to be her new Dad, or worry that he is going to take her away from me. She has had so much of her life change in such a short space of time, and she has coped amazingly with it all. I guess I'm just worried this will be the thing that she doesn't deal with."

"Rachel, she asked to meet him didn't she?" I nod. "And she has been so excited to meet him. She hasn't stopped talking about it all morning. She can't wait to meet the man that makes her Mummy so happy." I can feel some of the unease melting away already. "Your Mum and I were talking about this last night. After everything Ami has been through- everything you have *both* been through, you aren't going to be doing this unless it is something you are really sure about."

"Thank you Daddy." I walk over to him and kiss his head.

"He is really something special isn't he?" Dad grins at me and my cheeks flush even more.

"He really is." I sigh.

"I'm happy for you princess."

Just then Ami bounds through the door. She looks so grown up, it's almost scary. Skinny jeans and little black booties with a smart jacket and a new hat and scarf set she bought specially for the fireworks tonight.

"You look lovely." I beam at her.

"Thanks Mum! Can we go now?"

I look back over at my Dad and he gives me a reassuring nod.

"Let's go."

We have parked up and are walking towards the seafront. I decided to go somewhere Ami really likes, just to make sure she is totally comfortable; so we have come to a little American style diner on the beach. We come here at least once a month, and then go to the arcades down the road. This kid has an obsession with the two pence machines. I joke with her that I am going to have to keep an eye on her gambling when she is older.

The cool sea breeze is usually so relaxing, but it is doing absolutely nothing today to calm my nerves. Ami is skipping along beside me, completely oblivious to the inner meltdown I am having. I take a deep breath in.

Stop being such a drama queen. This is going to be fine! You stressing is going to be what fucks it up.

"Is that him Mummy?"

There in the distance, stood outside our little diner, is Tad. He is nervously shuffling on his feet, tapping away at his phone. He looks gorgeous. He is dressed in smart jeans and brown shoes, with a dad style jumper on. I laugh silently to myself.

"That's him baby."

"Wow…"

"Wow?" I look down at her.

"He is fit!"

"Amelia!" I laugh!

He must hear our giggles as he looks up and puts his phone away.

His eyes catch mine, and that beautiful smile creeps over his face. My insides just melt at that smile. He starts to walk towards us, and looks at Ami. I can feel her hand tighten slightly around mine.

"Hey." I say nervously as we meet.

"Hey." He leans in and gently pecks me on the cheek.

I look at Ami and she is smiling nervously at me.

"Ami, this is Tad."

"Hi Tad." She blushes.

"Hello Ami, it's lovely to meet you." Tad holds out his hand and I desperately try not to snigger out loud as nerves get the better of me. Ami takes his hand and shakes it. As she is about to pull her hand back, Tad gently lifts it to his lips and gives her the softest kiss on her knuckles. She giggles and pulls her hand back.

I don't think I could love this man anymore if I tried.

"Shall we go in then?" Tad says as he interrupts my swooning.

We walk into the diner and it is quiet. In fact I think we may be the only people here. This place is absolutely amazing, the food is great, and you are right on the seafront and can see the ferries coming in and out of Portsmouth. But it's always so quiet in the winter. Oh, I tell a lie. There are two other people in here. Tommo and one of Tad's other security guards. They are sitting at a little table in the corner and look they are on a very romantic date!

"Ami!" Mickey the owner comes out from behind the bar to greet us. He has always been so friendly to us, even when Ami ran in front of a server and smashed an entire order. "I was wondering when I would next see you!"

"Hi Mickey!" They high five and Mickey grabs some menus.

"Rachel, lovely to see you, how are you?"

"I'm really good thank you." I can see him trying to eye up Tad, without being too obvious. "This is my boyfriend, Tad."

"Lovely to meet you." Tad holds his hand out right on cue.

"Ah boyfriend eh? Rachel, I am heartbroken! I thought we were waiting for each other!" He fakes a hurt look and shakes Tad's hand. Ami and I both laugh and start to walk over to our usual table.

Tad pulls out a chair for Ami, and the one next to her for me. He sits opposite me and smiles across the table.

I catch Tads eye as Ami takes a menu and starts to look through it.

"Am I doing ok?" He mouths silently at me.

I just smile and lean my hand out on the table and he grabs it with his.

"So what's good here?" He asks.

"We always get a cheeseburger with chili cheese fries. It's amazing!" Ami says very enthusiastically.

"That does sound good."

I can see Mickey walking over with a bottle of wine and a huge ice cream float.

"On the house my dears, now what can I get you to eat?"

"Oh Mickey, you can't do that!"

"I'll let you in on a secret, it's my restaurant, I can do what I like." He winks at Ami and she laughs as he puts her drink in front of her.

"Thank you." She says before taking a huge gulp.

"Thanks Mickey! Can we both have our usual? Tad?"

"And me please."

"Coming up." He skips back off to the kitchen and Tad starts to pour us both a glass of wine.

"Only a tiny glass please, I've got to drive back."

"Come back in the car with me?"

"But my car is here?"

"It's ok. I'll get one of the guys to drive your car back."

"Oh go on then."

Tad pours me a glass of what is the nicest red wine I have ever tasted in my life. I always treat myself to a glass when I am here. And then I tend to ask Mickey to put the cork back in the bottle so I can finish it at home once Ami is in bed!

"So do you two come here often then?" Tad asks.

"We come here loads on Mummy daughter dates." Ami says. "Then we always go to the arcade after. You should see Mum on the dance machines." She laughs.

"The dance machines eh?" Tad smirks. "Now that I would pay money to see!"

"Not happening!" I laugh back.

"Don't be a spoil sport Mum!" Ami chimes in.

"Shush you, and drink your float!"

We've finished our food, and I am ready to be rolled out of here. God only knows how they have the room but Tad and Ami have ordered huge ice cream sundaes for pudding.

"Ami, I think you have more of that ice cream around your face than you do in your belly!" I say when she has finished.

"Can I go to the toilet to clean my face?"

"Of course you can baby."

She jumps off her chair and skips off to the toilet.

"She likes you." I say to Tad through the biggest grin.

"Does she? How do you know?" He asks nervously.

"I'm her Mum! Plus it's obvious. If she doesn't like someone she just won't talk to them."

Tad smiles at me and reaches across the table to grab my hands.

"I love you Rachel."

Oh, those words.

"I love you too."

"And you have an incredible daughter. Not that I expected anything less of course."

How have I ended up here? How is it even possible to be *this* happy? I feel like I am floating.

Ami comes back to the table with a lollipop poking out of her mouth.

"Where did that come from?"

"Mickey gave it to me." Of course he did!

"How do you even have any room left?!"

She shrugs at me and smiles.

"Mummy, why is Freddie here?"

"Freddie?"

"Freddie. Over there with the other man."

I shoot a confused look at Tad.

"How do you know his name?" I ask.

"I see him around school lots, and outside Nanny and Gramp's sometimes so I asked him what his name was."

"Oh... Well, he works for Tad. He is just here to keep an eye on us, that's all."

"Cool."

That bloody word! How does nothing at all phase this kid!

"Where are we going to watch the fireworks?" She asks.

"Well the display in Portsmouth is always great, and I have a bit of a surprise for you both." Tad answers through a mischievous grin.

The very thought of being out with all those people fills me with dread. We have been to watch the fireworks there before, and yes they are amazing, they set the fireworks off from some of the boats that are docked there, and it is incredible. But it gets so busy. There are hundreds, if not thousands of people, all crammed into a tiny space overlooking the water.

"What's the surprise?!" Ami asks eagerly.

"Well it wouldn't be a surprise if I told you would it!" He pokes his tongue out slightly at Ami and she laughs. I must admit, seeing those two getting on so well does do something to help ease my nerves just a little.

Mickey comes over with the bill.

"Don't leave it so long next time!"

"We won't, don't worry!" I say as I rummage around in my bag for my purse. Before I have found it Tad is pulling out his wallet.

"This one is on me."

He takes the card machine from Mickey and types in a tip before entering his pin number. When he hands it back, Mickey checks the receipt that has printed and his eyes widen as he hands it to Tad.

"I think you pressed one too many zeros when you entered the tip."

"No, that's for you. You have a lovely place, and you treat my girls so well." Tad's eyes widen suddenly, as if he is second guessing what he just said. But Ami grabs hold of my arm and whispers "he called us his girls!" in my ear and I see Tad relax instantly.

"Oh wow, you can definitely come again!" Mickey grins wildly at Tad.

We are walking along the beach back to Tad's car. Ami is off kicking the pebbles while Tad and I walk hand in hand.

"I don't even want to know how much you tipped do I?"

"No, probably not!" He looks at me and smiles.

CHAPTER NINE

Tad

'm sitting next to Rachel in the back of the car. The traffic heading into Portsmouth is awful. Looks like everyone is coming to watch the fireworks here tonight. I can tell Rach is stressed out about something.

"What's wrong?" I whisper.

"Nothing really, just worried a bit about the crowds."

"I already have two guys there. Tommo will be joining us once he's parked your car. I promise you, everything will be fine." I squeeze her hand and she smiles at me, although I can tell she is still nervous.

She is definitely going to love my surprise.

"Ami, it's going to busy out there, and I know it's not *cool*, but I don't want you to let go of my hand at all once we have stepped out of this car. Ok?"

I see Ami roll her eyes from the other side of Rach and laugh to myself. They are so similar it is unreal. They look and act more like sisters than they do mother and daughter.

I can't believe how easy this afternoon has been. I was so worried about how Ami would be with me, but she has been incredible. In all honestly I was most worried about how I would be, but I actually think I'm doing okay.

I never saw myself settled down with kids of my own, let alone meeting a girlfriend's child. But, somehow, this just feels totally normal. There have been no awkward silences or hushed whispers about me. Ami really is incredible, she is smart and funny, just like her Mum. And she is so grown up, this whole situation is a hell of a lot for anybody to take in and I just can't get over how mature she is for nine!

"We are here boss."

"Cheers Freddie. Come on ladies."

I slide out of the car and hold my hand out for Rachel. She follows as Freddie helps Ami out of the other side of the car.

It really is busy outside. I grab Rachel's hand and I see her grab Ami's.

Walking towards the car are George and Alex, two more of my security team.

"Wait here with Freddie a second, I just need to speak to the guys a minute." I say to a very wide eyed looking Rachel. "Hey," I lift her chin slightly, "it's going to be fine, I promise." She smiles weakly at me and I walk over to speak to George.

"Boss." He greets me.

"Hey, so what's the best way through this crowd?"

"We've found a little back alley that is quiet. We can cut through there, then it just gets a bit busier the closer to the Spinnaker you get."

"Sounds good, I'll get the girls."

I walk back over to them and see that Rachel is watching Ami and Freddie having a full blown conversation about something or other.

I'm feeling really nervous. I hate this feeling. It's not me at all. I'm really hoping they both like what I have planned.

Shit. What if they don't like heights?

"Let's go beautiful ladies, this way." I signal for them to follow George, and can see Ami smile at me.

We get to a little deserted road and walk up it.

"Where are we going?" Rach asks. "Aren't the fireworks the other way?"

"You'll see in a minute."

We get to the end of the road and people are filling all around the entrance to the Spinnaker Tower. The tower was built for the Millennium, and stands at almost 600 feet above the ground. Me and Seb abseiled down the side of it once before. It's really an incredible building. From the top deck you can see views over the entire harbour and most of Portsmouth. I imagine the fireworks are going to look spectacular from up there.

I shoot Rachel a look and she looks puzzled.

"Neither of you have an issue with heights do you?"

"No... Why?" Rach asks suspiciously.

I just wink at her and continue walking to the entrance of the tower.

When we get there we are greeted by a smartly dressed woman with a clipboard.

"Ah, Mr. Turner! Lovely to meet you. My name is Mia and I'll be taking you up. If you would like to follow me."

"Tad...?"

"Are we going up the Spinnaker?!" Ami asks excitedly.

"Maybe." I grin at her.

We walk through the doors and I look back to see Rachel smiling. Not her forced smile when secretly I know she is stressing out inside, but a genuinely happy, relaxed smile.

Mia is talking about the history of the tower, or something, but I'm not really listening. All I can focus on is Ami excitedly jumping around next to me.

My nerves have gone, and instead I just feel happy.

Freddie and Mia are talking just outside of the lift. I have booked the whole of the Sky Gardens for us, so we don't have to worry about crowds, or bloody photographers.

"Now, do we want to go up one hundred meters in just under thirty seconds, or are we going up the stairs?"

"How many steps are there?" Ami asks.

"Five hundred and sixty." Mia smiles.

"Lift!" Ami and Rachel almost shout in unison.

We all walk into the lift and the doors close.

"We are about to go at about four metres per second, so you might want to hold on!" Mia smiles at Ami.

Ami's face lights up as she holds on to the rail at the side of the lift.

I catch Rachel's eye, and she comes to stand next to me and holds my hand.

"You are amazing." She whispers in my ear and then rests her head on my shoulder.

The lift starts to move and I think my stomach is momentarily left behind.

Ami starts squealing in delight from the side of the lift and Rachel and I burst out laughing.

Before our stomachs have a chance to catch up, the lift has slowed and the doors have opened onto the view deck.

"I'm afraid we do have a few stairs to go up to get to the second viewing deck." Mia says and heads off in the direction of some steps.

Ami is already bounding ahead.

"She has wanted to come up here for ages you know." Rachel says.

"Has she? How come you've never taken her?" I ask.

"I don't know really, think I kept making excuses as I was a bit nervous."

"You don't seem nervous now."

"That's because I'm with you."

The familiar fluttering starts back in my stomach at her words and I smile at her.

"Welcome to the Sky Garden." Mia says. "We are currently standing at one hundred and ten metres above sea level. The Garden offers three hundred and sixty degree views around Portsmouth and the harbour, and on a good day you can see up to twenty three miles out. Luckily it isn't raining today, as I am sure you have seen there is no roof!" Ami and Rachel both look up.

"The fireworks are going to be amazing from here!" Ami squeaks.

"Are there going to be other people up here?" Rachel asks looking around.

"No," Mia replies, "Mr. Turner booked the whole deck."

"Of course he did!" Rach smiles whilst giving me a slightly exasperated look.

"Only the best for my girls." I wink at her and she laughs.

"The fireworks are due to start in about twenty minutes, and I have ensured the sound system here will pick up the music, so you can get the full effect. I'll be just outside the doors if you need anything else."

"Thank you so much Mia."

Ami is at the window, looking out over the sea of people underneath us. Rachel walks over to me and wraps her arms around my neck.

"How did I get so lucky?" She asks me.

"You? What about me?" I gently stroke her hair out of her face and tuck it behind her ear. "I feel like the luckiest man on the planet right now Rach."

I lean my head in and touch my forehead against hers. I see her eyes close. My arms sneak around her waist so I can pull her in close to me.

She is the one. There will never be any woman on this entire planet that will ever come close to this one. She has broken me, in the very best way. Love was never in my plan; Marriage and a family were about as far down my bucket list as having a colonoscopy. But now, standing here... I want this. I want her, and Ami, forever. The good, the utterly shit. All of it.

I want to marry her.

Might need to get her divorced though first eh?

How the fuck does someone even go about getting divorced to a spouse who is on the run from the police after murdering someone?

I make a mental to speak to my lawyers in the morning to see if they have any words of wisdom and then put all thoughts of that cunt to the back of my mind.

Rachel

I have a glass of champagne in my hand, Ami is sitting one side of me and Tad the other, and I can honestly say the only moment that has ever topped this one was when I first got to cuddle Ami after she was born.

Ami has not stopped smiling since we stepped foot in the lift, and I don't think I have either. Tad has thought of everything. Next to Ami is a little table, filled with sweets, popcorn and toffee apples. And on the floor next to my feet is a bucket of ice with a bottle of champagne chilling in it.

A voice starts talking from the speakers overhead.

"ARE YOU READY FOR SOME FIREWORKS?"

From below us the crowd erupts into loud cheers and applause.

"Let's start the countdown! Ten, nine..."

"Aahh! They're starting!" Ami shouts and jumps from her chair to stand at the window. She is shouting along with the countdown.

Music starts to play and the first firework goes up. It sends shivers all through me, I have always loved fireworks. I recognise the song as "Firestone" by Kygo, and the fireworks start to shoot up in sync with the beat of the song. Sparkling tails of red, blue, and green, erupting into huge showers of silver and gold rain.

I can almost feel my eyes start to well up. This experience is nothing short of utterly incredible. I pull Tad up and we stand behind Ami at the window.

The music changes and so do the fireworks. The way the music and the display is choreographed is just incredible.

The display has been going on for at least ten minutes and Katy Perry's "Firework" is just ending, as are the fireworks.

Ami turns around and wraps her arms around Tad.

"That was AWESOME! Thank you so much!" She says.

Oh, my heart... Tad looks taken aback for a split second, but very quickly composes himself and hugs Ami back. Those tears are back. I am just so happy.

Ami lets go of Tad and hugs me tight. She pulls my face down to hers and whispers in my ear. "Mum, don't mess this up. He's amazing."

"I don't plan to baby." I laugh at her.

The sea of red lights stretching out in front of us seems endless. Every single car in the area seems to be heading in the same direction as us.

Tad is explaining the ins and outs of fireworks to Ami, and she is listening to him intently. I didn't realise before just how intelligent Tad actually is.

"It's all to do with what goes into the firework and how it is put together. All fireworks have to have gunpowder in them, or they wouldn't go *bang*! But there are different things in them that give off different effects and colours. Different metals and salts are used depending on which colour is wanted, and tiny explosives are put inside of shells to create the stars and sparkles we see."

"Woah." Ami says.

As if on cue, another display starts to go off in the distance. Bright orange tails of light fly up into the sky. An explosion of white stars light up the sky, and each star crackles before fading away.

Our usual half hour drive home has taken over an hour and it's well past Ami's bedtime. I can see her yawning away next to me and her eyelids look heavy.

"Bed straight away when we get in okay babe?"

"Ok Mummy. Tad where do you live?"

"I don't live far from you."

"Remember the glass house?" I ask "That's Tad's house."

"No way!" Ami is suddenly wide awake again. "That house is amazing!"

"You can come round and see it one day if you'd like?" Tad says.

"Can we go now?"

"Uh I think it's a bit late, you have school in the morning." I say.

"Oh please Mum!"

"I'm away next week Ami, but how about you come round for dinner one evening when I'm home? If that's okay with you Rach?"

"That sounds like a good idea."

"Hmph, fine."

"Rach," Tad whispers to me, "I'll drop you both off at your parents, and I can come back for you if you wanted to stay at mine?"

"Of course I want to stay at yours."

I want to jump on you!

"So I know this is a hell of a lot for one day, but you fancy just popping in for two seconds while I get Ami to bed and you can just say hello to my parents? Please feel free to say no! And you could wait in the car for me? I'll only be five minutes."

"No, that sounds like a plan. Let's meet the parents too, get it all out of the way in a day!" He laughs.

"It will get my Mum off my back at least! Thank you babe."

"For what?" He kisses me softly on the forehead.

"You know, for being you."

The car pulls up outside my parents'. Tommo gets out and opens Ami's door and Tad helps me out of his side.

"Let me just run in ahead and prewarn my Mum." I give Tad a quick kiss and run to the door.

Tad

Well I didn't plan for this today!

"Come on Tad!" Ami gestures for me to follow her into the house.

Breathe.

There's those fucking nerves again.

I follow Ami inside. I can't help but remember the last time I was here. Searching for Rachel, going out of my mind worrying. And then seeing the needle in the middle of the kitchen floor. I quickly shake the thoughts from my head and as I walk through the door, I can hear Rachel talking.

"Mum, stop being silly!"

"I'm not being silly." Her Mum replies. "A bit of notice would have been nice, that's all!"

"Well ok, I'll tell him to wait in the car then!"

Phew! Saved by the–

"Mary! Stop being so ridiculous, you look fine, the house looks fine. Let the poor boy in from the cold and make him a coffee!" That must be Rachel's Dad.

Rachel walks into the hallway and jumps when she sees Ami and I standing there.

"Mum's freaking out because she hasn't dusted the ceilings, or something equally as insane." Rach's lips curve into a smile as she speaks and Ami starts laughing.

"Ami, go get your pj's on please." Ami turns and skips up the stairs.

"Dusted the ceilings?" I lean in and whisper. Rach just laughs and grabs my hand. "Come on!"

We walk into the front room. In my head, I remembered this room as cold, and dark. But under much nicer circumstances I can appreciate just what a lovely room it is. The fireplace is lit, and soft warm light is coming from lamps in the corners of the room. The crackling of the fireplace is being drowned out by some soap or another on the television. It feels so welcoming, and homely that instantly I feel some of my nerves subside, just a little at least.

Rachel's father is sitting on the sofa reading a book, and I can hear clattering coming from the kitchen. Her Dad sees me walk in, takes off his glasses and stands.

"Mr. Bennett, Thaddeus Turner, it's lovely to meet you." I say as I hold out my hand.

I can't quite read his face, and there go my nerves again, in full force.

He reaches his hand out and shakes mine.

"Please call me Leo. It's lovely to meet you Thaddeus. We have heard quite a bit about you."

"Please, call me Tad, and all good I hope." I laugh.

"Believe me, you wouldn't be standing here now unless it had all been very good." He laughs, but I definitely sense an underling threat there. And too right, after all Rachel has been through.

"Please, sit down, Mary is in the kitchen making some coffee. Rachel says you are about as much of an addict as she is?"

"I'm not sure anyone is *that* much of an addict." We both laugh and look over at Rachel who rolls her eyes and walks into the kitchen.

Well this isn't quite so bad. Now don't fuck it up...

Rachel

Mum is pouring coffee into four mugs by the time I get into the kitchen. And not just any mugs, but her really posh mugs with the gold paint that I thought she was saving for when royalty came to visit!

"What's with the fancy mugs Mum?" I ask and can't help but smirk at her.

"Just thought it would be nice to be a bit civilised, is that okay with you?" Jeez she is properly pissed I didn't give her any notice about meeting Tad. But she has been asking since I mentioned him, and he was here, so it made sense.

She hands me two mugs and I walk into the front room. Tad takes his coffee and winks at me, which just results in me smiling and blushing like a love struck teenager.

I can hear footsteps jumping down the stairs, and I turn to see Ami ready for bed coming to say goodnight.

Mum walks in, gives Dad his coffee then puts hers on the coffee table before walking over to Tad. He stands immediately, and towers over my poor little Mum. She looks up at him, takes his hand and shakes it very delicately.

"Very nice to meet you Mr. Turner." Ami and I both look at each other and desperately try to stifle a laugh. Mum has put on the most posh accent I have *ever* heard! It sounds like she is trying to impersonate the queen!

"Lovely to meet you too Mrs. Bennett." Tad raises Mum's hand and gently kisses it. God he is just swoon-worthy.

Mum goes to sit next to Dad and Tad sits back down. He takes a sip of his coffee.

"I do hope your coffee is ok." Mum says, sounding more and more posh with every word that comes out of her mouth. Dad looks over to me and Ami and we all burst out laughing.

"What is wrong with you three?" She asks, and I want to shout at her to please stop talking, but I am laughing so much I can't breathe.

Ami slides down the wall on to the floor and is clutching her stomach where she is laughing so hard. I'm desperately trying to ask her if she is ok, but just keep wailing with laughter.

"Honestly, girls, you are being ever so silly."

"Please, Nanny! Stop!" Ami screams mid laugh.

"Stop what?"

Tad and Mum are looking totally confused and I take a deep breath and compose myself.

"Sorry Mum, too much caffeine I think. Ami, say goodnight to everyone, I'll take you to bed."

Ami kisses Mum and Dad and gives Tad a hug. Mum and Dad look at each other and smile.

"Take it you had a good day then Ami?" Dad says.

"I had the best day ever!" She says as she skips out of the room. My face actually hurts from all the smiling, and now laughing, I have done today.

Ami jumps into bed and her eyes look as if they are about to close as soon as her head touches the pillow. I stroke her cheek gently, brushing the hair off of her face.

"I really like Tad, Mummy."

"I really like him too." I smile at her.

"Night Mum."

"Night baby." I kiss her and head back downstairs to find Dad and Tad engrossed in a conversation about how the Spinnaker was built.

"It was incredible to watch, they would add a layer of concrete, then wait a few days for it to fully dry before adding another. It took forever to get to the height it is." Dad gets so excited when he talks about building, it's like he is a little kid talking about what he got for Christmas. "It's just incredible, did you know it is taller than the London eye?" He asks.

"I didn't, no. I actually abseiled down it last year. It was incredible."

"Really? Mary and I see them coming down and it terrifies me even from the ground!"

"It's not all that scary when you're doing it. My brother had a real thing about heights, which is why we did it. He used to break out in a sweat even if a film showed someone on a tall building. After going down the Spinnaker though, he was so much better. We had planned to do the Millennium Dome in London next year..." I can see Tad trail off and his face drops a little. I quickly go and sit next to him and change the subject. As I sit, Tad gives my leg a gentle squeeze. I think he is trying to thank me for rescuing him from what might have been an uncomfortable conversation with my Dad.

The feel of the soft cushions under me makes me realise how utterly exhausted I am. I lean my head onto Tad's shoulder.

"It's late babe, shall we get a move on?" I say softly to him.

"Sounds good to me." He turns and kisses me on the head.

"You'll have to come round for dinner one day Tad?" Mum says in that bloody accent again, she is lucky I am so tired or I'd be on my arse laughing again. Definitely need to have a word with her about that! I think she is trying to impress Tad, but he isn't royalty! Her normal accent is just fine!

"That sounds lovely Mrs. Bennett."

"Mary, please."

Tad stands and gently pulls me up. I can't believe how tired I suddenly feel. I think I have been running on nerves and adrenaline all day. Now it's over and it has all gone so well, I feel like I have run a marathon.

I give Mum and Dad a kiss, and Tad and I walk back out to the car.

CHAPTER TEN

am very aware of heavy breathing next to my ear. But I can't see anything. I can't move. I am back here.

Panic sets in and I feel the bile rise as I realise he has got me again.

I try to move, to shout, or scream but I am paralysed with fear.

"Don't worry Rach. I'm done with you." My skin pricks into goosebumps all over my body as he growls in my ear. "But I'm not letting you have Ami."

I feel like I have been submerged in ice as my entire body starts shaking uncontrollably. I have got to get out of here, I have got to get Ami!

My alarm wakes me from yet another nightmare. I am drenched in sweat and still shaking. My dreams feel so real, it's awful. I must call that councilor again today and chase up an appointment.

I grab my phone and silence my alarm. Tad is already out of bed. I can hear the shower running, and I can see a suitcase packed and ready by the bedroom door.

I really don't want him to go. I just don't know how I will cope without him around. And that is insane, because I have always been so incredibly independent. I never ever wanted to have to rely on anyone else, yet here I am, on the verge of tears at the thought of Tad being away for just a week.

That feeling is back in the pit of my stomach. That one that doesn't normally let me down. The one where I know something bad is going to happen.

I shake my head a little and try to clear these crappy thoughts from my head.

Think positive!

I check my phone and have a text from Celine.

"Hey babe, I hope yesterday went ok. Dan says he has text you an address for R&R, the estate agents his Uncle owns. His Uncle is Chris, pop along there this morning for a chat, but you pretty much have the job anyway. Give me a call when you're done, let me know how it went. Love you xx"

Shit, the job. I had completely forgotten about that.

I briefly worked in a shop around my college hours before Ami, but apart from that I haven't ever worked. It's not that I didn't want to, Kevin just wouldn't let me. Said my place was in the house, looking after him and Ami.

I hear Tad shuffling into the bedroom. I turn to look and he is naked, except from a towel around his lower half. His skin is glistening with water from his shower. He is roughly drying his hair with a smaller towel, and I swear it looks like a scene from a movie. I tilt my head a little and smile at him.

"What?" He says as he catches me staring at him.

"Nothing." We were so tired last night we didn't even manage to have sex. I think that is the first time we have ever gone to bed and just slept! And now I'm not going to see him for an entire week. Damn!

He walks over to his drawers and drops his towel revealing his gorgeous, smooth backside. My stomach starts to flutter a little, and I have to remind myself that he is supposed to be on his way to London very soon, and I have a job interview I need to get ready for.

He turns and catches me staring, biting my lip, and laughs as he pulls on a pair of boxer shorts.

"You going to miss me?" He grins at me.

"Meh." I shrug. "Gonna miss that view though." I smile and he walks over to me.

"Well, I'm going to miss you." He says as he sits next to me and pulls me in to that special little crook where only I fit. The smooth skin on his face feels totally weird as he nuzzles his face against mine.

"I've got an interview this morning." I try to change the subject as I don't want to cry because he is going.

"Oh yeah, at the estate agents?"

I nod as he stands to finish getting ready.

"Are you nervous?"

"Uh, a little. I've never been for an interview before. Although Celine said it's more of a chat as I already pretty much have the job."

"Well that's good then. They will love you, how could they not?"

Tad

don't want to go. I don't want to leave her. We are laying on my bed having one last hug before I leave. My fingers are weaving through her beautiful hair, and I'm savouring every last second I get with her.

God she has turned me into a right wimp!

A buzzing interrupts us, as Rachel's phone starts ringing. She reaches over and we see *DCI Robins* light up her screen.

"Hello?"

I can hear Robins on the end of the phone, but I can't make out what he is saying.

Shit. I bet he is telling her about the possible sighting. That is the last thing she needs when I'm not going to be here this week.

I notice Rachel's face suddenly turn white. Yep, he's told her then.

"Ok... Uh"- He carries on talking. I grab her hand and she squeezes it tightly.

"So you don't know for sure if it actually was him?"

She is going to be pissed off you didn't tell her...

"Ok, well thanks for the update." She hangs up.

"So apparently Kevin was seen at some B&B in Leicester somewhere, but when the police went to speak to the owners, they had never seen him before?"

"Well, that's ridiculous. Why make you worry like that when it probably wasn't even him?"

"Oh my God, you knew!" She stands suddenly. "You knew and you didn't tell me!"

How the hell does she know?

"Rach, if I had for one second thought that there was anything more to it I would have told you." I stand and pull her in close to me. "Tommo called me and told me, I had my guys look into it and it turned out to be nothing. I saw no point in worrying you, especially when we still have to be careful about your blood pressure."

Her face softens a little.

"I promise, if it was anything important I would tell you. You trust me don't you?"

"With my life Tad, you know that."

"Then trust that if I don't think something is important, if I think it isn't worth stressing you over, then I won't bother telling you. But if it's something, even something tiny that I think you need to know, then I will be the first to tell you."

She leans into my chest.

"I am going to miss you really you know?" She looks up at me.

"I thought you might." I kiss her gently on the lips, but pull back before either one of us have the chance to get carried away.

"Here, I have something for you." I go to my drawers and pull out a little square box. As I turn, she catches sight of the box and her eyes widen.

"Don't get too excited, it's not jewellery!" I joke.

She opens the box to find a key.

"It's to here. So you can come and go whenever you want. Even this week, when I'm not here, if you wanted to." The words sort of tumble out, and they sound like they are coming from someone else. Fuck, why do I feel so nervous? Her smile makes my nerves disappear in a second.

"Thank you." She wraps her arms around my neck and kisses me, and no amount of me trying to hold back was ever going to be effective against the way this woman makes me feel.

My car is driving away from the house, and already I feel shitty. A month ago this was my everyday life. A month ago I wouldn't have given a second thought to going off to London whenever I needed to. And now I actually feel like I have had to leave a little part of myself back at home.

My phone starts buzzing and I see it's Scott.

"Hey Scott."

"Hey man, where are you?"

"I've only just left. I'll be with you by about ten."

"Slacking mate! I'm already here having a coffee!"

"Well you can make a start on some work then can't you?!"

"God not you as well, Suze is already up my arse about something or other this morning. Castle has left a load of shitty voicemails about this meeting we have planned. He is definitely banking on us settling out of court."

"Well he is a fucking idiot then."

"Couldn't agree more. Anyway, see you in a bit?"

"Yeah, see you soon."

Rachel

I have thrown on the closest thing to smart clothing I have. Fitted navy trousers and a white short sleeved shirt. I have dug out my most sensible pair of heels and I am making a mental reminder that I must go shopping for more suitable clothes.

I arrive outside the address that Dan sent me.

Roberts & Robinson, Luxury Property Agents.

I walk up to the glass door and take a deep breath to steady my nerves as I push the door.

And I walk straight into the fucking door. Of course it's a pull door. Why wouldn't it be? I take a step back and pray my cheeks aren't as red as they feel. I pull the door and walk in. It is very bright in here, white walls, white desks, chrome picture frames on the wall. There are four desks in here, two on each side of the room. To my left is a young looking man on the phone, he is nodding and agreeing a lot with the person on the other end of the line, and he looks completely exasperated. He waves for me to walk through and points towards a door at the back of the room. I smile my thanks at him and start walking towards it. I walk past a young woman on my right who is intently tapping away on her keyboard, she doesn't raise her head and I'm not sure if she hasn't noticed me come in, or if she is a bit of a bitch...

My hand is poised, ready to knock on the door, when suddenly it swings open and I find myself very nearly knocking on the very large stomach of a man in a suit.

"Oh, sorry." I squeak as I jump backwards.

"Rachel! Lovely to see you again!" He leans in and gives me a big kiss on the cheek.

Again? Shit when did I meet him before?!

"It's lovely to see you too. You're looking really well." I am wracking my brain, desperate for some memory of this man. He is Dan's uncle so I must have met him through him... He had a birthday party earlier this year...

The one where you and Celine each drank about twelve bottles of wine and lost an entire weekend from the hangover? Good luck remembering anything from that!

Shit!

"Please take a seat." He says as he points towards a white leather chair sitting in front of his desk. He is a very large man, both in height and stomach! Very friendly looking, his hair looks like it used to be dark brown, although most of it is covered in light greys now. If his hair was greyer and he had a beard, I can imagine him playing a good Santa at Christmas time!

"I was so sorry to read of all your troubles in the paper Rachel." He says as we both sit down.

"Oh, uh, yeah. Thanks." I never ever know what to say when people say that to me. A slightly awkward silence creeps over the both of us and I shuffle nervously in my seat.

"Anyway, I have an opening, and I think you would be perfect for the job. Essentially I just need you to meet clients when they come in, take their jackets, make them coffee, and potentially engage in a bit of chit chat."

"Coffee and chit chat I can do!" I say, smiling.

"Yes I remember! That's why I thought of you, that joke you told me about the cucumber had me and my wife laughing for weeks!"

Cucumber? What...?

I just laugh along with him even though I genuinely have no idea what he is on about. I must phone Celine later!

"So we need you Monday to Friday, nine till four, starting pay is £22,000 a year, but there is always the possibility for you to work your way up through the company. Does that all sound ok?"

"Yeah, that sounds great." I can't believe he is just giving me the job off the back of some dodgy joke I told him while very drunk on a night I don't even remember!

"I'll just introduce you to everyone, then I have some paperwork for you to fill out if that is ok?"

"Yeah, great."

It's coming up to lunch time, and I've been introduced to Kenneth and Elaine. I still haven't made my mind up about Elaine, but maybe she is just having a bad day. I've filled out all the paperwork Chris gave me and he has shown me how the phone and computer works.

"James is really the tech wiz, and he is out at meetings all day. I'm going to get him to sort out your computer log in and things and you can start tomorrow? If that's okay with you?"

"Yeah, tomorrow sounds great. Thank you so much for this."

"Not a problem. See you at nine then."

CHAPTER ELEVEN

C*el, give me a call when you've finished work. Why does Chris remember me? And what bloody joke did I tell him about a cucumber?! Apart from that all is great, I start work tomorrow. Thank Dan again for me xxx*

I found a nice little coffee shop a few doors down from R&R, and I'm now sitting having a latte.

My phone starts to ring, I answer it straight away thinking it is Celine calling me back.

"Cucumber?" I ask grinning.

"Uh, hello. Is this Rachel Bennett?"

It's not Celine.

"Oh, sorry, yes it is, I thought- Sorry, who is speaking?"

"This is Dr. Ross, I'm sorry I haven't been in touch sooner."

"Oh hi, sorry I thought it was my friend calling me back! That's not a problem."

"So, I have a cancellation this afternoon at four if you are available?"

"Oh, yeah, I'm free."

"Ok, great."

I make a note of the address she gives me and hang up. I can't believe how quickly she can see me.

A lady brings over my ham and cheese toasty while I am writing a message to Tad.

Missing you already. I start working tomorrow. 9-4 Monday to Friday. I'll work even less than you do ;) I'm seeing Dr. Ross this afternoon, so hopefully I won't punch you anymore. Love you xx

Before I have even had a chance to take a mouthful of my sandwich, my phone pings with a reply.

I told you, it was a slap! What's the place like? Nice people? I'm glad you're seeing Dr. Ross. She is great. Love you xx

Wait- She is great, as in he knows from experience? It didn't even occur to me that he might have known her because he had been a patient himself. I suppose he has gone through a lot in his life, with his Dad and his brother. It must have been hard, even more so as his Mum seems not to care about any of them. I can't imagine growing up in a home without being showered in love daily from both my parents.

I'll ask him about Dr. Ross when he is home. I don't think that is the kind of conversation for a text.

As I put my phone down, I notice a man walking towards me. He looks overly familiar, but I can't remember where I have seen him before. He half smiles and sits at the table opposite me. I try to sneak a look while he is busy on his phone. He is dressed in light blue jeans, a dark blue roll-neck top, with a light brown, tailored blazer. He looks young, but his face is plagued with worry lines, and he has deep crow's feet next to his eyes, which are framed by dark circles. He catches me looking at him and smiles weakly at me. It looks like he has gone through the mill a bit, but his smile looks genuine, and friendly. And then I remember where I have seen that smile before. The other night in the club with Celine, he was the man who rescued us from the dancefloor.

"Sorry, I was just trying to work out where I knew your face from." I blurt out as I start to feel a little awkward that I have been staring at this man for the last couple of minutes.

"Ah, yes, the club." He says as he puts his coffee down. "You're lucky, I was just leaving when I saw you and your friend, but I couldn't well leave you two alone. Best thing to do next time is stick to the walls." He laughs.

"Well thank you again."

I turn to go back to my coffee, and notice that he is still staring. I get my phone out and try to ignore him, as I'm starting to feel uncomfortable.

"No boyfriend today then?" He asks.

"Uh, no he is working." I reply while still looking at my phone.

Why is he still staring? Time to leave Rach.

I quickly take another bite of my sandwich and drain the last of my coffee.

"Was nice to see you again." I say as I stand and put my jacket back on.

"And you. I hope to see you again soon." I just awkwardly smile and hurry out of the door. Friendly turned to creepy quite fast there.

"So tell me, what brings you here?"

Dr. Ross is sitting opposite me, on a high backed leather chair, with a notepad and pen in hand. Her fringe hangs so low over her glasses, I am not entirely sure she can actually see anything. I am sitting on a sofa, with a coffee table in front of it, and a box of tissues placed just within reach.

"Well, uh, I'm not sure where to start."

"Start at the point where you realised you needed to speak to someone. We can work back and forth from there."

"Ok, well I have been having awful nightmares recently, and I accidentally punched my boyfriend in the face in the middle of one as I was still dreaming."

"And what has bought on these nightmares?"

I take a deep breath in and prepare myself.

"Well, my husband of almost a decade drugged, kidnapped and tried to kill me, after killing a woman he had been sleeping with for the last few months behind my back."

She is making notes on her paper, and nodding along. I am guessing she already knows about this from the press, as anyone who heard that would react, even slightly. But she just carries on as if I told her my goldfish had died.

"And your nightmares are about this event?"

"Yes, and no. Sometimes I dream I am back there, other times he has got me where I am at the time."

"So let's go back a little. What was your marriage like?"

"Awful. He was controlling, and just an awful person. He had been since even before we were married. I just didn't really realise it until it was too late."

"Too late?" She stops writing and looks at me.

"He messed around with my pill and I ended up pregnant. That was why we got married."

"I see. And you felt you couldn't leave because you had a child together?" She picks up her pen and paper again and starts to write furiously.

"Yes, he told me that he would drug me and report me to the police if I tried to leave him, then he would have my daughter taken away from me."

Dr. Ross doesn't say anything as her pen is scrawling on the page at lightning speed.

I take a moment to look around her office. It is exactly how I thought it would be. A book case lines the back wall with hundreds of books. Some are clearly to do with her profession, but there are loads of hard backed, fabric books, that look really old.

"So, you say he was controlling; was he also abusive? Either mentally or physically?"

My stomach starts to twist. I don't want to go back here. I don't want to think about it. More than anything I am embarrassed. The second people know what he put me through, none of them can understand why I didn't just leave. They give me looks of pity, like they think I am stupid or weak. But once someone is that deep under your skin, once you have lived daily being told you are useless, being told nobody else would ever have you, being told that your daughter would be taken from you, and you would never be able to see her again. It has an effect. I couldn't just leave.

After about an hour of talking, crying, sniffing and generally letting every emotion possible spill out into that poor woman's office, I finally leave.

My head is spinning. Dr. Ross didn't say much at all. Just kept writing and writing. I thought at one point she was going to run out of ink.

She wants me to come back on Wednesday as we ran out of time today.

I check my phone and see a missed call from Celine, and a text.

A cucumber?! What the fuck?! I honestly have no idea! He was at Dan's party, so you must have met there... I'll ask Dan when he gets home! You free to come round one evening? Xx

Ah, well she is no help!

I'm free all week babe. Tad's in London, so I'm flying solo. Let me know when is best for you and I'm there. Xx

Tad

his meeting feels like it has been going on for hours and hours. We are going over the same shit and it is starting to wind me up.

"Can I just interrupt?" Scott and the legal team are going over notes from our last meeting with Castle for the hundredth time. "We have been here hours. Everything we did was completely above board. Castle has absolutely nothing on us, because we have done nothing wrong. Let's call it a day, and just see what that little weasel has to say tomorrow."

Everyone nods in agreement and starts to gather up their papers. I snatch my phone off of the table and walk towards my office.

"What's wrong with your face?" Suze asks as I pass her office on the way to my own.

"Nothing. Coffee please Suze." I don't even stop. I just shout through her door at her as I walk into my office and slam the door shut behind me.

I cannot seem to shift my shitty mood today. I'm away from Rachel, she's got a job now, and soon she will have her own place with Ami. I just feel like once she starts to live her life after being suffocated all of these years, she will get her own space and not want me anymore. Whereas I have been waiting for her my entire life. I am ready to settle down, and live out the rest of my life with her. But I just have this awful, gnawing feeling inside of me that she is going to realise that she prefers being free, and will leave me.

My door opens and Suze storms in with a mug of coffee. She puts it down on my desk and just stands there, hands on hips.

"Thanks Suze." I say without even looking up.

She clears her throat so I look up at her.

"Why are you in such a mood?" She asks.

"I'm not... I'm just stressed about all this bullshit."

"No you aren't. You know Castle has no case and is just trying his luck. This is something else." The problem with knowing Suze most of my life, is she is able to see right through me.

"Rachel got a job this morning." I sigh as I run my fingers through my hair.

"As a prostitute?" Suze asks slowly, as if confused.

"What? No! Of course not! Why would you think that?!"

"Well I'm just struggling to see why that would put you in such a bad mood?"

"Well, she's going to move out of her parents' and into her own place..." She just looks blankly at me.

"I'm sorry, I'm missing something?" She finally says.

"I just feel like we should be moving forwards, together, not separately. If she wants to move in with me one day in the future, then why not now? Why go through the hassle of renting her own place first? Maybe she is having doubts but she doesn't want to tell me."

"Thaddeus Turner, stop being such a child." She pulls out the seat on the other side of my desk and sits. "This woman has just got out of what I can see was an absolutely terrible marriage. Men should be the very last thing on her mind, especially settling down with one. Yet, here she is, with you. From what I can see, she has spent every free moment with you since everything happened with her husband. Now trust me. If she was just *testing the waters* or what not with you, she wouldn't have stuck around. And she most certainly wouldn't have introduced you to her daughter. Don't push too hard Tad, or you will push her out."

"Thanks Suze." She's right. I know she is right.

"I'm going home now. Go home, have a glass of wine, and relax. I'll see you bright and early in the morning."

"See ya Suze."

"Hey you." I can hear her smile on the other end of the phone, and it is enough to melt away all the stress I was feeling earlier.

"Hey beautiful, how are you?"

"I'm good. How were all of your meetings?"

"Tedious. How was Dr. Ross?"

"Uh, intense. There was lots of talking, and crying. But she wants to see me again Wednesday as we ran out of time."

"The first session is always the hardest. Next one will be easier, I promise." I just want to hold her close to me. I hate that we have to be apart.

"Tad?"

"Yeah?"

"You sound like you speak from experience with Dr. Ross?"

Shit, I guess I should have seen that coming.

"Oh, yeah. Uh, Suze insisted I saw her for a few sessions after Seb died."

"I see..." She sounds like she is waiting for me to talk more about it. But I can't. I can't get into this now. I don't want to talk about him now, not with his birthday so close.

"Anyway, what's the job like?"

We end up talking for ages before there is a knock on my bedroom door. I know it's Scott. I said I'd only be a minute as he wanted to go out to get something to eat.

"Dude!" He bangs on the door. "I'm hungry, what the hell have you been doing in there?!"

"Ah shit, hang on a minute Rach." I walk over to the door and open it.

"Dude, you're not even changed yet, let's go!"

"Sorry I was on the phone, I'll be down in five minutes."

I hear him muttering to himself as I close the door behind him.

"Sorry, that was Scott, we are supposed to be going out for dinner."

"I won't keep you any longer then babe. Have fun. I love you."

"I love you too."

"Tad?" I'm just about to hang up but hear Rachel's voice.

"Yeah?"

"I'm going to sleep at yours tonight, if that's ok?"

"Of course that's ok." I can't help but smile. "I miss you baby."

"I miss you too."

CHAPTER TWELVE

The bags under Castle's blood shot eyes are big enough that he'd need to check them in separately on a flight. His hair is a mess and he looks pale. Under any other circumstances, I think I would feel sorry for the guy, but try to fuck me over? Then I lose all sympathy.

"The very fact that your own lawyers aren't here today to back you up says everything I need to know. They know you have nothing to go on."

"They aren't here because I hoped we could sort this out in a more civilised manner. I hoped we could end all of this silliness today, instead of having to drag it through the courts."

"And why, exactly, would I settle out of court with you, when I have done nothing wrong?"

"Well, that's what you say. However, it seems too coincidental, that as soon as I start to run into trouble, there you are, ready and waiting to pounce on me and make me an offer for my company you know I had no choice but to accept at that time. It's like you knew it was coming..."

"I'm sorry," Scott starts speaking. "Are you trying to blame our company, for you sniffing crack off of a hookers, uh crack." Trust Scott to lower the tone of what is supposed to be a professional meeting.

Castle's cheeks turn a rosy shade of red.

"It just seems strange that there was a photographer around at that precise moment."

"I am not in the habit of having people followed by photographers, waiting for them to slip up Mr. Castle. That is not how I work."

"So you say..." He sneers.

I can feel my temper rising.

"Mr. Castle I believe this meeting is over. I offered you a good price, and you accepted, no questions. To be honest I offered you more than I probably should have considering the dire state your company was in when I purchased it. Through *my company's* hard work, we have built the website back up, and it is finally successful again. Everyone in this room knows that you have no evidence of extortion or any other bullshit claim you are trying to make. I don't do well with people trying to con me out of money."

"Then I will see you in court Turner, and we will see how well *your* businesses do while there is a load of bad press floating around about *you*."

"How dare you." I stand with such force that I almost knock my chair over behind me. "Without me, your company would have crumbled, you wouldn't have been able to pay off that photographer you beat up, you would be bankrupt and in prison right now. I know for a fact you have nothing on this company, or on me. And so do your lawyers, or they would be here with you now. Take it to court and see how far you get. And if even one false allegation ends up in the papers, I will sue you for libel and you will lose every single thing you have managed to cling on to. Don't fuck with me Castle. You will lose." And with that I turn on my heel and leave the room, with Scott following me.

I push the button for the lift and the doors open immediately. Scott follows me in.

"Well, I think that did it." He laughs.

Rachel

Celine is pouring me another glass of prosecco, to celebrate my first day at work. She has treated me to a curry from our favourite take away and we are washing it down with our second bottle of bubbles.

"This really is my last Cel, can't show up for work hungover on my second day!" I laugh.

"Pah, you can't get a hangover on prosecco, it's impossible!"

"Look, that wine tasting guy also told us that the calories in all alcohol are halved if you drink it upside down, I don't think you can believe everything he said!"

"No, that one was definitely true. I tried it. And was sick, so you know, at least half the calories were gone." It feels so good to be here, laughing and joking with my best friend. Last night was hideous. I couldn't face staying in my room at Mum and Dad's. I didn't want to be alone, but I didn't want to wake the entire house up having a nightmare. I hoped that being at Tad's, with his smell on the bedsheets would help me sleep. But I just ended up tossing and turning all night. It was the first night we have spent apart since we have been together, and every time I closed my eyes, my brain would go into overdrive with ridiculous thoughts. Everything from there being someone hiding in the closet, to Tad cheating on me.

"So Ami likes him then?" Celine says, interrupting my ridiculous train of thought.

"Oh my God, she loves him! Cel, it was like they had known each other for years. There was no awkwardness, or radio silence. And Tad seems to love her too. He has decorated a bedroom for her."

"What?"

"Yep, he redecorated one of his spare rooms for her. All pink, with unicorns and a beautiful bed with a slide!"

"Oh my God..." Celine stares off into space, smiling the same way I do every single time I think about how amazing he is. "You got so lucky Rach."

"I know." I grin at her and take another sip of my drink. "He also turned his basement into a room for us..."

"Oooh like a sex dungeon?!" She turns to face me with a big grin on her face.

"No! I mean, sort of... But it's not like a dungeon! It just looks like another bedroom if you were to stumble upon it, but he has a rather large chest of, um, well, toys and that sort of thing... And it's soundproof." I over exaggerate a wink.

"Jesus you kinky fuckers! What's in this chest? Whips and paddles and that sort of thing?"

"Yes." I take another sip to hide my smile as I remember the nights we have spent in that room, doing things with the contents of that chest...

Fuck, I miss him!

"You two were made for each other, in every weird little way!" We both laugh. "So, I must say, hearing about your exciting sex life made me a bit- curious..."

"No way! Go on..."

"I mean nothing quite as depraved as you two! But I ordered one of those bondage for beginner kits, and- well. It was fun!" She blushes and grins into her glass.

"I'm clearly a bad influence!" I chuckle.

"Yes, you are!"

My phone starts ringing from the table and I see Tad's name lighting up my screen.

"You take that, I'll get more wine." Celine says as she passes me my phone.

"Cel! Now who is the bad influence!" I swipe to answer his call. "Hello gorgeous."

"Hey beautiful, how are you?" His voice just trickles the whole way through me, like an ice cold drink, sending chills throughout my entire body.

"I'm really good baby, you? How was your meeting?"

"I'm ok. It was stressful, but nothing I can't deal with."

"Sorry you're having a shit time."

"It was always going to be shit, I'm away from you."

I close my eyes tightly as I hear the sadness in his voice.

"I couldn't sleep last night." I say softly.

"Me neither. I mean, even if Scott hadn't been snoring loudly enough to shake the walls, I still wouldn't have been able to sleep." He half laughs, but I can hear through it. He really does miss me.

And there was you worrying he was with some other woman.

Celine walks back in clutching a bottle of white wine.

"Hey Tad." She shouts down the phone.

"Is that Celine?" He asks.

"Yeah, we were overdue a catch up."

"Tell her I say hi. I'll leave you two to it. Call me when you get in if you want. I want to hear about your day at work."

"Ok baby. I love you."

"I love you too, so much." His voice sounds like it breaks slightly, and he hangs up. It occurs to me that something else must be going on. He doesn't sound himself. I thought that the meetings this week all had to do with a deal that was already done. He shouldn't be this stressed about it.

"What's wrong?" Celine asks as she pours me more wine.

"Oh, nothing. Well- I don't know. He just sounds a bit, off."

"He is probably just stressed with work babe."

"Yeah, you're probably right." But I can't help but shake the feeling there is something he isn't telling me.

"Evening ladies." A voice calls through from the hallway as Dan gets home from work.

"Hey babe." Celine says as he walks through the door and over to the sofa.

"Hey Dan."

"Rach, how was your first day?" He says as he sits down and takes Celine's glass out of her hand.

"It was good thanks. Answering phones and making coffee all day is pretty much what I do every day anyway! I don't suppose you remember some joke I told Chris at your birthday party do you?"

"Joke?"

"Yeah, he said I told him a joke that he and his wife couldn't stop laughing at. Something about a cucumber?" Suddenly Dan almost spits his mouthful of wine across the room as he starts laughing!

"Fuck!" He laughs while wiping wine from his chin. "Oh God! I can't believe you told him that!"

"What?!" Celine and I both ask in unison.

"You were both going around telling everyone this stupid joke that wasn't particularly funny, but you two were almost dying laughing, so everyone else ended up cracking up too!"

"What bloody joke?" Celine asks again.

"How can you tell if a woman is hungry or horny?"

Oh nooooo!!!

"Oh fuck!" I don't know whether to laugh or cry as I suddenly remember not only the joke, but also exactly why everyone found it funny.

"I still don't remember!" Celine laughs. "How can you tell?!"

"Well, give her a cucumber and see which hole she stuffs it in..." I bury my head in my hands, covering my ever reddening cheeks as embarrassment creeps in while I remember what happened next.

"That's not that bad?" Cel laughs.

"No, but then you two went to find a cucumber and were attempting to demonstrate!" Dan is laughing hysterically while I am just completely devastated that my now boss saw me try to deep throat a cucumber...

I look through my fingers at Celine and we both burst into hysterical laughter.

"No wonder you got the job Rach!" Tears are streaming from Celine's eyes and she has almost fallen off the sofa from laughing so much. The sides of my stomach are killing me and I am clutching on to them desperately trying to catch my breath.

The sun is setting over the horizon, and the sound of the sea lapping at the shore is interrupted only by Ami and Tad, laughing and joking. It is warm out, but the breeze feels cold on my skin. A shiver runs down the side of my face, and I wrap my arms around myself. Tad comes over and kisses me gently on the forehead. I close my eyes and take a deep breathe in. My nostrils are filled with the sea air, Tad's beautiful scent, and the smell of fish and chips in the distance... I open my eyes and search for Ami, but I can't see her. I quickly get to my feet and run towards to sea, but she has gone.

"AMI!" I scream at the top of my lungs. "Tad, where is she?" But he has gone. The breeze has picked up and is now blowing gale, my hair is whipping around my face, and I can feel the sea spray, freezing cold on my skin.

"Tad? Ami? Where are you?" I cry out, but my voice is carried away in the wind and I make no sound.

I try to turn and run back to find help. But I can't move. Something has hold of my shoulder. I twist, and pull, and hear that laugh. I freeze, and every cell in my body turns to ice as I remember that laugh. That hysterical, crazed laugh.

I sit bolt upright and jump straight out of bed. The soft carpet under my feet helps to bring me back, and reminds me that I am safe. I am in my room at Mum and Dad's and Kevin is not here. I slump down against the wall and try to steady my breathing to calm myself down. I can hear my heart beating in my ears where it is pounding so hard.

Thank God I have another session with Dr. Ross today. I can't go on like this. I thought maybe being at home, and knowing that Mum, Dad and Ami were in the rooms next to me would comfort me and keep the nightmares at bay. But clearly not.

It's almost six, so I cancel my alarm, grab some towels and head to the bathroom for a shower.

I turn the lights up and examine my face in the mirror. My skin looks blotchy, and the black, purple rings under my eyes are so deep that they almost like more like bruises than bags. I need Tad to come home before I start to look even more like a zombie.

"Oh, morning Princess. Did you stay here last night?" Dad is up, having coffee and cornflakes at the table while reading the newspaper.

"Morning Daddy, yeah I did." I yawn as I walk past him to the kitchen for coffee. I'm going to need lots and lots of that today.

I walk over to my coffee machine and see that there is a freshly brewed pot already made in it. I find the largest mug in the cupboard and fill it to the brim, leaving just enough space for sugar.

Dad is eyeing me as I sit down at the table, he folds his newspaper and puts it down in front of him.

"Black coffee? You slept that well then hey?"

"Uh don't..." I say as I take a long sip.

"Nightmares again?" He asks.

"Yeah." I sigh as I put my mug down on the table. "I can't stand that he still affects me this much Dad. I am finally away from him, and yet he is still impacting my life just as much as before, if not more so."

"Once he is locked away you can finally start to heal properly. It's hard at the moment, not knowing where he is or what he is doing. But he will be caught, sentenced, and put away for life."

Yeah, and a life sentence here is about fifteen years. He will be out before Ami is thirty...

I quickly shake that thought away. Although the thought of him ever being free to roam the streets again completely fills me with dread.

The pattering of footsteps down the stairs signals that Ami is up. She skips into the room and over to the table.

"Morning Gramps." She kisses him on the cheek and walks towards the kitchen.

"Oh, Mum, hi!" She runs towards me with her arms open and gives me the biggest hug. I give her a big kiss on the head, and close my eyes as I hold her close to me. I can feel her try to wriggle out from my grip but I just hold on tighter.

Stop it. It was just a dream. She is here, and safe.

"Mum! I need to get breakfast!" She laughs as she manages to squirm out of my arms.

Mum follows her into the front room, she sees me and stops in her tracks.

"Good Lord Rachel, what happened to you?"

"Gee, thanks Mum." I say as I roll my eyes at her. "I just didn't sleep very well that's all."

"I have a lovely cooling eye roller on my dressing table darling, might help to shrink those a little." She gently pats my cheek as she walks past me into the kitchen. Bless her, she means well but she can be so abrupt!

CHAPTER THIRTEEN

After twenty more minutes of me talking about my past with Kevin, Dr. Ross looks like she is finally about to do some talking, which I must say I am very happy about. I don't think I have many more words left in me.

"So, from everything you have told me about your ex-husband, about how your life has been for the last ten or so years and what recently happened to you. I would say that you are suffering from post-traumatic stress disorder."

"PTSD? The thing that soldiers get when they come home from war?"

"It is not just something that members of the forces get. You have been through an extremely traumatic event, and that event is now having a major impact on your life. It is far more common that you would think, and like you, most people think it is only something that soldiers get." She puts her pen and paper down in front of her on the table, looks up at me and smiles. "We have spoken at length about the past. But let's speak about the present. How is it that you know Mr. Turner?"

Part of me wants to ask how it is that *she* knows Mr. Turner, but I think better of it.

"He is my boyfriend." That sounds utterly pathetic when I say it out loud. "Although, he is more than just a *boyfriend*. I know this sounds lame, but it feels like we were meant to be together. We met the day that Kevin killed that girl, and we have hardly been apart since. I can't describe it, but once I saw him it was kind of like I realised that he was who I had been looking for, without actually realising I was looking for anyone at all. All the time I was with Kevin, and fantasising about the day I could leave him, it wasn't ever because I wanted to be with someone else. In fact, the thought of putting myself in the position where I could be controlled again was something I promised myself I would never do. I would have been perfectly happy to be alone for the rest of my life. I had my family, and Celine, I didn't need a man, or anyone who would tell me what to do. So when I realised I was in love with Tad, a guy whom I barely knew. It was scary. It still is terrifying. I can't sleep without him next to me, and I feel like part of me is missing when he isn't around. I never wanted to rely on anyone like that."

"Do you think that if you hadn't been through all you have with Kevin, you would still feel this intensely about Tad?"

"Yes. Without a doubt. I don't want to use the term soulmate... But..." I trail off as Dr. Ross picks up her paper and pen again and starts scribbling. It wouldn't surprise me if she is just writing *Crazy* in big letters.

She looks at me again and smiles.

"I am a therapist, I am supposed to tell you that love at first sight doesn't exist, and how love takes time. I am supposed to explain to you the effect of hormones rushing around your body mimicking love. However, I am also a bit of a romantic at heart. I think that if pouring yourself into this relationship genuinely makes you happy, then you should go with it. But, please be cautious. You have never been alone, and your only experience with relationships, is one that was completely toxic. I am wondering if some kind of couple's therapy might help you both a little. Maybe not now, but some time down the line. You have been through more in one month, than most couples have in their first year. What about your daughter, what does she think about you having a new partner?"

"She actually met him recently. They got on so well, and Ami loves him. I was so surprised. I mean, Tad is amazing, but it's all so much change for Ami that I had no idea how she would be. But that girl constantly surprises me. She just takes everything in her stride. I have no idea how she does it."

"She sounds like a testament to you Rachel, I don't think you realise how incredibly you have coped with this entire situation either. Does your daughter have someone to talk to?"

"Yes, she sees a school counselor."

Dr. Ross nods and writes some more.

"Ok, so I think the best thing we can do for you is try some cognitive behaviour therapy. Essentially I want us to focus on your thoughts, feelings, beliefs; the things that make you panic, or scared. I want to focus on your nightmares. And then when we have identified your triggers and the way they make you feel, I want to rewire your brain a little." She laughs, and I nervously laugh along with her. "At the moment, when you hear something, or see something, it triggers a memory, or a sense of fear and panic. I want to change that so that when you see those same things, you think of a different memory, you feel a different feeling. You say that when you enter your parents' kitchen now you immediately panic? I want to change that. I want you to remember the hundreds of other times you have been in that room where nothing bad at all has happened. Did you bake cakes with your Mum? Maybe help cook Christmas dinner one year? Have chats with your Dad over coffee? None of those memories make you scared do they?"

I shake my head.

"So, over the next week, I would like you to write a sort of journal. Every time you feel panicked, or scared, I want you to write it down. I want you to make a note of the date and time, the source, or reason for the feeling you have. How intense it is, whether it is just a slightly uneasy feeling in your stomach, or if it is a full blown anxiety attack. And I want to know how you respond to it, do you take deep breaths, ignore it? This includes when you wake from your nightmares too, try to remember them and write down as much of the details as possible."

"This is a lot to remember!"

"Don't worry, I have it all written down for you." She stands and walks over to her desk where she picks up a sheet of paper laying on it and a little note book. "And if you are out and about, you can always use your phone to make a note, so you don't forget by the time you are home."

I thank her as she passes me the little book and paper. It looks like a worksheet and I half laugh to myself that it feels like I am getting homework.

Tad

F uck this.

I have been tossing and turning for absolutely hours. I've never had problems sleeping like this before. I throw the covers off of me and swing my legs out of bed. I run my fingers through my hair and can't help but be really pissed off with myself. I have a meeting first thing in the morning with the management team at Serenity. I need to make a good first impression, they need to like me and to trust that I am not there just to lay them all off. Harris has put the fear of God into all of his staff that I am some monster who plans to come in and strip the staff down to the bare minimum.

I grab my shirt from the end of the bed, pull it on and grab my phone. I sigh as I realise it's not even four yet.

The chill as I open my bedroom door makes me shiver. It is absolutely freezing. I turn back into my room to grab a sweatshirt out of my chest of drawers.

The floor feels like an ice rink under my feet. The whole apartment has under floor heating, and I have absolutely no idea how it works. There is a manual in one of the drawers in the kitchen, but I decide instead on a hot cup of coffee and turning the fire on in the front sitting room.

I must admit, the views from here are spectacular. I think they are the only reason I have kept this place. It's not really very *me* at all; but sitting here, in front of the fire, with views of Buckingham Palace, and all the hustle and bustle of London right under me, I just love it. Rachel will absolutely love it too. From my kitchen you can see right over Hyde Park, and from the bedroom is a gorgeous view of the Thames. This building is in the perfect place to see out over all the best bits of London.

I get out my phone and skim through the ton of notifications I have, one catches my eye. It's a notification that *"The End"* has sent me a message on Facebook. Usually I just ignore shit like this, it's probably some stupid spam message. But for some reason this one has me intrigued.

I open the message, and it sends a chill down my spine.

"I am coming for you."

Immediately my mind flashes to Kevin. But in reality, this could literally have come from anyone. I don't even bother checking the profile. I just delete the message and forget about it.

Suddenly a little notification pops up telling me I have a new message, from Rach.

Can't sleep either? X

I close down Facebook straight away and call her. She answers before I even hear the phone ring out.

"Hi you." She half whispers.

"Hey beautiful. I miss you."

"I miss you too."

"Why are you whispering?" I whisper too.

"I stayed at home again tonight. Ami and I made dinner for my parents, then she crashed out on the sofa on me"

"That sounds nice." My stomach twists. An image of Ami, Rach and I cuddled up on the sofa watching rubbish on TV, flashes in my head. Everything I want, right there in one little picture.

"It was. Until I couldn't sleep that is."

"One more sleep babe, well one more night. I'll be home Friday afternoon. I was going to ask if you wanted to spend the night here, but I've been invited to a friend's restaurant opening nearer to home. Will you come with me?"

"Of course I will. What restaurant is this?"

"It's called Miel. It's Pierre Bouvant's new place."

"Wait– Pierre Bouvant? *The* Pierre Bouvant?! He is your *friend?!*" She squeals at me, clearly forgetting she is supposed to be whispering.

"I take it you have heard of him then?!" I laugh.

"Are you kidding me? He is incredible! I have all of his books!"

"Well, do you think you can get all of your squealing out of the way before then?" I hear her take a deep breath on the other end of the phone.

"Yes, well, probably." She giggles.

"Good." I laugh. "How did your session go with Dr. Ross?"

"It was ok. I got homework!"

"Homework?!"

"Well she wants me to write a diary and gave me what looked like a worksheet to fill out."

"Do you think it will help?" I remember the diary well from my own sessions with Dr. Ross. But I still haven't discussed those with Rachel yet...

"I have no idea, she said she wants to *re-wire my brain!*"

"That's not as scary as it sounds, I promise!" I laugh, and I hear her questioning how I know that in her silence. "Anyway, how was work been?" I quickly change the subject before she asks me about my own sessions.

"It's been good. The work is easy enough, and everyone there is really nice."

"That's good." A slightly awkward silence follows and I know it's because she knows I am hiding something from her. I just can't go into any of that now. "How's Ami?"

"She's good. She keeps talking about you, it's really quite sweet. Oh, I've just remembered, my Mum asked if you were free on Sunday to come round for lunch."

"That sounds really nice."

"Great. I'll let her know. What time do you think you will be home Friday? I finish at four."

"I will probably be back around then. We don't need to leave until about seven, so at least we will have a bit of time together before we go out."

"And what are you planning on doing in that time?" She asks, I start to feel something stirring in my shorts as I can imagine the sexy smile on her face.

"Well, I won't have seen you for a whole week. I'm not sure I will be able to contain myself when I finally do see you..."

"I hope not..."

"Suddenly I'm missing you even more Rach."

"And why is that?" She teases. All I can imagine is her sitting there, barely dressed, biting her lip, waiting for me.

"You know why..." I growl down the phone at her.

"Hmmm, I'm not sure I do..."

"You're a little tease and you know it." I laugh.

"Oh, I could tease you much worse than this, *Sir...*"

Suddenly I am very aware that this underwear does not have much space, as I am feeling very confined and uncomfortable.

"Oh Rach, stop! I have to work in a couple of hours, and I can barely think straight when I'm horny and thinking about you."

"Oh ok. I was just about to tell you that I am laying naked on my bed, and my hand is wandering because your voice alone is sending tingles all the way through me. But forget I said anything..."

"You are cruel..." I smirk.

"Cruel would be this"- I hear her take a sharp breath in and then she moans as she exhales.

I am suddenly rock hard and cursing being so far away from her.

"Rachel?"

"Yes, Sir?"

"Where are your fingers?" I grab hold of my cock and squeeze tightly, imagining Rach laying there, playing with herself.

"They are exactly where you think they are." She says breathlessly. "Mine aren't as good as yours though..."

"You'll have me and my fingers back tomorrow..." I growl at her. "Now take your fingers out, and no more touching until I am home." I want her to be utterly desperate for me, completely at my mercy.

"That's not fair!" She complains.

"Rach, I am going to make you come so hard tomorrow that you won't recover for days. But only if you are a good girl, and do as I say."

"You're so bossy."

"And you love it!"

CHAPTER FOURTEEN

Rachel

drain the last of my coffee and lock my computer before heading into the little kitchen at work to pour myself another mug.

"Does anyone want a coffee?"

"That's like your fifth one this morning! I'd be buzzing around the room if I drank that much!" Elaine says.

"Ah what can I say, I'm a pro!" I laugh. After getting to know Elaine over the last couple of days, I've realised she's a nice enough woman. Just don't get on the wrong side of her!

"Seriously though, how do you sleep at night with all that caffeine whizzing round you?" She shouts through at me as I get to the pot of coffee.

"Uh, usually I sleep ok. But I haven't been sleeping at all this week, hence the massive amounts of coffee needed." Once I've stirred my sugar in I walk back over to my desk.

"Yeah, I didn't want to be rude but I did notice the um"- Elaine points to under my eyes, obviously she has noticed my beautiful bags, despite me applying half of my make-up bag to my face this morning.

"Yeah, there isn't enough make up in the world to hide these bags." I sigh.

"Stick a couple of used tea bags on your eyes for half an hour or so tonight. Works a treat."

"I'll give that a go, thanks." I smile over at her as I check my phone for the hundredth time this morning. I'm annoyed with Tad. He is obviously deliberately hiding something from me to do with Dr. Ross. He knows absolutely everything about me and it pisses me off that he feels the need to hide things from me. I get that there is a whole stigma attached to mental health, especially for men, but this is me! I look at the photo I have set as my background and feel some of my annoyance ebb away slightly. It's a photo of Tad, Ami and I that was taken on fireworks night. We are facing the window, watching a beautiful red and gold firework exploding in the sky. I am standing in the middle, with Tad's arm draped over my shoulders, and Ami standing the other side of me, holding my hand while pressing her nose up against the glass. That was honestly the most magical night of my life.

The door opens and in walks a man dressed in a very smart suit. Not just any man, but the man who rescued me in the club, and who got a bit creepy at the coffee shop on Monday. He doesn't seem phased by me sitting there at all, just smiles at me and walks right towards me.

"Hi, I have an appointment with James." He says while taking off his jacket.

I quickly open up James's calendar and see he does have an appointment for this afternoon.

"What's your name please?" I ask.

"It's Theo. Theo Peters." He smiles at me, as if he has just realised who I am.

"If you'd like to take a seat Mr. Peters, I will let James know you are here." I stand and point towards the little black sofa next to the front window. "Can I get you a coffee?"

"Black please, one sugar." He is still staring at me and hasn't made a move towards the chair yet. Something about this guy just makes me nervous, but I can't put my finger on why.

I walk to the back of the office and knock on James's door.

"Yes?" I hear from inside. I open the door and poke my head around.

"Theo Peters is here for your appointment."

"Oh yes, lovely, bring him in please."

"No problem, can I get you a coffee?"

"Oh you are a doll, yes please."

I close the door and walk into the kitchen to make the two mugs of coffee. I can hear Elaine and Theo, deep in conversation as I walk back through with two steaming mugs.

"Mr. Peters? James will see you now, if you'd like to come through."

He stands and nods at Elaine, who flutters her eyelashes at him in a rather obvious attempt at flirting with him.

He is staring right into my eyes as he walks up to me.

"Please, call me Theo." He says as he takes the mug of black coffee out of my hand.

I half smile and turn towards James's office.

After I have closed James's door I walk over to my desk and catch Elaine looking starry eyed.

"You okay over there?" I smile at her.

"He's gorgeous!" She whispers with a huge smile on her face.

I roll my eyes at her and laugh. I suppose I can see where she's coming from, but I just find him slightly creepy for some reason. But maybe I have just been spoiled with Tad, and I'll never look at any man the same way again!

I check my phone and find a text from Tad.

I haven't been able to stop thinking about you all day. I daren't stand up to meet any of my new staff because I am worried they will file a sexual harassment complaint against me! Oh, what you do to me Rachel baby...

I smile as I write a reply.

Just wait for what I am going to do to you tomorrow night...

Just as I am putting my phone down it buzzes again.

Oh Rach. I am going to have to spank you tomorrow for being such a tease.

Christ I shouldn't be texting him like this here. My insides are clenching and I can feel my cheeks are turning red.

Ok, this isn't fun anymore. I am too turned on and need to be professional at work.

"Afternoon ladies." Chris has just walked back into the office after being out at meetings all morning. He makes me jump so much that my phone slips out of my hand and hits my desk with a loud thud. He and Elaine both turn to look at my bright red, flustered face.

"Everything okay Rachel?" Chris asks.

"Oh, yeah, um yes. Sorry." A school girl type giggle erupts from my lips and Elaine smirks at me as Chris walks into his office.

I pick my phone up to check for any damage and see a reply from Tad.

You professional?! How professional does it look that I'm meeting my new staff members with a raging hard on?

I can't help but burst out laughing. I can see Elaine peering over her computer screen at me again.

"Seriously, what is up with you this afternoon?!" She asks.

"Oh, nothing!" I say absentmindedly while replying to Tad.

Please don't talk about your hard on...! I can't concentrate on anything and just made a tit out of myself in front of my boss.

My work phone starts to ring and I can see it is James calling from his office.

"Hey James."

"Rachel, my printer has died, I'm sending some documents to your printer, I need you to bring them in to me please."

"No problem." He hangs up the phone without another word and I can tell he is stressed. Right on cue the printer next to my desk whirrs to life. Once it is finished I pick the pile of paper up and take it to James.

As I get closer to his office, I can hear raised voices.

"She never put a penny in. Not one fucking penny. How is any of this fucking fair?"

"I told you, there is absolutely nothing I can do. Go back and speak to your lawyers, they will be the only ones with any power." James answers.

I knock on the door and wait until James calls me in.

The tension in the room is obvious the second I open the door. Both men sit in silence and watch me as I walk over to James's desk. Theo looks stressed beyond words. I offer him a kind smile before I hand the documents to James.

"Thanks Rachel."

I walk out, and they wait until I have closed the door until they start speaking again.

"What's going on in there?" I whisper to Elaine as I walk over to my desk.

"Poor guy. His wife left him and has put their house on the market. Apparently her lawyers are going after 65% of the house due to *emotional suffering.* He seems like the nicest man though."

"How much is the house worth?" I ask, purely because I am nosey.

"Almost two million I think. James is dealing with this as it's a bit sensitive, so I'm not sure of the details."

"Two million! Bloody hell!" I walk back over to my desk and I'm not sure whether to feel sorry for Theo or not. I have absolutely no idea who he is, and as much as I get a weird vibe from him, he did look utterly broken in that room with James. However, there were plenty of times when Kevin could pull off the broken look to get the sympathy vote.

"What's going on with you anyway?" Elaine asks as I sit down.

"What do you mean?"

"Well you've been glued to your phone, and keep going all red and giggly!"

"Oh." I smile as I feel my cheeks burning again.

"Only a man could make someone look like that..." She probes and stares at me, waiting for me to spill.

I just shrug and smile at her.

"Forgive my snooping, but is it true what the papers are saying? That you and Thaddeus Turner are a thing?" I have completely avoided all papers and magazines since they started writing stories about everything going on with Kevin. And then after Tad and I were spotted out together, the papers realised who I was and started creating these absolutely ridiculous stories. One paper suggested that I had been having an affair with Tad which sent Kevin into a jealous rage, which is why he killed that girl. I don't know the rest of the stories out there as I refuse to even acknowledge them, but I imagine they are equally as insane.

We haven't publically confirmed we are a couple, Tad wanted to, but I just don't see why it is anyone else's business.

"Uh, I'm not sure what the papers are saying, but we are a thing I suppose, but a very recent thing."

"You lucky cow!"

I can't help but laugh. I forget sometimes that he is a something of a minor celebrity. I'm not sure how I didn't know who he was before I met him. Celine forwarded me a load of newspaper and magazine articles as well as TV interviews that she found while Googling him. He seems to be in the news every week or so for something or other.

I check my phone to see another message from Tad.

It's not nice when someone is teasing you and there is nothing you can do about it, is it? I have to go into a meeting now, I'll call you later. Xx P.S Just imagine me sinking my hard cock inside of you tomorrow, and then fucking you until you scream... P.P.S. Love you x

Oh... My cheeks are burning scarlet and I am chewing on my lip, trying to suppress half a moan. I don't know how I can wait another day to see him. God I need him, now!

I look up and Elaine is staring at me.

"I wish I could meet a man as good looking and rich as Thaddeus Turner, who made my face go that shade of red just with a text message!" We both laugh and I try to compose myself.

James's door opens and a deflated looking Theo walks out. His eyes catch mine, and for a second it looks as if he is furious with me. His face quickly softens and he walks up to me.

"Lovely seeing you again Rachel." He smiles at me.

"And you." He turns to walk out and then seems to change his mind. "I don't suppose you fancy a drink some time, do you?"

Fuck.

"I'm sorry, like I said, I have a boyfriend."

"Pity." He turns and walks out without another word.

CHAPTER FIFTEEN

Tad

Fuck! I am so late! I was supposed to be home hours ago, but there had been a huge accident coming out of London which saw us stuck in the middle of hundreds of cars for over two hours.

So much for getting to fuck Rachel's brains out before we have to head out.

I walk through my door and into my lounge to see Rachel perched on the edge of the footstool. She looks absolutely stunning. But mad. Really mad.

"Where the hell have you been? I've been worried sick!"

"I'm so sorry, there was a huge accident and we were sat in traffic for so long! My phone died and then the car charger wouldn't work."

I pick her up off of the stool and my stomach does a somersault.

"I'm sorry, don't be mad."

"I was just wor"-

I can't wait any longer. I lean in and kiss her with such force I almost knock her backwards. Immediately her hands are running through my hair, pulling, sending electricity from my head throughout my entire body. She pushes herself into me, her breasts are squashed up against my chest, and my cock is getting harder by the second as it rubs against her.

"Fuck, I missed you." I whisper through our kiss.

She doesn't need to say anything back. Her tongue searches deeper into my mouth and I know full well she has missed me too.

Suddenly the doorbell goes and I remember that we have somewhere we need to be tonight.

She pulls back.

"The door..." She says as she tries to catch her breath.

"Fuck the door."

"What if it's important?" She says as she takes a step back and flattens her dress.

"It's just the car to take us out. But we don't have to go."

I take a step towards her and she holds her hand out to stop me.

"Well I'm going! I want to meet Pierre Bouvant!"

"And I want to stay here and make love to you." I say in my sexiest voice as I cup her face with my hand.

"No you don't. You want to fuck me senseless!" She teases and I laugh. She can see right through me.

"Ok, fine, either way. I don't feel like going out."

The doorbell goes again and I get my phone out to text that we don't need the car anymore.

"Tad, if you make me stay in tonight, and miss seeing one of my heroes, then I will not be having sex with you." She folds her arms across her chest and gives me a look that says she is deadly serious.

"Fine." I sigh. "Go and get in the car, give me two minutes to, uh, sort myself out and I'll be there." Her face lights up and she gives me a kiss on the cheek. She grabs a little bag and skips off towards the front door.

I groan loudly to myself as I try to rearrange the bulge in my trousers.

We are sitting in the back of the car and I am willing the night to be over already. Rachel has her head buried in my neck, and every breath on my skin leaves me tingling, and wanting more. Every so often she kisses my neck and it takes everything in me not to just lay her down and fuck her right here.

"How was your week?" She asks.

"Long, and boring. I just wanted to be home with you." I reply as I wrap my fingers around hers. Her breath hitches as my thumb brushes against the bare skin, peeping out from the bottom of her dress.

"Don't get any ideas." She whispers in my ear. "I have underwear on tonight." She nips my ear before pulling away and I feel it right down in the pit of my stomach.

"Damn." I growl at her before I lean in and kiss her beautiful soft lips.

I feel the car slow and stop as we arrive at *Miel*.

Before we have even stepped foot out of the car I can see a frenzy of flashes as photographers are snapping pictures of everyone walking in.

"I think it is safe to assume that everyone will know we are together by the time the papers come out tomorrow..." I say to her through a nervous smile.

"Good." She beams at me and kisses me briefly on the cheek before the driver gets out and goes to open my door.

I step out, turn and offer my hand to Rach.

I didn't get a chance to appreciate just how beautiful she looks tonight. She is dressed in a short dress, covered in bluey silver sequins. It has long sleeves and, unfortunately for me, her cleavage is not on show at all tonight. But the back of the dress dips right down, and shows almost all of her back. Her hair is down and has a slight curl at the ends, she just looks stunning.

She looks up at me and smiles as she takes my hand. I pull her out of the car and wrap my fingers around hers as we turn into the blinding flashes of the press. I feel her hand tighten around mine, and I give her a reassuring squeeze as we start to walk forwards.

As we get closer to the doors, I see Pierre standing there greeting all of his guests. I nudge Rachel's shoulder with my own and nod my head in his direction. She turns to look and suddenly squeezes my hand and turns to look at me with wide, excited eyes.

"That's Pierre Bouvant!" She silently mouths at me through a huge grin, and I can't help but laugh. I lean in close to her.

"Come on, I'll introduce you." I'm sure I hear a squeal as I start walking again!

"Pierre!" I say as I hold my hand out.

"Tad! Comment ça va mon ami?" He reels off in his perfect French.

"Je vais bien merci. Et toi?" Rachel shoots her head around and looks at me with an open mouthed smile.

"Tres bein! And who is this beauty?" He grabs hold of Rachel's hand and brings it to his lips. She is doing an impressive job of keeping her cool, even if I can see her feet shuffling around nervously under her.

"This is my wonderful girlfriend Rachel." I say as I pull her in close to me.

"Girlfriend?!" He looks surprised at me and then takes Rachel's hand to his lips once more. "C'est un plaisir de vous rencontrer!" This time she visibly blushes and I feel the need to snatch her hand from his. Luckily I don't need to as he lets go and points us in the direction of the bar.

"Please, go and enjoy a drink and I will catch up with you in a little while."

As we walk over to the bar Rachel turns to me with the biggest smile on her face.

"You speak French?!"

"Mais bien sûr!" I wink at her.

"Oh God, stop that or I won't be held responsible for my actions!" She laughs.

We get to the bar and a server hands us each a glass of champagne.

"To us." I say as I clink my glass with hers. "I don't think I told you tonight how incredibly beautiful you look." The edges of her ruby lips curve into a smile that makes my stomach flutter.

"Thank you. You look pretty hot yourself." She takes another sip of her drink, and leaves a perfect imprint of her bottom lip on the glass. My mind wanders and I suddenly have an image of those lips wrapped around my cock, leaving her mark in lipstick.

"So how do you know Pierre Bouvant then?" She says bringing me back from my fantasy and I curse my inability to keep my penis under control.

"He was actually one of my first business ventures. He worked at a restaurant that my Dad would take us to quite often. He was so talented, but the owner was a bit of a prick, thought he knew it all and wouldn't let Pierre put his creative mark on anything. Anyway the place got less and less popular and the owner eventually sold. I got together every penny I could for a deposit and managed to buy it. I had absolutely no idea what I was doing! Only that I wanted Pierre to be head chef because I had complete faith in him. Somehow we made it work, and he bought the restaurant from me less than a year later as it was so successful."

"I had no idea he had ever worked around here! I just remember seeing him on the telly one morning, he made the most incredible looking pie! And then he seemed to be everywhere."

There is a tap on my shoulder and I turn to find a young man with a camera.

"Mr. Turner, could I get a photo please?" I pull Rachel in close to me and turn to look at the camera. The flash is almost blinding so close up. I turn to look at Rachel and her whole face is glowing. I can't help but smile back at her. I see another flash from the corner of my eye.

"Thank you Mr. Turner, and...?" He waits for Rachel's name.

"Rachel Bennett." She smiles at him.

The guys face lights up as he makes a note on a piece of paper.

Rachel

We are on our ninth course of food and I feel like my stomach is about to explode! They have only been tiny plates as it's a tasting menu, but with all the wine and champagne, it feels like I have eaten a weeks worth of food in one sitting.

Pierre walks out of the kitchen straight over to us.

"How has the food been mes amies?" He asks in his incredible French accent.

"It's absolutely amazing! But please tell me there isn't much more. I am stuffed!" I laugh.

"Ah just the dessert and some petits fours with coffee ma chérie."

Oh my God! Mum's face will be a picture when I tell her that Pierre Bouvant just called me his *chérie!*

"Tad, can I borrow you pour une minute?"

"Bein sûr!" Tad says as he stands. "I'll be back in a minute baby." He gently strokes my cheek as he walks away with Pierre and I feel it, right in between my legs. Hearing Tad speak in what has to be the sexiest language on the planet has done absolutely nothing to calm the fire that's been raging inside me since he first stepped back into his house.

I had been sitting there for hours, waiting for him to walk through that door so I could jump straight on him. I'd be fantasising about every other time he had kissed me, touched me, fucked me... I was getting myself so wound up I had to go for a cold shower to try to calm myself down. And then he turned up too late for us to be able to do anything about it. The effects of the cold shower wore off the second he touched me.

I shake my head in a vain attempt to stop thinking about naked Tad and reach down for my bag so I can check my phone.

There's a text from Ami saying goodnight and asking me to say Hi to Tad for her, and a couple of missed calls from a withheld number. They must have left a voicemail, and my finger hovers nervously over the icon to call my messages. Realistically, it's probably some sales call or some other innocent albeit rather annoying phone call. However as I go to check, my heart starts pounding in my chest and my stomach starts to knot. I make a mental note to add this to the diary for Dr. Ross, but before I'm able to call my voicemail Tad appears back at the table. I quickly put my phone back in my bag and leave it until later.

"Everything ok?" Tad asks, looking slightly concerned as he sits down at the table.

"Yeah fine, Ami says hi." I smile.

"You looked stressed when I came back over?" He pushes.

"Honestly, I'm ok." I grab his hand over the table and smile again.

He gently strokes his thumb over my knuckles and it makes my stomach jump. I look up at him and he is staring right at me. His eyes are burning with the same desire that is coursing through my body, and I feel it in every inch of me. The chatter and music around us seems to soften as we continuing just staring at one another. It feels as though everyone around us has disappeared. It's only me and Tad in the room. I sneak my foot forwards under the table until I feel it touch his leg, and I gently stroke it up and down. His eyelids look heavy and he half closes his eyes. Our hands tighten around each other's. His lips part slightly as my foot travels further up his leg, and the only thing stopping me from throwing my chair backwards and jumping across the table to him is the sudden appearance of dessert. I blink and pull my hand from Tad's and it's like someone has unmuted the restaurant. The music and talking is blaring in my ears again, and the waiter puts our plates down, while looking slightly uncomfortable.

Dessert is a selection of profiteroles, served with cream and three different sauces. I wolf it down without any appreciation what so ever for what I am eating. I just need this night to end now so I can get home and have mind blowing sex with the gorgeous man sitting opposite me. Tad has finished his in record time too, and it seems we are on the same page.

"It's not like me to ever turn down coffee, but what are the chances of us being able to sneak away, like, now?" I lean in and whisper to him.

The corners of his lips turn up into a devilish smile.

"Why are you so eager to get home?" He says as he slowly licks some cream from the end of his finger. My whole body tingles so much it makes me noticeably shudder.

"You know why..." I say in a voice so husky I barely recognise it as my own.

"Let me say bye to Pierre and then we can go ok?" I nod as I don't trust my voice at the moment.

My fingers start to strum on the table as I wait for Tad to come back. He walks through a set of doors with Pierre and they both walk over to the table.

"You cannot go yet ma chérie, I am just finishing up and I would like to have a drink with you both."

Never in my life did I imagine I'd want to tell Pierre Bouvant to fuck off! However, I fake my most polite smile and agree to one drink.

Tad walks up beside me and holds his hand out. I take it and he pulls me up and towards a door to the side of the room.

"Where are we going?" I ask, intrigued.

"You'll see." He says as he winks at me.

We reach a set of stairs and he climbs them two at a time, I curse my decision to wear heels as I end up taking far longer than him to get up the two flights of stairs.

He has disappeared by the time I reach the top.

"Tad, where are you?"

"Over here." His voice calls through an open door.

I push the door open enough to walk through and am immediately hit by the freezing cold night air. I wrap my arms around my chest and see Tad sitting on a stool, next to what looks like a bar. Above his head is a heater, so I quickly race over to him and he wraps his arms around me to warm me up.

"Have my jacket." He says as he starts taking it off.

"No, I'm fine here babe." He has his legs wrapped around mine and his arms around my waist and I can feel the heat radiating from him.

"It's nice up here." I say as I look around. There are wooden benches scattered under a huge canopy, covered in grape vines. The bar is beautiful, but mostly empty.

"Pierre wanted to open this tonight too, but he has had issues with builders and electrics or something or other. But it means we get a bit of time alone..." I turn to look at Tad, he is running his teeth along his bottom lip and his eyes are darting between mine and my lips. I feel my insides clenching as I realise why he has bought me up here. I trail my hands up his back to his neck, and see his eyes close in response. Our breathing starts to speed up, and I can feel a growing bulge from within his trousers.

I lean in and gently touch my lips to his, and I swear I feel a spark. I go to pull my head back but he pulls me in closer and locks his lips on mine. His tongue begins flicking at my own and I open my lips over his. God, I have missed his. Our breathing is heavy and fast. One hand is grabbing his soft hair, the other is trailing around from his back, and I move my hand lower until it reaches the top of his leg. His kiss becomes rougher, and his grip on me tighter. I slowly move my hand across and he moans deeply into my mouth as I skim across the swelling in his trousers.

Without warning he stands and lifts me up. I wrap my legs around his waist and he turns and rests me on the bar stool.

"I need to fuck you Rach." He growls into my lips.

"Fuck me then." I whisper between kissing and trying to catch my breath.

He starts to fumble with his belt, and then I hear the sound of Tad's zip quickly being pulled down.

"Lift up." He demands as he grabs both sides of my knickers from under my dress. I do as I am told and he pulls them down and off in one quick flick.

He grabs my arse and pulls me forwards so I can feel him right there. I rest one hand on the bar and one on his shoulders to try to steady myself. He pushes forwards, painfully slowly. His eyes close and his mouth opens wide as we become one again. The feel of him filling me up, stretching every inch of me is incredible. I whimper as he slowly pulls out again, his cock passing my swollen g spot. Suddenly he quickly thrusts forward, almost knocking me off the stool. I grip him and the bar so tightly that my knuckles have turned white. He starts to fuck me hard and I can already feel my world falling apart.

His eyes are clenched tightly closed and his brow is furrowed, and I know he is as close as I am already. He brings me closer and closer with every thrust, and then I start to tumble. Reality stops, the only two things in existence right now are me and Tad, there is nothing else. My moans are getting louder, and I know I need to be quiet but I have no control over any part of me right now. I throw my head backwards as I explode from the inside out and I scream. Tads hand pushes my head up and I open my eyes just in time to see him close his as he stills and groans. I can feel him pulsing as every last drop of come gushes inside of me.

He rests his head on my chest and I wrap my arms around him as we catch our breath.

"We should go back down." He says as he lifts his head.

He pulls out of me, and I immediately clench my legs together as hard as possible to stop his come from spilling out of me.

"There's a bathroom just inside the doors babe." Tad half laughs as I try to slide off of the stool without opening my legs at all.

"Could you pass me my underwear please?" I point in the direction of a bench where my knickers have landed next to it.

I shuffle over to the door and Tad opens it for me.

"You go down, I'll meet you in a minute." I say as I waddle sexily into the bathroom.

Tad

Pierre is at the bar when I get back downstairs.

"Ah, there you are! I thought you had left!" He says as he hands a glass of whiskey to me.

"I was just giving Rachel a tour."

"A tour eh?" He laughs as he taps his glass on mine. I take a sip and look around just as Rachel is walking out of the doors. She sees us and walks over.

"A girlfriend huh? Never thought I would see the day mon ami!" I just laugh as I watch Rachel walk towards us, looking absolutely perfect.

I pull her in close to me and I can't seem to wipe the smile off of my face.

"A drink ma chérie?" Pierre asks Rach.

"White wine would be lovely thank you." Her voice has that slight huskiness to it that she gets after we have had sex and it just makes my smile even bigger.

Rachel thanks Pierre as he hands her a glass of wine.

"This is my own wine, I save it for special guests, enjoy."

She takes a sip and closes her eyes.

"That is incredible!" She says before taking another sip.

"The grapes up on the roof I had brought here from my vineyard in Bordeaux. I'm not sure how they will fare with the cold weather here but nous verrons."

We all talk for a while and Pierre invites us round to his house one night soon for dinner. Rachel has just finished her second glass of Pierre's wine, and I can tell she is eager to leave.

"Pierre, it has been absolutely lovely, but I'm afraid we must be going."

"Ah bein sûr! I will let you two love birds head home. Thank you so much for coming." He leans in and gives Rachel a kiss on both cheeks, and he pulls me in for a big hug.

"Elle est tres belle. Je suis content que tu aies trouvé quelqu'un."

"Merci beaucoup Pierre."

He pats me on the back as we walk off.

"What did he say?" Rach asks when we are out of earshot.

"He said you are beautiful and he is glad I have found someone." I smile at her.

"Pierre Bouvant thinks I am beautiful?!" She half squeals and I roll my eyes and laugh at her.

CHAPTER SIXTEEN

Rachel

I open my eyes and see Tad sitting next to me with a tray full of bacon sandwiches and coffee. In a vase next to the bed are a beautiful bunch of sunflowers.

"What's all this for?" I ask puzzled.

"Well, as pathetic as this sounds, today is our one month anniversary. I thought I'd do something special."

Fuck!

"Shit! I didn't even realise!" I say feeling incredibly guilty.

"It's ok! You have a lot going on! I only realised a couple of days ago myself. Then I thought I'd worked it out wrong because I can't believe it's only been a month."

"I know... It feels so much longer."

A month? Four weeks? How?! I feel like I have known Tad for years.

"Thank you Tad, this is so sweet." I sometimes wonder if it is in any way possible for a heart to just be so full of love for someone that it bursts. Every day, every little thing this man does for me makes me love him more and more, and I don't know how one heart can hold so much love.

"How do you feel about booking a little holiday for us today?"

"Ooh really? Where were you thinking?" I ask excitedly.

"I'm not sure, where is somewhere you have always wanted to go?"

"Anywhere really! I've only ever been to Paris, and that was only to Disney."

"You've never been abroad?" Tad says in shock.

"Well, no... When I was a kid, Mum and Dad always stayed here when we went away. I've been all over the UK, but that's it."

"Well how about a cruise then? We could do a Mediterranean one, France, Italy and Spain?"

He looks so excited, but that sounds expensive. I can't afford that, and I hate the thought of him having to pay for everything.

"We could just do a weekend in Paris or Rome or something?"

"Why do just a weekend in one place when we can spend a week seeing loads of different places? The world is a big place Rach, you have a lot of catching up to do!" He chuckles and strokes my face softly.

"It just sounds really expensive." I chew my lip anxiously as I really don't want to have this conversation now.

"Oh Rach! You have to stop making the money thing a big deal. I have lots of money, so what? If I want to spend it on you then that's my choice right? And one day it will all be our money anyway so don't even"- My head quickly turns to face him. He is scratching his head and his cheeks have gone red.

"What does that mean?" I smirk at him.

"Well... Uh just- you know..." He stutters.

"No, I don't. You'll have to enlighten me." I tease.

"Well, I want to marry you Rachel. I mean not now- don't take that as a proposal. But, you know... One day."

Just the small matter of me being married to a psychopath to deal with first hey?

I have absolutely no idea what to say. I just sit in stunned silence for a moment while I try to process that this beautiful hunk of a man wants to marry me. Yes, crazy me with stupid amounts of baggage, both emotional and in the form of a child... And yet he wants to marry me.

"I mean obviously I'm thinking way in the future... I mean I don't even know if you would ever want to get married again, or married to me... I"-

I lean in and kiss him on the lips to shut him up.

"Of course I want to marry you, one day, you dope!" He kisses me back and I feel his body soften as he relaxes.

"So, a cruise then?" I say softly.

Later that evening, I am sitting in a glorious, hot bubble bath, being fed strawberries by Tad, who is sitting behind me. We spent hours in the travel agents, Tad wanted everything to be just perfect, and every cruise we found, there was something missing. Eventually we found one that sounds perfect. We fly out to Barcelona, then spend a day in Palma de Mallorca, a day in Marseille; where Tad has booked for us to go snorkeling. Then a day in Florence, with a trip to see the leaning tower of Pisa. The next day is Rome, and I am so excited to see the Colosseum! Then a day in Naples before spending an entire day on the ship on the way back to Barcelona.

I can't even put into words how incredibly excited I am that I get to see so much of the world in just one week, after thinking I would never really get to go anywhere.

Tad has booked us a suite with a private balcony. It looks incredible. He sent me away when it came to pay though, so I absolutely dread to think how much it cost. But I suppose if this is going to work between us I am going to have to accept that Tad does, and will always earn far more money than I could ever dream of...

Tad's smooth hands snake across my stomach under the water, interrupting my thoughts.

"What are you thinking about?" He asks huskily.

"Just how much money you have..."

"Huh, an odd time and place to be thinking about that but ok!" He laughs and starts to stroke my stomach with his fingertips.

"It's just all new to me that's all. I mean, I've never struggled really for money, but if I wanted anything over my *allowance* I'd have to beg, borrow or steal. I had to save up for months and months just to get a new phone after my one died. But I'm betting now, if I even mentioned to you that my phone was on its way out, you would buy me some new snazzy one without me even having to ask."

"Are you saying you need a new phone?" Tad says and I turn to see him smirking at me.

"That is not what I meant!" I say as I playfully splash water at him.

"Just stop worrying about it babe. It's only money." His hands start to trail further up my skin until his fingertips are brushing the bottom of my breasts. His touch makes tiny little bumps erupt all over the skin on my chest, and my nipples harden as his hands move higher.

"You're so fucking sexy Rachel." He growls in my ear, which sends a sudden rush of blood downwards, and I start to feel heat radiating out from in between my legs.

My chest flushes a shade of pink as Tad's hand changes course and starts to trail down under the water. I part my legs slightly, in anticipation of what is to come. He traces his fingers around the top of my leg, before skimming all the way across to my other leg, teasing me, and leaving me desperate for his touch. I turn my head to look at him, his eyes stare hungrily into my own and he holds my gaze as his hand finally moves to where I desperately want it to be.

"Mmm." He sighs. "I don't think I will ever be able to get my fill of this."

Tad and I are recovering on the sofa, wrapped in towels, with a giant pizza each. He had planned for us to go out, but the thought of having to get ready was just too much effort. A nice quiet night in with him seemed like a better idea to me anyway.

"This was a much better idea than going out." He says as he closes the lid of his pizza box.

"It really was. I don't think it would go down very well if we turned up at a restaurant half naked." I laugh.

A soft buzzing interrupts us and I realise it is coming from my phone on the other end of the sofa.

I stretch out to grab it and hear Tad sigh. I turn around and he is staring at me, half biting his bottom lip.

"Behave yourself!" I laugh.

I check my phone and see another missed call from a withheld number, and a voicemail. A shiver runs through me as I remember the voicemail I didn't listen to yesterday.

I can feel my heart start to race and I suddenly feel full, on the verge of sick.

"Babe, what's wrong?" Tad shoots up from the other side of the sofa and comes to sit next to me as he tries to look at my phone.

"It's honestly nothing, I'm just being stupid that's all."

"Rach, you are not stupid, tell me."

I show him my phone, the missed calls are still lit up on my screen.

"Who are they from?" He asks, concerned.

"I don't know. I haven't listened to the messages yet..." I say as I stare blankly at the screen.

"Do you want me to listen for you?" He gently tucks a wayward strand of hair behind my ear and lets his hand trail all the way down to my shoulder, which he squeezes gently.

"No, it's ok, it's probably nothing..." I say as convincingly as I can manage.

I hold down my voicemail button and put the call on speakerphone. The familiar female voice begins telling me that I have two new voicemails. The voice that follows turns my blood ice cold. It is tinny and echoing, unnaturally deep and has clearly been altered by some sort of voice changer.

"Please pass along my regards to your boyfriend. He has been ignoring me, and I don't like to be ignored. The end is coming Rachel."

My heart is racing and I am finding it hard to slow my breathing. Even through the voice changer it is obvious exactly who the message is from.

Tad has pulled me into his chest and tries to take my phone from me.

"No, I need to hear the other one." I say as I snatch the phone away from his hand.

"I'm just curious. Does he really think he can take everything from me, ruin my life, and then sail off into the sunset with his little ready-made family? I have news for you both. Life doesn't work that way. I will take it all from him, leave him with nothing, the same way he did to me."

Tad

A loud bang echoes around my kitchen as I slam my phone down on the counter in sheer frustration.

"What was that?" Rachel comes running in from the front room, clearly panicked.

"Sorry babe, I dropped my phone." I lie.

"What did Robins say?" Rachel asks as she leans into me.

"Nothing. The guy is a useless prick. He said he will send someone over when he can to listen to the messages... Seems to think it is more likely to be a prankster than to be Kevin." I can feel my blood boiling as I am telling her this. "Fuck!" I slam both my hands down hard on the counter and feel Rachel stiffen net to me.

I turn to look at her, and she is wide eyed.

"Shit, I'm sorry Rachel, come here." I pull her into my arms and wrap them tightly around her while breathing in her soft, sweet smell. "I just get so angry. I can't understand why they won't take this more seriously. He already got hold of you once. I cannot let that happen again." I feel her nails digging into my sides as she holds me tightly.

"I'm sorry I've put you in this position Tad." She whispers.

"Hey, look at me." I pull her chin up towards my face. "Don't you ever apologise for any of this. None of it is your fault." She smiles weakly at me before resting her cheek against my chest.

"Why don't you go up to bed? I'll be up in a second. I just want to call Tommo to check in."

"Ok, I'm going to give Ami a call and say goodnight anyway." She pecks me on the cheek and turns to walk out of the kitchen.

"Tell her I said hi." I shout after her. She turns around and smiles at me before heading up the stairs.

I can feel my heart thundering in my chest.

Fuck!

How has that *thing* not been found yet? I swear if he ever lays a finger on Rachel again, or Ami, I will kill him. I will hunt him down for as long as it takes and end him and I will have absolutely no regrets about it...

"Yes boss." Tommo answers my call.

"Rachel has had a couple of calls from *him*. As much as I want to believe they are just empty threats, I want to make sure two of you are watching Rachel and Amelia at all times. And can you please organise for mine and Rachel's parents houses to have CCTV fitted and some sort of alarm system. I will speak to them tomorrow, I'm sure they will be fine about it."

"No problem boss."

"Cheers Tommo." I hang up and can hear a soft laugh coming from upstairs.

I turn off all the lights and double check the lock on my front door before walking upstairs.

I can hear Rachel talking on the phone with Ami. She sounds so relaxed and happy, she really can be a good actress. Sometimes it's easy to see how she managed to hide Kevin's abuse for so long. But other times she is like an open book. I can just look at her and know almost exactly what she is thinking.

I walk into my room and see Rachel laying on her stomach across my bed. Her perfectly round behind is swaying gently from side to side, barely concealed behind a small towel. I pause for a second, purely to admire the wonderful sight in front of me.

"How's Ami?" I ask when she has said goodnight and hung up the phone.

"She's ok. She says hi. Apparently Mum has scrubbed every inch of the house and lost her shit at Dad earlier for walking through the kitchen in his shoes!" She laughs. "I hope you like lamb, she's bought like an entire sheep!" I go to sit next to Rachel on the bed and she shuffles across to lean her head into me.

"Are you ok?" I gently pull her on to my lap and wrap my arms around her tightly.

"I'm ok. I have you looking out for me. He'll get caught." Her voice wobbles slightly. She doesn't sound convinced at all.

"Let's go to sleep baby. It sounds like we are going to have a pretty crazy day tomorrow."

She tilts her head up towards me, her eyes are incredible. An intense blue and grey that almost looks as if it swirling and twinkling right in front of my very eyes. I get completely lost for a moment, and something inside of me pulls my lips towards hers without any thought. I don't think I will ever get my fill of this beautiful woman.

CHAPTER SEVENTEEN

The wine and food are flowing, and Rachel's Mum seems to have finally dropped her pretend accent. She has gone all out; the table has been laid as if we were in a restaurant. Rachel says that her Mum is even using her wedding china, and she has treated me like royalty the entire time I've been here. It's incredibly sweet, if a little funny.

"That really was delicious, thank you so much Mary." I lay my knife and fork across my plate and lean back to try to allow the insane amount of food to settle in my stomach.

"I hope you aren't too full Tad? Ami and I made chocolate fudge cake for dessert!"

Jesus more food?! How is Rachel not the size of a bus?!

"I'm sure I can squeeze a tiny slice in!" I laugh, but I can feel my stomach protesting from under my increasingly tight belt.

"Mummy, after lunch can I go and see Tad's house?" Ami asks.

Rachel turns to look at me.

"It's fine with me if it's okay with you?" I say before Rachel can say anything. She takes a sharp breath in, as if she is about to say something. But then stops and smiles.

"Ok baby, I guess you can go see it, just quickly though ok?"

"Yes! Thanks Mum!"

"Where do you live Tad?" Rachel's Dad asks me.

"Tad lives in the big glass house!" Ami says excitedly before I even have the chance to open my mouth.

"Oh wow! We watched that huge glass wall go up. What a lovely house." Her Dad says.

"Thank you. The view is just amazing, and I felt I was missing too much having to look through small windows!"

I can see Rachel and Ami looking bored from the corner of my eye as me and her Dad sit and talk about the construction of my house. To be honest, it's not the most exciting thing we could be talking about, but he really does seem to love all things building and design.

"Here you go." Mary puts a plate in front of me, with a slice of cake. Ok, it is less of a slice and more like a quarter of the cake. My stomach groans at me and I hear Rachel sniggering from next to me.

"Didn't I say a small slice?" I lean in and whisper to her.

"Trust me, that is small!" She laughs.

Rachel

Poor Tad looks defeated by Mum's huge portions and copious amounts of wine. We are sitting on the sofa, and I can see that Tad has had to loosen his belt to accommodate all of the food.

"You doing okay there?" I ask.

"I think I have put on about four stone!"

"Don't worry, you'll get used to it!" I wink at him.

Ami comes bounding excitedly down the stairs.

"Ready!" She shouts.

"Mary, Leo, thank you so much for a wonderful lunch. I won't need to eat for the rest of the week now!" Tad laughs as he stands.

"Really Tad, it was our pleasure. Don't be a stranger." Mum says as she takes him by the arm and walks him to the door.

Ami is already standing at the door waiting for us.

"Come on slow coaches!" She says.

"Do you fancy walking back? I think I need the air!" Tad asks me.

"Sounds good to me."

"Thank you for today." I squeeze Tad's hand in mine.

"I had a lovely time. But next time, make sure I don't eat for a few days before hand!"

We get to Tad's house and Ami stands and stares up at the huge wall of glass.

"Woah!" She says as Tad opens the door.

"You coming in kid?" He calls over to her.

I walk straight into the kitchen to make coffee for me and Tad, while he gives Ami a tour of downstairs, before collapsing in a heap on the sofa.

"Your TV is huge!" Ami says in awe as she sits on the sofa opposite Tad.

"Has she been upstairs yet?" I mouth at him as I pass him his coffee.

"No, wanted to check it was okay with you first." I smile at him.

"Ami? Go upstairs and go into the last room on the left." I say while warming up my hands on my coffee cup.

"Why?" She asks, looking puzzled.

"Just go!" I laugh, and she jumps up and heads straight towards the stairs.

"I might have made a few additions since I decorated..." Tad says.

"Additions?"

"Yeah. Uh, a TV, and a PlayStation..."

"Tad! She doesn't even have those things at home..." Oh God, he's trying to win her over to make her want to live here isn't he. I open my mouth to tell him I'm not happy about this but hear a loud "WOW! Oh my God!" coming from upstairs.

I look over at Tad and he is smiling to himself, and I honestly can't work out if it's totally innocent and he is just happy that Ami is happy, or if he is secretly pleased with himself, that Ami loves it and will be more than happy if I said I wanted to live here...

He catches my eye, and his face drops.

"What?" He asks, almost innocently.

"Why did you get her that stuff? Truthfully..."

"Well, I just thought if she ever stayed over or anything then she would need something to do."

"Tad, she's not staying over. Not yet. And if she did I guess it would be because we had been out somewhere and it was late. She's not going to need a TV and a PlayStation for that..."

I hear Ami racing down the stairs and force myself to not look quite so pissed off.

"It's amazing! Is it for me?!" She squeals in excitement.

Tad turns to look at me.

Oh so now you want my input hey!

"It's just for if you ever come over, Tad just thought you might like your own space."

"It's amazing! Thank you Tad!" She runs over to him and gives him a huge hug. Normally this would melt my heart, and I would be so happy that they are getting on so well and that they clearly really like each other. However, I just feel like he has gone behind my back to try to force my hand by making Ami want to stay here.

"Can I go play upstairs Mum?"

"Uh, ok. But we can't stay long, you have school tomorrow and still have homework to do."

"Thanks Mummy!" She is half way up the stairs before I've even finished speaking.

Tad turns to look at me with a huge grin on his face and it takes everything in me not to launch my coffee at him.

I slam my mug down on the table and walk into the kitchen instead.

"What is wrong with you?" He says accusingly as he follows me into the kitchen.

I put both of my hands on the counter in front of me to steady myself, close my eyes and take a deep breath in, to try to calm myself down enough that I don't scream at him.

"You knew that she didn't need that stuff, yet you went and got it anyway because you're trying to get her on board with moving in here." I turn to face him and he looks a mixture of hurt and confused.

"Even if that was true, which it isn't, why is that such a bad thing? We love each other, we want to be together. Ami and I get on really well and I could protect you both better if you lived here with me."

"Tad that is not the point!" I'm trying to keep as calm as possible, but I can hear my voice getting louder and starting to shake slightly. "You do not go through Ami to get me to do what you want. I told you I wanted to take things slowly when it came to Ami. I told you that I didn't want to move in so soon. I thought we were on the same page."

"Yeah. So did I." He scoffs and turns to walk into his office.

"What is that supposed to mean?" I call after him but he ignores me. "Tad?" I follow him into his office where he pulls a bottle of some kind of whiskey out of a drawer next to his desk.

He takes a glass from a shelf and pours himself a drink, still ignoring me.

"Tad, what did you mean by that?"

"I dunno Rach. I'm meeting you parents, and your kid, and decorating a room for her. Fuck, I even find myself picturing our wedding and wondering the best way to propose to you." He puts his head in his hands and runs his hand over his stubble. "I just feel sometimes like I'm in this more than you are. I tried to do something nice for Ami and honestly there was no ulterior motive in it at all. I won't lie, if she did want to live here then that wouldn't be a bad thing, for me anyway, but that was never my intention Rachel."

You're being a bit of a prat, you should apologise...

"Why don't I believe you?" The words come tumbling out of my mouth before I even think about it. I risk looking over at Tad and he looks absolutely crushed.

Seriously, what are you doing?!

The look of utter pain on his face makes me turn mine away. I don't want to be arguing with him. And knowing that he thinks I'm not in this as much as him just devastates me. I risked absolutely everything for him, I can't believe he thinks that. Part of me wants to just go and sit on his lap and hug him and reassure him that I love him more than almost anything in the world. In fact most of me wants to do that. A tiny percentage of me however still doesn't believe him, and worries that this type of manipulation is just the start of another relationship like with Kevin...

And of course my stupid brain decides to listen to that tiny part of it. I find myself turning on my heel and walking out of his office. Even as I'm walking I am cursing myself for being such a stubborn twat.

I get to Ami's room and find her playing some sort of Lego game on her PlayStation.

"Come on babe. We need to go, you've got homework." I say.

"Oh Mum! Five minutes?" She pleads with me.

"No. I said now!" I snap and her little face falls. "Sorry babe, I've just got some stuff to sort at home and Tad has had to get some work done."

She turns everything off, and heads downstairs.

"Can I say bye to Tad?" She asks just before we reach the front door.

"He's on the phone babe. You can see him again soon ok?"

That's if he ever wants to see you again...

I've tucked Ami in bed, said goodnight and I'm now sitting on the sofa with Mum watching whatever soap she's got on.

"What's wrong darling?" She asks.

"Uh, nothing really..." I lie as I feel my eyes start to burn with tears.

"Rachel, please talk to me." Mum shuffles closer to me and puts her arm around my shoulders, pulling me in close to her.

I close my eyes to keep any tears from slipping down my face.

"We had a fight. I say we, but it was me, I just kept picking and I ended up kicking off for almost no reason at all, and then I just walked out, leaving him looking heartbroken." I bury my face in my hands as the tears start streaming at the realisation that I have completely over reacted and hurt Tad in the process.

"What did you fight about?" Mum asks softly as she strokes my hair, in a way that only Mums do with their children.

"Well Tad thinks I should just move in with him. He has for a while, but I've told him it's way too soon and I have Ami to think about. He decorated a room in his house especially for her, which I thought was really sweet. But then he went and put a giant TV and a PlayStation in there, without telling me, and it just felt like he was trying to almost bribe Ami into wanting to live there, to force my hand." I look at Mum and can tell she is deep in thought.

"Was that why he did it?" She asks finally.

"I don't know, he says he just wanted her to have her own space there, and something to do if ever she was at his."

"But you felt like he was trying to trick her into wanting to move in?"

"Yeah, something like that. I don't know Mum. I'm so confused." I start to feel frustrated. At Tad, at Kevin, at my whole bloody life right now, but mostly at myself.

"It's a really tough one honey. Only you know how fast or slow you want to go, and Tad needs to respect that. But, in saying that, Kevin has left huge scars. He tricked and manipulated you into most of the last ten years of your life. It is completely understandable you are going to be wary, but from what I can see, and from what you have told me, Tad is absolutely nothing like Kevin."

"Oh God Mum, he's nothing like Kevin at all! I've messed up haven't I?"

"No, honey you haven't messed up. All relationships have ups and downs. This is still new. You are still figuring out how to make it work, and learning about each other. But you can't do that by walking away and letting things stew. I know you can be stubborn, but go to him. Talk to him. Work it out."

I check my phone again, hoping he has sent me a message, but nothing.

"I'm not sure he wants to see me Mum, he looked so hurt when I left." Fresh tears sting in my eyes at the memory of how he looked as I turned my back on him and walked out. He didn't call for me to stop, or try to follow me.

"Then call him darling. Don't leave it too long ok. He loves you, it's obvious. And the fact he is willing to accept Ami so soon is wonderful. Plus, you know, he is a bit yummy..." She blushes.

"Mum!" I laugh as I wipe away my tears. "I'll call him now. Thanks Mum." I give her a kiss on the cheek and walk into the kitchen with my phone. This conversation may need wine.

Tad

The cold air stings my face and I can feel the dampness from the sea breeze on my cheeks.

I had to get out of the house. I felt like I was suffocating inside those four walls. There is just too much going on right now, and I am so tempted to pack up and go to London for a few days.

The last thing on my mind when I got that stuff for Ami was some back hand move at trying to get them both to move in. I honestly thought I was doing something nice. I ordered it all before I had even met Ami, and I guess in my mind I was hoping that if she didn't like me much when we met, maybe she would like me more if I got her something nice. Luckily, it turned out she liked me anyway, but I thought she deserved what I had bought anyway. She's been through so much, and I know a TV isn't going to fix that, but I didn't think it would cause any drama.

I walk over to a large rock not far from where waves are crashing onto the shore, and my mind travels back to when I sat Rachel here last month. When things seemed simpler.

I lean against it and realise just how cold it is out. I can barely feel my hands and I can see my breath in front of my face.

In the distance over the water, I see flashing lights from boats and ferries, and somewhere overhead I hear the rumbling of a plane.

I should be on that plane, ok, maybe not *that* plane. But a plane. Seb and I should be together, drinking champagne on our way to Vegas to celebrate his birthday. Which is in two days' time. I had no idea how hard it was going to hit me, but I just want to run away from everything right now. I had hoped that spending the day with Rachel would be enough for me to at least put it to the back of my mind... But I'm not sure when I will hear from her again. She looked so angry. And I get it, in some ways I really do. But she should know me better than that.

It's only been a month. She has only known you for thirty days...

I put my hands on the back of my head and lean forwards. The urge to scream into the night is overwhelming.

I'm not sure how much time has passed but I am suddenly aware of someone standing behind me. I turn to look and see the silhouette of a person standing in the shadows. They are stood statue still, just staring at me.

I quickly stand as I feel my pulse start to speed up.

Everything inside me, all of my instincts are telling me to run. Something is not right. Nobody comes to a beach in the dead of night to stare at a random stranger. Yet I find myself frozen to the spot, waiting for the figure to move, or speak. But they just stay completely still. I can hear the blood pounding through me and my heart is racing.

"Can I help you?" I shout into the darkness. I strain my ears to listen for anything they may say.

Suddenly they laugh. It is a man's laugh and it sounds almost deranged. That laugh travels straight through me and chills me from the inside out. I slowly move my hand around to reach for my phone, only to feel nothing except an empty pocket. My stomach drops as I realise I left my phone at home. I start to pat down all my pockets, almost frantically, in the desperate hope that my phone jumped into one of them without me realising.

Suddenly the figure steps forward. Just enough into the light that I can see he is dressed in black, with thick gloves and a hood covering his face.

I look around to figure out the best way out of this. The gap in the bushes is just behind the hooded man and to the left, if I make my way over that way he will be able to block me off. I'm going to need to climb the rocks and get to the beach on the other side.

My heart is slamming into my chest and he must be able to hear it. He goes to take a step forward when suddenly a loud voice cuts through the breeze.

"Boss?" It's Freddie. He is standing at the gap, and before I have the chance to do or say anything, the hooded man runs in the opposite direction and straight into the thick bush surrounding the beach.

Freddie must hear the rustling and rushes forwards.

"Who was that?" He shouts to me.

"I don't know, get the guys, find him!" I shout at him as I make my way off of the sand. He fishes about in his pocket for his phone and I can hear him shouting at the others to get here now.

"Make sure you leave two guys outside Rachel's. He wasn't here for me." I say as I walk past him and back over to my house.

As I get to my front gate Tommo races over to me.

"Boss, what happened?"

"Kevin. It must have been him. Find him."

Without another word he runs off in the direction of the beach.

I walk into my house and slam the door shut behind me. I lock the door and take my stairs two at a time. Like I don't fucking have enough going on in my life, I'm now being stalked by my girlfriends ex-husband, who just so happens to be a murdering psycho.

I pull my jumper over my head in one swift move and throw it somewhere. As I walk into my bedroom I undo my jeans and let them slide down my legs so I can step out of them. I go straight into the bathroom and turn my shower on full blast. The room quickly fills with steam and starts to warm me up. The water almost burns my skin as I step under it. My skin turns red from the stream of roasting hot water, but I'm not bothered at all.

I step under the shower, and tip my head forwards to let the water run down my face. I can feel my heart racing in my chest and I'm finding it hard to catch my breath. I'm so fucking wound up, so angry with the world. I slam my hands against the wall and can feel my eyes stinging. More than anything I want to talk to Seb. He was my best friend, he always made me feel better. Why the fuck is he not still here. I can't talk to Rachel, because she's pissed off with me. The memory of her walking out earlier leaves my vision blurry, and I have to tightly close my eyes to stop tears from spilling out.

The sound of a door closing makes me turn around so fast I almost lose my footing. Through the steam on the shower door I can make out the shape of Rachel. I wipe my hand along the cold glass door to check my eyes aren't playing tricks on me.

She is standing there, her chest noticeably rising and falling as if she is breathing heavily. Her eyes are red, and she looks broken. I shut off the water and push the shower door open so hard that it slams into the wall behind it, causing Rachel to jump.

I step out into the cold, and feel the water dripping from me and pooling at my feet.

"I'm sorry." Fresh tears start streaming down her face as she catches sight of my own.

"I know." I say curtly. I don't mean to be as angry as I must look. But if I let my guard down, if I open my arms to her and feel her soft skin on my own, I will break down. And I can't let her see that side of me.

She takes a step towards me. "Let's talk, please."

"I don't want to talk." I hold my hand out to stop her coming any closer. I need to compose myself before we talk, before she touches me. She stops just short of my fingers, and her bottom lip almost trembles as she looks at me.

My fingertips skim Rachel's top, and without thinking, I grab it in my hand and pull her roughly towards me. Her eyes widen in shock, but close quickly as my other hand lifts her top and my fingers graze across her stomach. I drop my other hand and it grabs her top and pulls it over her head. She is standing in just her bra and trousers, and she looks nervous. Her teeth are pressed hard into her bottom lip. I take a step closer to her, lean in and push my lips against hers. Immediately she throws her arms around my neck and pushes her hands into my still wet hair. Her mouth opens and her tongue pushes into my mouth. My hands run up her back until they reach her bra strap. I quickly fumble with the clasp and once it is undone, I slide my fingers across her skin, around to her chest where I grab hold of it and tug. She lets go of my hair and drops her arms, allowing the bra to land at our feet.

My hands are holding onto her sides, keeping her steady beneath me. Her hands are dangling right next to my cock, and I can feel it getting harder by the second as all my blood rushes to it. The back of her hand brushes it, which sends shivers all over my body, and makes my grip tighten on Rachel's skin. She whimpers slightly, but then it just seems to spur her on. Her hands move to her jeans, where she is undoing her buttons. Abruptly, I stop kissing her and turn her around in front of me. I grab hold of her waistband and pull so forcefully, Rachel's arm shoots out to grab my own to steady herself. She steps out of the jeans and kicks them into a corner, then starts to turn back to me.

"No." I stop her and turn her back around. "Stay there- Actually..." I bend Rachel all the way over so her arse is right up in the air and her head is dangling somewhere close to her feet. "Stay there."

I walk out of my room and run down the stairs. I am mildly aware that my house is absolutely freezing compared to my bathroom, and I am totally stark naked, but I don't care. I open the door to my basement and quickly walk down the stairs and straight over to the chest at the foot of the bed.

I pull out an unopened pack of cable ties and quickly take two out, before running back up to the bathroom. I can help but half smile as I walk in to find Rachel in exactly the same position I left her in.

I kneel down in front of her. "Grab your ankles."

She immediately does as she is told, without any questions asked. I pull the cable tie behind one leg, and tighten it over her wrist, so she can't move her hand. I move across and do the same to the other wrist. While I am still kneeling in front of her, I put my hand under her chin and turn her face to look at me.

She smiles at me, and that is all I need.

I quickly stand, and walk around behind her. Her breathing starts to speed up in anticipation for what is to come.

I grab hold of my cock in one hand, and her hip with the other. Without warning, I thrust forwards and push hard into her. Her head flies backwards as she cries out. I still for a second, both to catch my breath and to give Rachel a chance to steady herself.

Then I slowly pull out before slamming back into her again. I pound into her with everything I have, gripping both of her hips tightly to keep her upright.

I fuck her like never before. This time it's purely for me, I need this, I need to fuck her. I need to try to forget about all the shit in my life right now, just feel nothing, but

Rachel. She starts to tighten around me and her heavy breathing turns into loud moans as I thrust even harder. She clenches so tightly around me that it almost tips me over the edge, but I keep fucking her hard through her orgasm. She is screaming with every thrust and her legs start to shake, but I push deeper, and deeper, holding her tighter. I am right on the very edge, part of me wants to slow down, so I can make this incredible feeling last longer, so I don't have to come back to reality. But this feels so fucking good. I pound into her faster, and the only other noise apart from Rachel's cries and moans, is the slapping of my body against hers.

I feel myself explode inside her as her pussy tightly grips my cock from another orgasm. I slow and try to catch my breath before I pull out.

I can't help but stand for a second and admire the beautiful sight, of Rachel stood there, arse completely up in the air, with my come spilling out of her and down her leg. Rachel's head pokes out from the side of her leg. Her cheeks are bright red, and she looks spent.

"Uh, can I have some help?" She smiles at me.

"Yeah, I'm coming."

I walk over to the medicine cabinet and grab a pair of scissors to cut through the cable ties.

Once her hands are freed she slowly stands and turns towards me. I walk to the shower and turn it on for her.

"I'll meet you in bed ok?" I kiss her on the cheek and walk out of the bathroom.

CHAPTER EIGHTEEN

Rachel

The dress in front of me is beautiful. Snow white, and covered in gems that sparkle in the light. I feel the lace under my skin and know I have chosen the right dress. I slide it on and struggle to do the zip up on the back.

Suddenly a hand grabs my hip, while I feel my zip being pulled up.

"Tad, it's bad luck for you to see the bride before the wedding."

I feel lips touching my back, and my neck, but they feel strange. Not soft and warm like Tad's usually are, but cold and rough...

"It's lucky I'm not Tad then..."

I try to spin around but the hand on my hip tightens it's grip, and another hand grabs hold of my hair tightly. My breathing speeds up and I can feel fear rising in my chest.

"Kevin, please let me go." I sob. "Where's Tad?"

"Tad's gone. He didn't want you anymore. He said I could have you back." His warm breath against my ear makes me cringe.

"No! Tad would never do that!" Tears spill from my eyes, and I start to feel lightheaded from where I am struggling to breathe.

"Of course he would. I always told you nobody else would ever put up with you..."

I wake suddenly, tears still streaming from my eyes and my chest tight from feeling so panicked.

I'm in an empty bed and I can't hear Tad anywhere. By the time I had finished in the shower last night, he was already asleep.

I desperately wanted to talk to him, to explain, to apologise properly. I know he is still upset with me.

I wipe the tears from my face and check my phone. I've woken before my alarm so I have enough time to quickly talk to Tad.

As I turn to get out of bed, a dull pain comes from my hip that makes me jump. I pull my pyjamas down just enough to see small purple bruises forming on my hips that match the shape of Tad's fingers perfectly. I trace my fingers along the marks and almost smile at the memory of how they got there. It may have been rough, angry sex, but it was still amazing.

I can hear Tad on the phone as I am walking down the stairs, and he sounds furious.

"And I already told you I don't want to rearrange just cancel the whole damn thing!" I have no idea what he is talking about, but he sounds so stressed. I walk towards the kitchen and he is stood at the sink, with his back to me, in just a loose fitting pair of pyjama bottoms.

"I don't care about the money just fucking cancel it!" He shouts so loudly that it makes me stop dead in my tracks.

He takes the phone from his ear and throws it roughly on the kitchen counter. I have never seen him like this before and I have a suspicion that this isn't entirely about my outburst yesterday. I start walking towards him when he grabs a cup from in front of him and launches it half way across the kitchen. It smashes into tiny pieces on the floor and I don't know what to do. I want to turn around and run away. Part of me is suddenly terrified.

He's not Kevin. Something is obviously wrong.

I walk to island in the kitchen and stop just in front of it.

"Tad?" I call out nervously to him.

He spins around and the look on his face makes me want to go and hug him. His eyes look red and puffy, and he doesn't look like he has slept at all.

"I didn't hear you come down." He looks across at the smashed mug on the floor and runs a hand through his hair.

"Yeah, I heard you on the phone." I start walking towards him. "Please talk to me, I know this can't all be about me being a dick yesterday."

"I've just got a lot on my mind right now that's all. I'm sorry I'm being like this."

"Hey, everyone is entitled to a bad day. But I can't help if you don't tell me what's going on?" I go to put my arm around him, but he walks away and towards a cupboard, where he pulls out a broom and starts to sweep the broken ceramic scattered across the floor.

I can feel myself starting to get frustrated. I know he has a stressful job, and I've upset him, but if he would just talk to me, I'm sure he would feel better.

"Tad?" I say again, in a slightly less soft tone than before.

"Rach, I just don't want to talk. Not now. I can't. I'm sorry." He doesn't even turn to look at me.

"Ok, well I have to get ready for work." I turn and walk straight out of the kitchen without another word.

Tad hasn't replied to any of my messages today, and by the time I was ready for work he had locked himself in his office.

I'm sat at my desk trying to work, but I am so worried about him. My phone vibrates on the desk, and I reach for it so quickly I almost knock it off the edge. My heart sinks a little when I see it's a text from Celine.

Hey babe, what's new? I need to book in to go and try on some wedding dresses. The place I like has an appointment late Friday afternoon, can you make it? Xx

I quickly reply.

Friday should be fine, I'll just check later that I don't already have anything planned and I'll let you know tonight xx

My finger hovers over Tad's name on my phone and I debate trying to call him again, but Celine replies before I have the chance.

Call lover boy and check for me now babe, I don't want to miss this appointment. I'm cutting it fine anyway! Xx

I lock my computer and take my phone and empty coffee mug into the kitchen.

Only a few hours until I can be done with work and get round to Tad's to find out what the hell is wrong. Unless he doesn't want me there? Maybe it is just me, maybe he's changed his mind and doesn't want to be with me anymore?

I take a deep breath and call Celine.

"Hey you!" She answers, sounding extremely chipper.

"Hey, how you doing?"

"I'm great thanks babe, how are you?"

"Uh- don't ask!"

"Why, what's up?"

"That's kind of why I'm calling. I can't really ask Tad about Friday at the minute. He's not talking to me." I have to blink away the sudden sting of tears in my eyes.

"What's happened?"

"I don't really know. We had such a great weekend, he went for dinner at Mum and Dad's, but then Ami came back to his house and it all turned to shit. I sort of over reacted a bit to something, and stormed off, and now he's hardly spoken to me since."

"Well that seems slightly ridiculous. Did you apologise?"

Suddenly I hear the front door swing open.

"Give me two seconds Cel, someone has walked in." I put my phone down on the counter and walk out of the kitchen to see Theo Peters standing in front of my desk looking really wound up.

"Mr. Peters, how can I help you?"

His eyes travel up my body and by the time they have reached my face he looks somewhat calmer.

"Please call me Theo." He smiles and pauses.

"Oh, uh Theo, how can I help you?" I laugh slightly awkwardly and I am suddenly very aware that the office is empty apart from myself and Peters.

"I have a meeting with James, he called me about half an hour ago and told me to come in."

"Oh, James isn't here right now. He should be back, maybe he's stuck in traffic. I'll quickly call him and find out how long he will be."

I walk over to my desk and can feel Peters' eyes burning into me.

I quickly dial James' mobile number.

"Rachel?"

"James, Mr. Peters is here for a meeting. He said you called him"-

"Shit, I didn't think he would be in that quick. Get him a coffee and I'll be back in ten."

"Ok, see you then." I hang up my phone and look at Theo. "He apologises and says that he will be here soon. Please take a seat and I will get you a coffee."

One side of his lip curves into a sort of smirk as he walks over to the sofa by the window.

I walk into the kitchen and see my phone laying on the counter, still on a call to Celine.

"Shit, Cel, sorry, someone is in for a meeting." I whisper.

"Ok." She mocks me and whispers back. "So did you apologise?"

"What?" I've completely lost where our conversation was.

"To Tad? After falling out?"

"Oh! Well I tried last night, but he didn't want to talk, although I thought things were ok. But this morning he completely lost it. He was screaming at someone on the phone about cancelling something and not caring about not getting the money back."

I start to make Theo's coffee, remembering he takes it black with one sugar. I might not be able to remember my own name at times, but I can always remember how someone drinks their coffee.

"Ooh, what do you think he was cancelling?"

"I don't know. I might have some sort of an idea if he would just bloody talk to me." I can hear my voice getting louder and I have to remind myself that someone is sitting just a few feet away from me, and I am at work. "Something has been bothering him for ages, but he has just dismissed it. Anyway babe, I have to go. I'll give you a call later, is that okay?"

"Yeah of course, hope you get everything sorted out."

I put my phone in my pocket and pick up mine and Theo's coffee mugs. As I walk out of the kitchen, I see Theo standing right next to the door and I very nearly walk straight into him. He seems to be looking at some framed newspaper cuttings on the wall.

"Black with one sugar?" I say as I hand him his cup.

"What a good memory you have!" He laughs as he takes it from me.

"Not for most things, but coffee making is a particular skill of mine." I laugh as I walk back over to my desk.

I hear his footsteps following behind mine and when I sit, he stops right in front of my desk.

"So, boyfriend troubles?" There's that lop sided smirk again.

"Excuse me?"

"I couldn't help but over hear you on the phone..."

You probably could have helped if it you weren't being a nosey bastard and hiding around corners listening to private phone calls.

"Oh, I didn't realise you heard that. Sorry I shouldn't have been"–

"It's ok, I don't want to pry. And don't worry, I won't tell your boss you were slacking on the job." He winks at me and then puts his coffee cup on my desk. "But really, don't put up with anyone not treating you right. You're a beautiful lady, anyone would be lucky you have you. My offer for a drink still stands if you're interested?"

I can feel my eyes darting from his to anywhere else in the room, I can't put my finger on it, but something about the way this guy behaves around me just makes me feel on edge.

Just as I am about to decline his offer, again, I hear the door open and I honestly have to suppress an intense urge to get up and hug James as he walks into the office.

"Sorry I'm late Theo"– He looks at the both of us and stops in his tracks, possibly noticing just how close Theo is to me and how uncomfortable I must look. "Come straight through."

"Until next time." Theo says quietly to me before following James into his office.

I feel my shoulders relax and I let out a deep breath.

I try to focus and get some work done, but not more than a few minute later, James' office door opens again. He closes the door behind him and walks over to me.

"Was everything okay when I walked in there?" He says in a hushed voice. "It's just, you looked really uncomfortable..."

"Oh, it was nothing. He has asked me out before and I've had to decline, that's it." I smile but can feel my cheeks reddening, this is not the best conversation to be having with your boss.

"I can have a word if you'd like?" He suddenly looks very protective, slightly how I can imagine Dad looking in the same situation and I half laugh to myself.

"It's ok, he's harmless. But thanks."

"Ok. There's hardly anything to do this afternoon Rachel, if you could just make me a coffee then you can go early." He says as he makes his way back towards his office.

"Are you sure?" I call over to him.

"Best piece of advice I am ever going to give you here; if your boss says that you can leave early, then run!" He laughs and walks back into his office.

The noise of the coffee machine is almost drowning out the sound of my phone ringing Tad. Voicemail. Again.

I check the time and work out I can go round to Tad's to sort all of this out now, and still be back in time for dinner at Mum's without missing seeing Ami more than I would have done if I had stayed at work.

I purposefully avoid making any eye contact with Theo when I give James his coffee. I walk out of his office and almost run to get my bag and coat.

Just as I am leaving the office I get a phone call.

"Finally, where have you been?" I say without even checking who it is.

"Rachel? It's DCI Robins."

Jesus, learn to check who's calling before you answer!

"Oh. Sorry. I was expecting someone else." My heart simultaneously sinks at the realisiaton it's not Tad calling, and starts pounding. Robins only ever calls with news.

"I haven't been able to reach Mr. Turner today, and I just needed to go over some more details of last night."

"Last night?" What is he talking about?

"Yes, I had some men search the area not long after I was called, but we couldn't see anyone fitting the description Mr. Turner gave. I just wondered if I was missing something."

"Sorry detective but I think I am missing something. Who exactly were you looking for last night?"

"Has Mr. Turner not told you?" He sounds genuinely shocked and I stop dead in my tracks. What the hell has Tad been hiding from me?

"Told me what!" I half shout down the phone.

"Well, I had a call from one of his security team, who told me that your husband was seen last night, in front of Mr. Turner's house..."

My phone almost falls from my hand and I can feel my coffee creeping its way back up my throat. How *dare* he keep this from me? I am more than angry. I am utterly furious. My entire body starts to shake as I go over in my head every opportunity he had to tell me about this, but he chose not to. He lied to me. He betrayed me. He told me that he would only tell me what was important and that I had to trust him. Seeing Kevin outside of his fucking house seems important to me.

"Rachel?" Robins' voice startles me as I realise I'm still on the phone to him.

"Sorry. Uh, I'm on my way over to his house now. I will have him call you when I get there." I hang up the phone before either one of us has the chance to say anything else.

CHAPTER NINETEEN

I am trying to calm down before I walk into his house, but I just can't. The noise of my car door slamming echoes around the whole street as I storm over to his front door.

I ring the doorbell, and no answer.

I ring it twice more and nothing.

Anger rises and I can feel I am completely on the verge of losing my shit in a way I've never done before. But then a thought stops me.

What if Kevin got to him?

I rummage around in my bag for his key and open his door.

"Tad?" I call out into the silence.

I walk slowly towards his kitchen and I can hear music coming from his office.

So he's okay then. *For now.*

I furiously throw the door open and take a deep breath in so I have full capacity to scream at him for being a total wanker.

But he is not sitting at his desk.

He's not anywhere.

Then all of the hairs stand on the back of my neck as I realise the room has been trashed. There are papers and photos all over the floor, smashed glasses, shelves hanging off the wall. And–

"Tad?"

Poking out from the side of the desk is a foot.

Tad's foot.

"TAD!"

I run in and see him laying lifeless on the floor. Every nightmare I have ever had is coming true. Kevin got to him.

I am frozen to the spot. I don't know what to do. The room feels like it is starting to spin, but then I notice that his chest is rising and falling very softly.

I fall to my knees and lift his head. "Tad. Tad! Wake up, what happened?"

I am suddenly hit by the overwhelming smell of alcohol, and I look around Tad and see two empty bottles of whiskey.

The relief that washes over me is almost as intense as the anger I am feeling at him putting me through this.

"Tad?" I gently tap him on the face and he stirs. His eyes open, but can't focus on anything. I suddenly let him go and stand up, fear courses through me.

This is how it all started with Kevin. The first time I found him drunk like this, he pushed me down the stairs. I stand over Tad, not knowing what to do as panic sets in.

Are you seriously comparing Tad to Kevin right now? Like right now, when he is going through something so awful he thought that this was the best solution?

I can't get hurt again.

Tad's eyes open again and seem to find me through his drunken haze.

"Rach?" He holds his hand out and instinctively I lean in and try to lift him. Man he is heavy.

"Tad, I can't lift you myself, you're going to have to help me."

"I can't." He scrunches his eyes tightly and let's go of my hand.

"You can, come on!" I grab him under one arm and pull him up with everything I have. I manage to get him sitting, and half drag him backwards to lean him up against the wall.

"I'm going to get you some water ok?" I say as I start to stand. Suddenly his hand grabs my arm.

"No, please don't leave me." His eyes are swimming with tears and he looks more broken than I could ever possibly imagine.

"Hey," I cup his face with my hand, "I'm not going anywhere. I'm just going to get you some water."

"No, please, you won't come back. You'll leave and you won't come back. I can't lose you Rachel. I love you." A tear slips from his eye and down his cheek and I start to well up. What is going on in this man's head that he would have rather done this to himself than just talk to me.

"Ok, but you need water." I say as I gently wipe the tear from his cheek with my thumb. "You're going to have to walk with me to the kitchen, can you do that?"

He nods, and I stand in front of him. I grab hold under both of his arms and pull. He seems more with it this time and is able to get up, although staying up might be slightly more of a challenge.

He puts his arm around the back of my neck and I grab on tightly around his waist.

We stagger along into the kitchen and I prop him up next to the counter.

"Stay there." God he looks in such a mess, I've never seen him any more than tipsy before, this is brand new territory for us. I guess it had to happen sometime. Although I definitely thought the first time one of us was stinking drunk and needed looking after, it would have been me!

I open the fridge and take a bottle of water before grabbing back on to him again.

"Come on drunkard. Bed now."

We struggle up the stairs, and for a split second at the top of the stairs he almost slips and brings us both down, but luckily something must have kicked in and he managed to grab on to the banister.

We don't quite make it to the bed before he gives up and just collapses in a heap on the floor. I turn to pick him up, feeling my frustration rising, but it melts away the second I see his face. He is in bits. Tears are streaming from his eyes and he starts to sob.

I drop down next to him and pull him in to my chest, wrapping my arms around him and stroking the hair out of his face.

"Tad, please, you have to talk to me. What is going on?" Just seeing him like this is breaking my heart. I can feel my own eyes swimming in tears as I watch him fall to pieces in front of me. My strong, beautiful, bossy Tad, breaking down in front of me.

"You're all I have. And you're going to leave." He whispers

"Tad, I'm not leaving, I promise you."

"Everyone leaves. My Dad, my brother. I have no friends, no family, nothing. You are my everything."

"Sshh, I'm not going anywhere, I swear. Hear me now Thaddeus Turner. I am not leaving you until the day you are fed up of me and tell me to go."

He smiles weakly at me.

"Tomorrow is- should have been my brother's birthday."

"Oh Tad. Why didn't you tell me?"

"There's just been so much going on, I didn't want to stress you out even more."

I wipe his tear streaked cheeks and pass him the bottle of water.

"Drink this. You're going to be so ill tomorrow."

He opens the bottle and takes a few sips.

"I feel like shit." He slurs slightly as he struggles to screw the lid back on.

"Come on, bed." I stand and pull him up. He puts his arm over my shoulders and we walk over to the bed. There's not a chance I am going to be able to get him undressed in this state so I just pull back the quilt and flop him on to the bed.

His eyes close as soon as his head touches the pillow, so I throw the blanket over him and turn to walk out of the bedroom.

"Rach?" He calls.

I walk back over to the bed. "Yes babe."

"I'm sorry, for everything."

"Ssh, it's all ok. Sleep babe."

"Ok." He says as his eyes close again.

I need to find out what happened last night, and what the hell is going on with Tad right now. I've swiped his phone from his office and made myself a coffee in the biggest mug I could find.

I've called Mum and told her I will be late home. She and Dad are going to take Ami out for something to eat, so at least I don't need to worry about them. I imagine that one of Tad's guards will be watching them, and they will be in a public place so they will be safe.

I'm scrolling through Tad's contacts and I find who I am looking for.

"Boss." Tommo answers.

"Tommo, it's Rachel. Sorry I used Tad's phone. Where are you?"

"I'm just outside, is everything ok?"

"Uh- yes. Well, I don't know, can you come in for a minute please?"

"No problem." He hangs up and immediately I hear a key in the front door.

"What's up?" He says as he strides over to the front room. "Is Mr. Turner ok?"

"Well," I absent mindedly look up the stairs. "He's not really himself at the moment, so he's gone to bed for a bit." Tommo looks confused for a split second, until his face returns to its usual stern, emotionless expression.

"Tommo, who's watching Ami?"

"Freddie and one of my other men."

"Ok, next question. What the hell happened last night?"

That stumps him.

"Mr. Turner didn't tell you?"

"No! Now will someone please tell me what actually happened? I've had Robins on the phone saying someone said they saw Kevin and I'm freaking out and now Tad is- well he isn't in a state to talk right now and I have no idea what the fuck is going on!"

Tommo's eyes widen at my outburst and I suddenly feel a pang of guilt. None of this is his fault. Me shouting at him is hardly fair. "Sorry, I'm just so stressed out." I brush my fingers through my hair and feel like ripping chunks of it out.

"From what I have worked out, Mr. Turner was on the beach last night, he said he needed some air. He'd been gone a while so Freddie went to look for him. When he got there, there was a man starting to walk towards Mr. Turner. He ran off the second he saw Freddie, and got away. But Mr. Turner is convinced it was your husband."

I can't even talk I am so shocked. I have a million questions, a million things I want to say.

Why didn't he tell me?

"We assumed that he told you when you got here last night?" Tommo interrupts the hundreds of thoughts thundering through my brain.

"So Robins wanted to speak to Tad to talk through some more details with him, but like I said, he can't right now. Do you think you or Freddie could call him and see if you can help at all?"

"Yeah, I'll do that now."

"Thanks Tommo."

I lean back into the sofa and feel utterly exhausted.

How the hell has my life become this much of a drama.

Tad's phone starts buzzing next to me, and I see Scott's name lighting up the screen. I know they are close, they have been friends for years. The both went through the loss of Tad's brother. Maybe he could help? Reluctantly, I answer the phone.

"Fuck sake man, I've been calling for days, why the fuck haven't you got back to me?"

"Oh- Uh, hi. It's Rachel."

"Oh, sorry, Rachel. Hi. Where's Tad?" He says suddenly sounding worried.

"Well, he's in bed at the minute..." I feel like I'm betraying Tad here, but he said he has nobody, no friends. Scott is his friend and maybe will be able to help pull him out of this mood he is in.

"In bed? Is he ill?" Scott asks.

"Listen, I feel bad telling you this, but he is a mess. He hasn't been himself the last few days, I assumed it was just stress at work. I got here a little while ago and found his office trashed, and him passed out on the floor after drinking his weight in whiskey."

"Shit."

"He managed to tell me that it is Seb's birthday tomorrow, so I assume that's what this has all stemmed from. I just wondered if maybe you were free to pop in at some point. I'm sure once he is conscious he would like to see you."

"Yeah, I'm not around at the moment, but I'll get there as soon as I can."

"Thanks Scott."

Tad

How the fuck did I end up in bed? And why do I feel like I have been smashed over the head with a brick?

I try to sit up and am smacked in the stomach by a wave of nausea so fierce I have to run into the bathroom.

Three times I have attempted to get up off of the floor and go back to bed, and three times I have just ended up throwing up again. I don't remember the last time I was so ill from drinking.

Once I have finally given up and accepted my fate is to die with my head in the toilet bowl, I hear a gentle tapping at my bathroom door.

"Tad?" Rachel's soft voice calls through the door.

"Don't come in. I'm okay."

"You're not ok, can I at least give you some water?"

"Okay."

I sit myself up slightly. There can't be anything left in my stomach anyway, so I should be safe. She opens the door and pokes her head around. Her eyes look red and tired.

"Hey." She smiles as she walks towards me and sits on the floor opposite me.

"Hey." She passes me a bottle of water, and I open it and take a cautious sip.

When I put the bottle down and look up, she is staring at me, and I can tell she is waiting for me to talk.

"I'm sorry." I say croakily.

"I know." She leans in and puts her hand on my leg. "Talk to me."

"I've been trying to forget about Seb's birthday. We had planned a trip to Vegas. Booze, gambling, a suite at an amazing hotel. Just some time to forget about life and enjoy ourselves. I'd forgotten about it to be honest until I got an e-mail a couple of days ago reminding me about my booking details."

"Is that what you were cancelling this morning on the phone?"

"Yeah. I just needed the fucking messages to stop!"

"You know you could have told me right?"

"You've got such a lot going on and"-

"No, Tad. We are in this together, if you're struggling or stressed or whatever, you tell me! I'm not a child, I don't need protecting. It hurts me to see you like this, and to know you've been all alone in it." Her eyes start to well up and if it's at all possible I feel worse than I did before. I have to look away from her before I end up a wreck in front of her again.

"I saw Kevin." I keep my eyes firmly glued the spot they have found on the floor. I know she is going to be utterly furious with me and I can't bring myself to look at her.

"I know." She says calmly, my head shoots up so fast I almost make myself dizzy.

"You know?"

"I know! Robins called me earlier, he said he needed to speak to you to go over some details."

"Fuck Rach." I bury my face in my hands. "I don't know why I didn't tell you. I was just going through so much. I half hoped if I ignored it, if I just forgot it happened then it would disappear. But I need to deal with this now. Kevin was here, right in front of this house."

"Did he say anything?" Her voice sounds shaky, I can't even imagine with she must be feeling right now.

"No. Just stared at me, laughed and then ran the second Freddie turned up. I don't know what he might have tried if he hadn't been disturbed though..." A shiver runs through my body at the thought.

"I'm so sorry Tad."

"Why are you sorry?" I ask as I shuffle closer to her.

"Well he was only there because of me. You've done nothing wrong, it's nothing to do with you, and now I've put you at risk."

"He isn't a risk babe. And now we know he must be nearby, we will find him and then he will be locked away for the rest of his miserable life."

I wrap my arm around her and she leans into my chest.

A few minutes pass and my eyes feel heavy, when suddenly I hear footsteps coming towards the bathroom door. Rachel lifts her head just as the door starts opening.

"Oh, by the way Scott called. I mentioned you were having a bit of a tough time and thought you could maybe use a friend right now..." Her cheeks flush a slight pink and she is looking at the floor as if she is nervous. I lift her chin so she is looking at me.

"Thank you."

"What are you two doing sat in front of the toilet?" Scott laughs in a voice so loud it makes me cringe.

"Right, I'm ordering pizza, or a kebab, or both? Something to soak up the rest of this booze anyway." Rachel says as she stands. She holds out her hand to me and I grab it as I pull myself up. She kisses me on the cheek and walks out.

"What the hell happened to you?" Scott says looking concerned.

"Uh, a bottle of Macallen happened to me. Maybe more, I'm not sure. I lost count." I walk over to the mirror to examine my haggard face.

"I've been calling you..." Scott says.

"I know. I'm sorry. I've just been trying to forget about tomorrow."

"Well that was a bit of a dick move." He is smiling, but looks pissed off too. I forget sometimes just how close he was to Seb. This must be hard for him too.

"Sorry I've been shit."

"I forgive you. I'll meet you downstairs."

I start to run the shower as he walks out of the door. I may not have many people in my life, but the people I do have are pretty damn special. I'd do well to remember that sometimes.

CHAPTER TWENTY

So I haven't spent Seb's birthday in any way how I had planned, but Scott has stayed with me all day and we have laughed and joked and talked constantly about Seb. Rachel said she would call in sick to stay with me but I didn't want her to do that for me. It's been really nice catching up with Scott, without any work needing to be done.

Suze has called to check in on us both as we are both skiving off work, but apart from that, most of the day has been spent slobbing on the sofa. Scott brought down the PlayStation from Ami's room and Rachel has nothing to worry about as I think I might keep it now!

"How are things with Rachel?" He asks, obviously trying to distract me so I will get blown to bits again.

"Yeah, they're good." I say, concentrating on the TV screen.

"Just good?" He presses.

"Well you know. It's been a bit tense the last couple of days. But she's amazing." I'm just about to go in for the kill, when suddenly the game pauses.

"Tense?" Scott puts the controller down and looks at me.

"Well you know. There's a lot going on..."

"I think that's probably an understatement. I'd call my girlfriends husband trying to murder me slightly more than *a lot going on.*"

"He didn't try to murder me!" I scoff.

"How do you know that's not what he was there to do?"

"Because he had ample opportunity to actually kill me if he wanted, instead he just stood there, and ran. He just wants to scare me. To scare us, and I'm not going to let him."

"Is she really worth all this though dude?"

"Yes!" I almost shout. "Scott, she's the one. I'm gonna marry her one day."

He just stares at me and eventually laughs. "You sap!"

Rachel

've stopped off at the supermarket on my way back to Tad's. Ami has gone to her friends' house after school so I'll just run back home to put her to bed. I swear that kid has a far better social life than I will ever have!

In my trolley there is a birthday cake, candles, a bottle of champagne and some party hats. Just because Seb isn't here anymore, doesn't mean his birthday shouldn't be celebrated.

Tad opens the door, looking much better than when I left him this morning. He is smiling again, and it melts my heart.

"Hey beautiful." He leans in and kisses me gently as I walk through the door.

"Hey you, you look better."

"I am, thank you." He goes to hold my hand and then sees the plastic bag I am carrying. "What's in the bag?"

"Uh, you'll see. Just go back to what you were doing, I'll be there in a minute."

He looks over his shoulder and leans in to whisper. "It's not kinky is it? Scott is still here?"

I burst out laughing and he joins me. It's so nice to hear that sound again.

"No, not kinky, I'm afraid!"

I walk past the front room and see Scott playing on the PlayStation, and I laugh to myself.

Once I am in the kitchen I get out the little chocolate cake I have bought and put three candles on it. I put a party hat on and then start to look for a lighter, finally I find some matches in a drawer in the kitchen and I set about lighting the candles.

Slowly, so the candles don't blow out, I take the cake into the front room, with a couple of extra party hats.

Tad turns his head just as I walk through the door, and I can't read his face. For a split second I panic. Maybe he just wanted to forget about today. Maybe he is going to hate this and be angry with me for reminding him about the fact Seb isn't here. I feel like running back into the kitchen and hiding. But then a huge smile creeps over Tad's face. He pokes Scott who turns his head quickly, so not to interrupt his game, but then does a double take back to me and pauses the PlayStation.

"I ain't singing Happy Birthday!" He laughs!

A little while later and we are stuffed full of chocolate cake and champagne. Tad and Scott have been telling me stories about their adventures with Seb. About the time they went to Amsterdam and Seb ended up thinking bicycles flew if you rode them fast enough, and ended up riding into a canal.

"He would have really liked you." Scott says to me and I smile.

The doorbell interrupts us and Tad goes to open it.

"Thanks for coming round yesterday Scott."

"Thanks for telling me what was going on. He's a nightmare for bottling stuff up."

"Yeah, so I see!" I take my last sip of champagne as Tad walks into the room with a small box.

"What's that?" I ask glancing over.

"No idea, a courier just dropped it off." He says as he starts to pull the tape from it.

"What the"- He drops the box to the floor and looks horrified.

"What?" I stand and walk over to see a dead rat. Its rotting flesh is falling away from its body and both carcass and box are crawling with maggots. A putrid smell travels up my nostrils and I have to take a step back.

"Holy shit!" I can feel my stomach turn and Scott walks over and kicks the box away.

"I'll go and see if the courier is still there." He says and he runs out of the front door.

"What the fuck?" I cry. "Why would anyone do this?"

Tad looks unbelievably calm, but I am shaking all over.

"There's something under it." He says as he looks back over at the box.

"Don't touch it!" I almost scream as I snatch his hand away.

"He grabs a pen from the side and pushes the rat out of the way. His face turns white and he steps back slowly.

"What is it?"

"Well it makes it obvious who it's from..."

I walk over and risk looking in the box. Under the rat, and all of the squirming maggots is a photo that has been cut out of a newspaper. It's of me and Tad from the opening of Miel. Red crosses mark each of our faces, and under the photo are the words "You're next."

I feel a chill run throughout my entire body, and then I feel- nothing. I just feel numb. I don't feel sad, or scared, or angry... I just can't take it in. My life has turned into a nightmare. I slowly walk over to the sofa and sit, in absolute silence.

Scott walks back in with one of Tad's guards. I can hear them talking in the distance, but their words aren't registering. The sofa dips next to me as Tad comes to sit beside me. His arms snake around me and I bury my face into his chest.

Robins has been and gone, and has been about as much help as a chocolate teapot. I am rapidly beginning to lose faith in him, and am so grateful, more than ever, to Tad for hiring guards especially to watch me and Ami.

Scott has left, so it's just Tad and I, sitting in silence.

"I need to go and pick up Ami from her friends." I say finally.

"Do you want me to come with you?" He asks softly.

"No, it's okay babe. I'll be back later. If that's ok...?"

"Why would it not be ok?" He grabs my hand in his and squeezes gently. "None of this is your fault." He smiles but I know that's a lie. He is only being threatened by Kevin because of me. If I hadn't come into his life, he would be getting on with his right now, without constant threats from a psycho.

"I love you." I say as I kiss him on the cheek.

"I love you too, so much." He kisses my hand as I stand. "Rachel?"

"Yeah?"

"Can you let one of the guys drive you in my car? I'll worry otherwise."

Any other day I would have laughed and said Tad was being over protective, but today, after all that's happened, I just smile and nod at him.

CHAPTER TWENTY ONE

The last couple of weeks have, thankfully, passed without incident. After knowing how close Kevin had come to us, I couldn't step outside without constantly checking over my shoulder. Poor Ami was pretty much put under house arrest. But, I am guessing that whatever Kevin had been planning has backfired. You see the problem with sending threats, is that it gives people a chance to be prepared. Tad has employed a whole envoy of security staff, and both my parents' and his houses have been kitted out in top of the range CCTV.

My sessions with Dr. Ross have been going well, and I am starting to feel much calmer about things. Tad and I have had no more stupid fights, and Ami actually ended up staying over one night. We compromised that the PlayStation would stay downstairs, and she and Tad were up playing until the early hours. They get on really well, it makes me so happy.

I still have this nagging worry about Kevin though. As each day passes where he isn't caught, I worry he is getting further and further away. Which is good in some ways, as I don't want him anywhere near us. But I do want him caught. I want him punished. More than anything, I want to look him in the eyes, and prove to him that he hasn't won. I'm not worthless, or any of those things he said I was. I will go on to live a happy life, with a wonderful man, and an incredible daughter, while he spends his days locked up behind bars.

Celine's wedding is coming up fast, and this weekend is her hen do. We are headed off to Brighton for a night out, and then a day at the spa. I had a feeling one day at a spa would not be enough to fully recover from our antics the night before, so she will have a week to recover before the big day.

Just as Celine predicted, she walked into a dress shop, tried on one of the first dresses she saw, and bought it on the spot. I don't know if she just settles, or if she has an absolute gift; but the dress does look absolutely stunning. While Celine was trying her dress on, I found myself wandering around all of the beautiful white gowns. Feeling the soft lace under my fingers, smiling to myself. Knowing that one day I will be in here again, but looking for a dress for me this time. Choosing the perfect dress to wear as I say "I do" to the perfect man.

Of course, for that to happen any time in the near future, I'm going to have to hope that Kevin gets caught, and that I can somehow persuade him to agree to a divorce while he is in prison.

You would think that if someone commits murder, and then attempts to murder his wife, you could automatically get divorced, without needing the offending partner's permission. However, it seems that isn't the case! I will still need to get Kevin to agree to a divorce, or wait two years and divorce on the grounds of desertion. I think I would have a better chance of winning the lottery and summoning a genie from a lamp, on the same day, than Kevin agreeing to a divorce. That's if he is even found any time soon.

"Mum?" Ami's voice makes me jump. "You've been in here ages, what are you doing?"

"Sorry baby, I was a million miles away!"

"Tad says have you gone to Columbia for the coffee beans?" I turn to look at Ami and she has a mischievous grin on her face.

"You tell Tad to shush or he can get his own coffee!" I laugh back at her and she skips back off into the front room.

Those two get on so well together, it's such a lovely thing to see. Ami has been round a few times this week. I've cooked dinner for us all, and it's just felt so natural. We all just get on like a perfect little family, and it's amazing. Ami seems happier than I've ever seen her, and in all honesty, it has stated to make me wonder about Tad's offer to let us move in...

I carry our coffees into the front room, to find Tad and Ami pretending to be asleep.

"Alright you two, very funny!" They don't budge. I put the mugs down on the coffee table and silently walk over to where Ami is laying back on the sofa. My fingers outstretched, I lean in and tickle her sides. She shoots up instantly, hysterically laughing and trying desperately to get my hands away from her sides. Next thing I know, two giant hands snake around my sides and pull me off of Ami. Tad pins me down on the sofa and calls to Ami "I've got her, tickle her!"

Ami's little hands start grabbing at my sides and I am trying to suppress the awful laugh that is coming out of me. It sounds like a cross between a dog yapping and a cat in heat!

"Okay! Okay! I give up! I give up!" I scream through the laughter.

Ami climbs off of me, and as she is walking she accidentally backs into the coffee table, sending one of the mugs flying off the side of the table.

Her smile disappears instantly, her eyes widen and her face falls. "I'm sorry. I'm really sorry." She looks scared. And it breaks my heart, because I know why she looks like that.

I go to get up to tell her it's ok, but Tad gets to her before me. He scoops her up and starts tickling her.

"What are we going to do with you, clumsy eh?" He laughs while she giggles uncontrollably. He puts her down on the sofa and ruffles her hair before he walks off into the kitchen.

"He's not mad." She almost questions.

"No baby, he isn't mad. It was an accident." I smile softly at her and she relaxes back into the sofa. "Here, find a film to watch, I'll help Tad clean up." I pass her the remote and walk into the kitchen. Tad has a dustpan and brush in his hand, and is grabbing a roll of kitchen towel from the side.

"Is she okay?" He whispers, while looking concerned. "She looked like she was about to burst into tears."

"She's fine now. I guess Kevin affected her more than I thought." My heart drops at the thought. "If she'd have done that at home, with him around, he'd have been furious with her. I thought he had been around so little that she hadn't been affected by him. Guess I was wrong..." I feel so incredibly guilty.

"Hey," Tad's strong hand gently pulls my chin up to look at him. "Don't you ever feel bad or guilty for not leaving him sooner. Who knows what he might have done if you had tried. You had to keep Ami safe, and one day she will understand that, if she doesn't already."

My weak smile doesn't convince him, and he pulls me into his chest, wrapping his free arm around me and kissing the top of my head.

"Come on, let's go and grab something to eat. Then we can take Ami back to your parents' and you can grab whatever you need for this weekend." He says as he guides me back into the front room.

"You sure you're going to be okay all by yourself this weekend?" I tease.

"Well, it will be hard, I won't lie. Very hard." He looks at me and winks and I can't help but burst out laughing.

"What are you two laughing at?" Ami peeks her head out of the front room.

"Nothing baby, want to get something to eat?"

"McDonalds!!" She shouts enthusiastically.

Tad

I can't stop worrying about Rachel going away for the weekend. We have just dropped Ami back at home, and we're walking back to my house.

"What are you thinking about?" Rachel asks.

"Nothing much. Just that I'll miss you while you're gone."

"It's only two nights babe. You got anything planned?"

"No, I have some work I've neglected this week. I'll probably just catch up on all of that."

"Living life on the wild side eh?" She teases.

As we are walking, tiny white flakes of snow begin to fall.

"Oh it's snowing!" Rachel squeals from next to me. "I love the snow! I can't even remember the last time it snowed properly here."

"My Dad took Seb and I to Scotland one year during one of the coldest winters ever. We stayed in this little lodge in the middle of nowhere, and ended up snowed in for a week before we could get the car out!" I smile at the memory of it. I've never felt cold like it, and I was sure that I'd get frostbite and lose all my fingers, but it was worth it. "We literally had just the food we had taken with us, and a little log fire to keep us going. We were at the bottom of quite a steep hill, and we found a way up it one day to sledge down. Honestly I thought I was going to die, I went down it so fast!" I laugh and it feels nice to be able to talk about Seb again without feeling like I'm going to break down.

"I've never even seen enough snow to go sledging." The flakes in front of us are getting bigger by the second, and I can see Rachel looking excitedly up at the sky, as if she is willing it to snow harder!

"Let's go somewhere snowy one day, maybe Lapland next Christmas with Ami?" She turns to look at me with a huge smile on her face.

"That sounds incredible." She leans her head into my shoulder, and I wrap my arm around her.

When I was a kid I heard a saying that always stuck with me, *"How lucky I am to have something that makes saying goodbye so hard."* I never understood that before. I couldn't get my head around the idea that anyone could love a person so much, that they would feel lucky being sad at them leaving. But as I'm standing here watching Rachel leave me for just a couple of days, I now totally get it. I will miss her, and she will only be gone for such a short amount of time. But knowing that she will be coming back to me, that I have someone that special in my life, is such a comfort to me.

I close the door behind me and head towards my office to make a start on some work.

Rachel

Even though things have been quiet the past few weeks, Tad isn't risking anything and has said that either two of his men come with me on Celine's hen do, or he doesn't want me to go. I get it, I totally do; but wandering around Brighton with two big burly men in suits babysitting is hardly how I imagined spending my best friend's hen do. Tad has hired a Limo to take us to the hotel though, so, every cloud!

The car pulls up outside Celine's house and before I have even stepped out, she has flung open her front door and is racing towards me

"Oh my God! A limo! You legend!" She throws he arms around me before I have even had a chance to step away from the car.

"Tad organised it. I'll pass along your thanks!"

"God you got so lucky with him!"

I can't help but beam at her. "I did, didn't I?"

"Mum!" Celine suddenly turns on her heel and runs back into her house. Seconds later she is half dragging her confused looking Mum outside. "Look what Rachel's boyfriend organised for us!"

"Oh very nice!" She walks over to me, holding her arms out for a hug. "Rachel my darling, I am so sorry to hear about all of your struggles. You are looking radiant though!"

"Mum, trust me, Rachel is done with the struggles. Wait till I show you a photo of her new man!" Celine laughs.

I roll my eyes and sigh.

We arrive at the hotel and Celine's other friends are waiting in reception for us. She introduces her mum and I to them all, and from the corner of my eye I am sure I see some elbow nudges and hear hushed whispers about me and Kevin. I expect it now wherever I go. The papers seem to find something else to write about every day. I don't read any of the articles, but Dad does, no matter how many times I tell him not to. The amount of times I hear him tutting and muttering to himself while reading the papers in the morning is rather annoying!

"I'll go check us in Cel." I say as she is chatting to her friends.

I'm greeted at reception by a woman, whose smile almost reaches both of her ears. How is it even possible to have a smile that big?

"Hi, I'm checking in. Rachel Bennett."

She starts typing on her computer. "Ah Miss. Bennett. It looks like your room has been upgraded since your booking. You are now booked into our golden suite for the duration of your stay and have access to the full range of services in our spa, all included with your booking cost."

I just stare at her for a second before it fully kicks in what that man, that wonderfully over generous man has done.

"It's also been paid for already, and I appear to have card details for any room service charges. So there's nothing for you to do. I'll just get your room keys."

I get my phone out as she turns away and call Tad.

"Don't be mad. I just thought you both deserved a treat." He answers sounding a little on edge.

"You are amazing you know that don't you?" I can't wipe the smile from my face and I can see Celine walking over to see what's going on.

"Well you deserve it." I can hear the relief in his voice that I'm not mad.

"I love you."

"I love you too, now go and have fun, just not too much fun." I hear him laugh.

I hang up just as the super smiley receptionist is handing me the room keys.

"I will have your luggage carried up for you. If you take the lift in reception to the top floor, your suite is the door right in front as you walk out."

I thank her as I turn to Celine.

"Suite?" She asks looking excited.

"Super Tad strikes again!" I laugh as her face mirrors smiley reception lady.

"Oh my God!" She squeals. "Seriously, he is amazing Rach!"

She practically skips over to the lift with me. I put one of our key cards into the slot in the lift and press the button labelled "Gold Suite."

The doors close, and I feel that familiar lurch in my stomach as the lift starts its ascent.

"So what's going on with you and Tad then?" She asks, suddenly serious.

"What do you mean? Nothing has changed, we're together and happy."

"Nothing has changed? Rachel, come on. You are there almost every spare minute you have, even Ami has spent most of the week at his house. They both get on like a house on fire. Is there any chance of your stubbornness giving way and you guys moving in?"

The lift slows and the doors open.

"It's too soon Cel!"

"Says who?" She pushes. "Stop worrying about other people, or society, or whoever these imaginary people are that you allow yourself to be judged by. You and Ami both love this wonderful man, and he loves you both too. It's not every day that people are given a second chance as amazing as Tad! Talk to Ami. If she is against the idea, then fine, but at least allow yourself the opportunity to think about it."

I know she is right.

It's about one in the morning, and I think I am on my millionth glass of wine. We have ended up in some trashy club, with weird looking men walking around in next to no clothes, but probably more make up than I have ever felt the need to wear! The music is pounding and I can feel the room starting to spin.

"Come and dance!" Celine shouts in my ear over the music.

"I don't think my feet are working! I'm just going to run outside for some air." I slur back.

"I'll come with you." She starts to lift my arm.

"No, it's ok. I've got the black in men to look after me. No, then men in- you know, them!" I point over to my two guards, they are being swarmed by a group of drunk women who seem to think they are part of the entertainment. "I'll be back in a minute."

I start to stand and feel the world move under my feet. The room around me starts to blur in and out of focus, and I fall back down onto my seat. I try to steady myself by taking a deep breath in, then suddenly feel a hand on my shoulder.

"Rachel are you ok?" Tommo has managed to escape the crowd of women and has made his way over to me.

"I need some air." I shout at him. He puts his hand under my arm and lifts me almost effortlessly. Once I am standing, I feel both of his arms on my shoulders as he guides me out of the club. When the freezing cold air hits me in the face, everything starts to spin even more, and I feel as though my legs are about to give out on me.

I try to walk but my legs just don't want to work, and I curse myself for drinking so much. Tommo half carries me over to a wall, which I almost collapse on to.

God I wish Tad was here. I only saw him this morning and yet I miss him already. This is so annoying! I start to try to open my bag to find my phone, but the zip is currently far too complicated for my inebriated brain.

"Tommo, can you call Tad and let me talk to him please?" I'm not currently sure which Tommo I am talking to, as there appears to be two in front of me, however one of them hands me a phone seconds later and after almost dropping it, I put it to my ear.

"Tommo." Tad's got his work voice on. That sexy, boss like, stern tone, and more than anything I wish he was giving me a spanking right now.

"Nope. It's me." I answer.

"Rach?" His tone softens, which almost disappoints me a little.

"No, it's Deirdre." I laugh.

"Oh, well Deidre you sound just like my girlfriend, except rather more drunk than her."

"It is me really!"

"Oh, Rachel, I never would have guessed." I can hear his grin down the phone.

"Soo, what you doing?" I ask, sounding like a five year old.

"Well I was in bed, what are you doing?"

"Just outside some club. I needed some air. I think I might have drunk just a little bit too much."

"Just a little bit hey?" He laughs.

"I wanna move in Tad." I blurt out.

"What?"

"I. Want. To. Move. In." I over pronounce each word, just to make sure he hears me.

"Rachel, let's talk about this when you haven't drank your bodyweight in alcohol."

"This isn't because I am drunk!" I half shout, annoyed that he is dismissing me so quickly. "I've been thinking about it for a while, just didn't want to admit that maybe I wasn't right."

"Have you spoken to Ami about it?"

"Not yet. But I will when I am home."

"Ok, well you know that I want you here. I want you both here, so if it's really what you want, and Ami is on board, then you can both move in whenever you want."

"I love you Tad."

"I love you too Rachel. Why don't you get Tommo to take you back to the hotel so you can sleep?"

"In a minute, I need to go and be sick first. Bye." I almost throw Tommo's phone back at him and then I turn backwards and throw up all down the back side of the wall.

I can feel myself starting to fall backwards, but a strong arm grabs my shoulder and pulls me back. As I turn back around I see Celine and her friends walking towards me but then everything fades to darkness.

CHAPTER TWENTY TWO

Tad

"**B**ut she is ok?" I ask for the tenth time.

"Yes, she is fine boss. She's sleeping now, with a bucket next to the bed and her friend is looking after her."

"Thanks Tommo, I know this isn't really in your job description." I half laugh down the phone.

"It's not a problem boss. I'll keep you posted."

I put my phone down and sigh. That woman definitely keeps me on my toes.

But she wants to move in. She actually wants to move in!

Well she told you she wanted to move in after drinking God knows how much alcohol, and before passing out, maybe hold off on getting the champagne out for now...

I look at the clock and its coming up to four. I don't think I'm going to be able to get back to sleep now so I grab my dressing gown from the end of my bed and start to walk out of my room. Through the gap in my curtains, I see something move outside and immediately my skin pricks. The hairs on the back of my neck stand upright, and I feel like something is off. I walk over to my window and hide just behind the curtains, slowly I peek through the gap. I can hear the blood pumping through my ears. It's pitch black outside, and it takes my eyes a few seconds to see through the darkness, but there, in my driveway, next to one of my cars is a hooded figure, dressed all in black. My fingers start to move slowly to my pocket, I need to get my phone to call one of my guards, or the police. Surely Kevin wouldn't be so stupid as to be here, right outside of my house, where I have CCTV and guards that can be here within seconds?

I pull my phone out, and I start calling Freddie. It starts to ring and I watch as the man bends down under my car and starts to pull himself under it.

Come on Freddie, answer the fucking phone. We've got him.

He pulls something shiny from his pocket and starts fiddling silently under the car.

"Boss." Freddie finally answers.

"Outside, now, under the Audi. He's here."

I hang up and call 999.

"Which service do you"–

"Police please, quickly." I give my address and watch as the figure pulls himself from under the car and starts to run.

No way, I'm not losing him now.

Without even thinking, I turn on my heel and sprint down the stairs. I slide a pair of trainers on in record time and then throw open the front door. The cold air stings my cheeks, but I can't let him get away. Not again.

I race out of my drive way and turn left at the road, I can't see him, but he can't have got too far. My dressing gown is flapping around in the breeze behind me and in the distance I can hear police sirens. I get to a fork in the road, turn both ways but can't see anything.

"Fuck!" I mutter, my warm breath turning to steam in the freezing cold air.

I hear footsteps behind me and see Freddie and George running to catch me.

"Boss we"–

"Where the fuck were you? He got away again!" I can't hide my frustration from them. "Where the hell are the others?"

"Boss, we had a call about half an hour ago from one of the guys outside of the Bennett's. A guy was hanging around their garage, and then their alarm sounded, so a group have gone out searching there."

"What is he playing at? He did something to the Audi. I don't know what, I've called the police, they should be here in a minute." I rub my head in sheer irritation. This guy is clearly doing a great job of evading the police, so why this? Why risk getting caught just to try to scare Rach and I? He clearly isn't half as stupid as I thought he was, and the feeling that he is doing all of this for some bigger purpose is incredibly unsettling.

I see a police car behind us pulling in at my house.

"You two have a look around, see if you can see anything. I will go and speak to the police."

I quickly walk back to my house and see two officers getting out of the car.

They see me coming over and walk towards me.

"Was it you who called for assistance Sir?"

"Yes it was, I need to speak to DCI Robins. He is looking for a man who I believe was tampering with my car a few minutes ago. He ran and I tried to chase him but I lost him. I have two men out looking now, but he has probably got away. He was also spotted earlier outside of my girlfriends' house." The woman looks puzzled at me and I feel my anger rising. I just stare at her and she turns to speak to her colleague.

A black car pulls up behind the police car, and Robins gets out of the driver's door. He looks haggard, his eyes are red with deep black circles under them and his hair is a mess.

"Mr. Turner." He says as he walks over to me. "It's been a busy night all around it seems."

"What do you mean?" I ask.

"Well this is the second call I have had regarding a possible sighting of Blackford in the last few hours." In the last few hours? He can't be talking about Rachel's parents, that was only half an hour ago?

"What do you mean?"

"It appears Mr. Blackford wants to add vandalism to his ever increasing list of crimes. I had a call from an officer to say that a property agency in Chichester had been broken into. All the glass was smashed, and the inside had been trashed, but nothing had been stolen. Turns out this is the estate agent where Rachel works, once the officer put two and two together he called me to have a look. A witness saw a man dressed in black running from the scene after the alarms sounded." He sighs and runs his hands through his thick hair. "I was just on my way home when I heard your address on the radio."

I scratch my head as I try to take this all in. Rachel is going to be devastated. Going after her work? She is going to feel so guilty.

"We think he was also seen at Rachel's parents too." I say quietly.

"What the hell is he up to?" Robins looks almost as confused as me. "What happened?" He asks.

I explain about the car and he immediately makes a call to have a team of specialists come over to see what he was doing under there.

"I'm going to need to clear the area I'm afraid." Robins turns to the other officers and gets everyone to move back while he blocks off the entrance to my driveway. "You two, make yourself useful and search the area will you." The two officers sprint off down the road.

"Can't I go back in my house?"

"It's probably safest right now if we keep the area clear. We need to see what he was doing with that car, Blackford is not stupid. It's a stretch, but if he wanted to, he could easily have made some kind of explosive device and hidden it under the car."

A bomb?! He can't be serious!

"Is there anyone else in the house?" He asks and I shake my head while I still try to get round the fact that there may be a bomb under my car.

"Where is Rachel?"

"She is at her friends hen do in Brighton."

"Ok, do you have somewhere nearby you can go? Or would you prefer to come to the station?"

Well I guess this is one of the downfalls of having no friends nearby. I could go to Rachel's parents. I'm sure they wouldn't mind. Instinctively I go to grab my phone to call Rach, but then I remember she is passed out in bed and even if she does wake up, I don't think she will be up to talking about this now. The last place I feel like spending however many hours is a police station, so I guess I can go and get to know the future in laws a bit better.

"I can go to Rachel's parents for a while."

"Ok, I'll have someone drive you there, and then they can have a look around."

Well, this is going to be fun. I check the time and it's just after five in the morning. I gently knock on the door, hoping that someone hears without waking the whole house up. I can see a light on in the kitchen, so I'm hoping someone is already up.

I hear keys in the lock on the door and it opens a crack, revealing Rachel's Dad, looking very confused and half asleep.

"Tad?" He asks as he opens the door. He looks me up and down and his face grows more confused.

"I'm so sorry to disturb you so early Mr. Bennett, there has been a bit of a situation at my house and the police won't let me in for a while. I don't really have anywhere else to go nearby, and I hoped I could wait here."

He takes a few seconds to process what I have said and then quickly opens the door for me. "Of course, of course, come in please. And please call me Leo." I walk in and he closes the door behind me. "Coffee?" He asks.

"Yes please. I hope I didn't wake you?" We walk into the kitchen.

"I was actually up already. The alarm for my garage went off a little while ago, and then I couldn't get back to sleep."

So whatever he did to my car, he was trying to do to Leo's car too? He must see the look on my face. "What?" He asks solemnly.

"I saw Kevin tonight, he was doing something to my car. That's why I can't get into my house, Robins is concerned he might have planted a bomb." Leo's face goes white and he has the exact same expression as Rachel gets when she is panicked. "My guys saw someone fitting Kevin's description running away from here about half an hour before I spotted him at mine, and before that, he went to Rachel's office and smashed it to pieces."

Leo just stares at me in silence, trying to take in everything I have said.

"I always knew that guy was a piece of work, but this. This is just unbelievable."

He finishes making our drinks in silence and then walks through to the sofa.

The front room is covered in tinsel and fairy lights, and a huge Christmas tree fills a corner of the room. There are Christmas cards hanging from string across the walls.

My house doesn't even have a tree. I hadn't even thought about it. When I was a kid Seb and I would decorate a tree with Dad the night before Christmas, but that was about as festive as our house got.

"Have you spoken to Rachel about this yet?" Leo's voice cuts through the silence.

"No, I spoke to her a few hours ago and she was, well, slightly worse for wear. So she needs a few hours to sober up." Leo's lips curl into a smile and a loud noise comes out of his mouth as he laughs.

"That sounds about right." He smiles. "Maybe we should hold off telling her at all until she is home, or she won't enjoy her day tomorrow and will want to leave early. There's no reason for her to be here, in fact, she is probably safer there for now."

I promised her I would keep her up to date with anything that happened, she will be furious with me if I keep this from her. Although it won't affect her at all not knowing now, and I will tell her when she is back.

"I agree."

"You're a good man Tad." Leo says out of nowhere.

"I am?"

"You are. Most guys would run a mile with the amount of drama that has come your way because of Rachel. It's hard enough just having an ex-husband and a child come along with a new partner, but add to it the fact the ex-husband is a murderer on the run from the police who has taken to terrorising you. Well, like I said, you're a good man." He drains the last of his coffee and puts his mug down on the table.

"I've never met anyone like Rachel. It wouldn't matter to me if she had ten psychotic ex-husbands coming after me. I still could never leave her." He smiles at me and picks up a newspaper from next to him.

I lean back into the sofa and my eyes start to feel heavy. I've had hardly any sleep, and now the adrenaline is calming down, I feel exhausted. My eyes start to close and I let them, just for a minute...

Rachel

O h my God. I don't want to open my eyes. Or move. Or breathe. The sun is already burning my eyes from behind my closed lids, and every breath I take is making my head pound.

I can hear laughter from somewhere in the room, and it sounds like someone is screaming in my ear. I manage to groan out loud, but that's about as much communication as I can manage.

"Rachel?" The bed dips beside me and Celine whispers softly, but her voice goes right through me, straight to my pounding head, inside my searing muscles, and wraps itself around my extremely delicate feeling stomach. It makes me tense up and physically want to be sick.

I manage to make a sshh sound and then I hear her giggle. The unexpected loudness of it makes me throw my hands over my ears, and I regret it instantly, as the movement wakes my entire body up, including my stomach. I open my eyes and sit upright so fast I hear Celine jump. I just about manage to locate an empty bin next to my bed that I loudly throw up into.

"Oh God." I manage to croak out a minute later once I have pulled my head out from the bin. "How much did I drink?" My voice sounds husky, my mouth and lips are bone dry, and I honestly wonder if death might just be the easier option than having to see this hangover through.

"Well, a lot!" Celine laughs. "How you feeling?"

I just look up at her with a face that says *how do you think I'm feeling?!* And she laughs again.

"What time is it?" I ask.

"It's almost lunch time babe, you missed the gorgeous breakfast Tad had sent up for us, and I've already had a massage and been down to the sauna."

"Isn't the hen supposed to be the one that gets completely shitfaced and has a three day hangover?" I half manage a laugh.

"Clearly not!" She giggles.

"I didn't ruin your night did I?" I say, suddenly concerned that I can't actually remember any details from last night. It all seems to be a blur of wine, naked men, more wine, drag queens and even more wine. Oh God, my stomach churns just thinking about that word.

"No babe, honestly you were the life and soul of the party! I'm guessing you don't remember jumping up on stage for a duet with a drag queen?" She is smirking at me and I feel my cheeks reddening.

"Oh fuck, I didn't?"

"Oh yes you did! And then you decided that she was holding you back, snatched the microphone off of her and did your best Frank Sinatra impression!" She is half falling off the bed where she is laughing so much and I just want to crawl under the covers and die.

"Maybe it's a good thing I don't remember any of that."

"Oh it's ok, enough people had their phones out filming you. You will no doubt be viral already!" She is laughing still, but my stomach drops. This is not good. I'm already in all the bloody tabloids and trashy magazines, all the stories about Kevin, and of course now Tad and I have gone public. This is really bad.

Celine sees my face and stops laughing. "Don't look so worried babe." She rests her hand on my leg over the covers. "Everyone was drunk, everyone had a great time and it was a great night."

"Yeah, but everyone knows I am Tad's girlfriend now, and of course that my husband is a murderer on the run. It's not going to be good for Tad to have me behaving like this in public is it?" I can feel panic rising in my chest. What if he has already seen a video that has undoubtedly ended up going around Facebook, what if he's angry that I've shown him up? My breathing stars speeding up and if there was anything left in my stomach, it would definitely be making an appearance.

"Hey," Celine grabs my hands in hers, "calm down! Stop worrying. Tad is not royalty, you are both normal people with normal, well normal ish lives, and if you want to go out and get drunk then who is to judge you? Honestly, after everything you have been through the last couple of months, I think everyone would agree you needed to let your hair down."

I fake a smile, but really I feel on the verge of tears.

"Where's my phone? I need to call Tad, and maybe check Facebook." I cringe at the thought of anyone seeing me in that state.

"Good morning Sleeping Beauty." Tad answers the phone and his deep sexy voice goes straight through me.

Good, so he isn't pissed off with you, yet...

"Morning." I say in what is probably equally as deep a voice.

"How is my little pop star feeling this morning?" I can hear the grin in his voice.

Fuck.

"Oh God. Is it everywhere?" I cover my face with my hand and will the ground to open and swallow me up.

"Just Facebook, Instagram, Twitter, that sort of thing!" He laughs.

"You're not mad at me?" I mumble.

"Mad at you? Why would I be mad at you?" He asks, sounding surprised.

"Well, everyone knows about us now, and me acting like that will show you up, I don't want anyone to judge you by my behaviour."

"Oh Rach, don't be daft! Have you seen the video yet?"

"God no!" I half shout.

"Well you should, you put on a very good show! Plus almost every comment is positive."

"I feel like such a twat." I say, shaking my head.

"Rach, don't be so hard on yourself!" He says.

In the background I hear a little voice, "is that mum?"

What is Ami doing with Tad?

"Is that Ami?" I ask surprised.

"Oh, uh, yeah, your Mum invited me for lunch." He stutters.

Lunch? She didn't say anything to me about lunch?

"Oh. That's nice. She didn't mention she was going to invite you?" I question. Something feels off.

"Think it was spur of the minute babe, here, Ami wants to say hi."

"Mummy! Hi, I saw you singing!" She shrieks excitedly down the phone and I have to hold it at an arm's length.

"Did you now." I half laugh.

"You were funny!" She laughs. "But really good!"

"Well thanks baby. Are you having a good day?"

"Yes! Nanny is doing banoffee pie for pudding."

"Ooh yum! Save me a slice, ok?" I say enthusiastically, even though the thought of eating anything right now is making me want to heave.

"Hmm, maybe." Ami giggles. "See you later Mummy. Love you."

"Love you too baby."

I hear her give the phone back to Tad.

"Hey." Oh, that voice. Something about it just has a way of making everything seem better.

"Hey." I reply, smiling my first genuine smile of the day. "So, what's really going on there?"

"What do you mean?" He answers, slightly too quickly and higher pitched than he normally sounds, so I know he is up to something.

"Come on Tad. Either you're up to something, or my Mum is!"

"Is it honestly too difficult to believe she just thought I might be lonely, and unable to cope without you for a weekend, so she invited me round to feed me up so I wouldn't need to eat for the next week or so?" He laughs and even though I know he is hiding something, I'm in no mood to push now.

"Hmm, ok. Well, have fun, and don't end up in a food coma."

"I can't promise anything." His voice changes to a whisper. "Honestly, it's as if your Mum thinks I don't eat at home." I can't help but laugh.

"I'll talk to you later. I love you."

"I love you too Rach."

I throw my phone down on to the bed and see Celine walking towards me with a pile of toast and a pot of what smells like fresh coffee. As hideous as I feel, something about the smell of hot buttery toast and coffee makes my stomach rumble.

"Here, eat this and then we can go for some real food." She says as she puts the food next to me.

"You are a good friend." I risk a tiny bit of toast and when I am sure it isn't about to come straight back up I have another couple of bites while Celine pours us both coffees.

CHAPTER TWENTY THREE

Tad

I put down my phone to see Mary and Leo looking at me with concern.

"He planted some sort of homemade explosive device under the car. Apparently, he had put it in the wrong place for it to have done serious damage, but it still could have caused a massive accident if it went off and I was driving."

Their mouths slowly open in unison as I speak and they stare at me, obviously not knowing what to say. I feel the exact same way. I mean, clearly the guy has issues, but a bomb?

"And they didn't find him?" Leo says after what feels like an eternity of silence.

"No, he got away. Again." Anger rises through me and I feel my cheeks start to burn. How do the police keep letting him get away? Why are they not doing more to actively find him? What if I hadn't seen him last night and I picked up Rachel in the car? Or Ami? That last thought sends waves of nausea rippling through me.

"They said I can go back to the house now."

"Are you sure you will be ok? You're more than welcome to stay here for a while if you'd like." Mary says kindly, she smiles at me in a way that my own mother never did, and it has such a comforting and calming effect on me. I softly smile back at her.

"That's very kind of you, but I really do need to get home. I think it's clear we all need to up our game a bit, and I will be making sure there is always at least one of my men on constant watch, for all of us."

I quickly fire a message to Freddie to pick me up. Rachel is going to be devastated about her work being targeted, I need to do something to soften the blow a little.

"And you can have it sorted by the end of the day?"

"Yes Mr. Turner, I'll have a team there in the next twenty minutes."

"Great, thank you so much."

"Not a problem. Have a good day Sir."

At least once Rachel finds out about the office it will have already been cleaned up and she won't be able to see how bad it was. And it was bad. I had one of my guys go to check the damage and the photos he sent me were vile. "whore" "slag" and "gold digger" had been scrawled on the wall behind Rachel's desk. Her computer and personal items had been thrown around the office, photos had been torn and drawn on. All the windows were smashed, but the other desks and computers in the office were untouched. So it made it painfully obvious that this was a personal attack on her.

Kevin must have completely lost the plot. Clearly, he wasn't right to start off with, but to go from petty vandalism, to planting a bomb within the space of a few hours is just insane. It's only six o'clock, but I feel utterly exhausted. The soft sofa cushions feel so good underneath me that I could just close my eyes and sleep here all night. I glance over towards my office and remember the pile of work that I needed to get done today, but the wave of exhaustion that flows through me wins, and my eyes close, just for a second.

A buzzing against my thigh wakes me. A quick glance at the clock tells me that my eyes closing for a second, turned into a three hour nap. I pull my phone from my pocket and see its Rachel calling me.

"Hey beautiful." I answer, still sounding sleepy.

"Hey, were you sleeping?" She sounds much perkier than this morning.

"Yeah, I fell asleep on the sofa. How you feeling now?"

"Much better thank you. I had a massage and spent an hour in the sauna with Celine. Pretty sure the other people in the room were getting drunk from the alcohol sweating out of my pores!" She laughs, it is the sweetest sound in the world, and it reminds me that she is completely worth all of this stress.

"I'm glad you're feeling better." I smile.

"What's up Tad? You sound off?" Her tone changes from happy to serious in a second.

"Honestly babe, it's nothing at all for you to worry about."

"Well, now I am worried." She huffs.

"Rachel, please, trust me. I will explain when you are home, but for now, just enjoy yourself, ok?"

"Tad" –

"Rachel," I interrupt using my commanding work voice. "I am telling you to trust me. You deserve to enjoy yourself, worry free, even for just a day or two. We can discuss this tomorrow, if you ask me again, you will not enjoy your punishment." I hear her gulp and she is silent for a moment.

"That's not fair." She finally says in a breathy, hushed voice.

"What isn't?"

"You can't use your bedroom voice on me like that."

"Well I just did baby, and you need to learn to trust me more."

"I do trust you."

"Good, then no more questions."

"Ok," She pauses, "but I am kind of intrigued as to what my punishment would be." I can't help but laugh.

"Oh Rachel, punishments are not supposed to be fun."

"But I like being spanked." Her barely audible whispers travel straight through me and I have to shuffle to make room for my growing cock.

"I know you do, and that's why I wouldn't spank you as punishment."

"What would you do then?" She's getting excited, I can hear it in her voice. My hand absentmindedly grabs the growing bulge in my trousers.

"You have to ask permission to come don't you baby?"

"Yes."

"What if I didn't give you permission? And tried my best to make you come anyway, with making sure I stopped just before you broke the rules again."

"You wouldn't let me come?!" She sounds shocked, but equally turned on, and fuck I wish she was here right now.

"No, I wouldn't. Not until I thought you had properly learned your lesson. So, will you be asking me any more questions that you shouldn't tonight?"

"No Sir."

"Good girl." I need to change the subject quickly before this call turns into a session of dirty talk and masturbating. "What are your plans tonight then baby?"

She clears her throat before she answers. "We are just going out for a couple of drinks. And I mean a couple, I'm never getting drunk again."

"Liar." We both laugh. "Have a good night, and I will see you tomorrow."

"I can't wait."

"Me neither baby." My cock agrees with me as it strains against my boxers.

"I love you."

"I love you too."

I throw my phone down next to me and lean right back into the sofa again. The hard bulge in my trousers makes me sigh.

I cannot wait to get my hands on her tomorrow.

Rachel

walk back over to the table where all the girls are sitting and I pull my chair out slightly more aggressively than I mean to. I sit with a huff and half throw my phone onto the table. When I look up, everyone is staring at me.

"Everything ok?" Celine asks from next to me.

"Oh, yeah. Sorry, just- you know, men!" I smile.

"No. Just no! You are not allowed to complain about Tad! He is perfect!" She swoons and I notice all of her friends are suddenly very interested in what I have to say.

"To be fair, he is gorgeous." One of them chimes in, I think her name is Sam.

"Yeah, if I had landed a hot rich guy like you have then I would never leave his side. Ever!" Says another, and they all laugh.

I fake a laugh so not to look like the odd one out. "Trust me, he isn't perfect! But let's face it, I'm not perfect either."

"No!" Celine laughs. "I refuse to believe he is anything other than perfect!"

I shake my head as I laugh, for real this time. I love how much Celine likes Tad.

"Trust me, he has his moments. Anyway, aren't we supposed to be discussing how perfect Danny is?" I nudge her with my shoulder and force myself to forget about whatever it is Tad is hiding from me.

Four or five glasses of fizz later, and I am feeling much better about everything. Tad promised that he would never hide anything important from me, and whatever it is he said we can talk about it tomorrow. Well later on today I guess. So I have just decided to trust him and enjoy my night. Though not as much as I enjoyed last night! I am never getting that drunk again. Celine looks so happy, I keep catching her sending little sweet texts to Dan and it just gives me so much hope that I was wrong all these years. That soulmates, and love at first sight do exist; and I should just embrace everything that life chooses to throw my way at the moment.

"You look deep in thought." Celine says to me.

"I'm going to move in with Tad." I blurt out.

"You are!" She wraps her arms around me and squeezes me tight. "I'm so pleased you have come around. He is so good for you babe, and Ami. Honestly I am so happy for you!" She goes back to squeezing me tightly and we stay hugging for a long while, until I feel something wet on my shoulder.

"Cel, what is it?" I pull her back to look at her and see tears rolling down her face.

"Oh, it's nothing! Well, I mean, you're like a sister to me. Seeing you dragged down for all of those years by that- that monster, was heartbreaking. I'm just so happy that you have finally found someone who deserves you." She cries, and I wipe the tears from her face.

"I love you Cel."

"Aw babe, I love you too. Although, if you don't make me your maid of honour when you get married, I will never speak to you again!" We both laugh and turn back to our champagne.

"To happy endings." I hold my glass up.

"To happy endings." She clinks her glass against mine and we both take a sip.

CHAPTER TWENTY FOUR

The car pulls up outside Mum and Dad's house and I start to feel sick with nerves. I'm going to speak to Ami today about the possibility of us moving in with Tad. I don't want to overwhelm her, and of course I will make it obvious that if she wants us to stay here then that is absolutely fine. This is entirely her decision, and whatever she decides I will be happy with. Although, secretly I am praying she thinks it is a good idea. The thought of waking up every morning next to Tad, making breakfast for us all, coming home to the two people I care most about in the world, just makes me so happy.

"Mummy!" Ami runs towards me before I have even put both feet into the house. I drop my bag and hold my arms out as she jumps on me for a huge hug.

"Hey baby! Have you missed me?" I ask in between kissing her head.

"I have. I'm so pleased you're home." She hugs me tightly. I let her go and she runs into the kitchen. Dad walks over to help me with my bags.

"Hi princess." He leans in and gives me a kiss on the cheek. "How was your weekend?"

"It was great, thanks Dad. How has Ami been?"

"A pleasure, as always."

I close the door and walk through to the kitchen to find Ami helping Mum make coffee.

"Hello darling, how was your trip?"

"It was good, thanks Mum. How are you?"

"I'm good. Ami is helping me make you a coffee."

"Ooh lovely, thank you."

I pull my phone out and send a quick message to Tad.

I just got back to Mum and Dad's. Just going to unpack and have a chat with Ami and then I will be round. Can't wait to see you x

Ami slowly brings me a mug of coffee which I take and sip gratefully.

"So, have you spoken to Tad yet?" Dad asks as I sit next to him on the sofa.

"Not this morning. Why?" I see Dad glance over at Mum, and when I look at her, she is glaring at him. "Why?" I ask again.

"Oh nothing, I just wondered that's all."

"God, you're a bad liar!" I sigh. "I'm going round there in a minute, I just wanted to chat to Ami first. But whatever has happened I am sure he will tell me when I see him." Dad just goes back to reading his newspaper, and I roll my eyes and take another sip of my coffee.

"What did you want to talk to me about Mum?" Ami comes and sits at my feet and rests her head on my leg. I brush my fingers through her silky hair and brace myself.

"Well, um, you like Tad, don't you?" Her little head shoots up, and she looks confused.

"Of course I do! He is amazing. Why?" Her eyes narrow, she is clearly wondering where I am going with this.

"Well, I was just wondering- and before you say anything just know that whatever you say I will be happy with. This decision is completely up to you, okay?" I see Dad put his paper down from next to me and I can feel Mum's eyes burning into me. "Tad has asked if we wanted to move in with him? I know it's a big step, and it's all very soon, and so much has happened recently, so I understand"-

"Yes!" She doesn't even wait for me to finish talking.

"Yes?" I question.

"Yes, definitely!" I can feel my eyes welling up.

"Really?" I squeak as I try not to cry.

"Yes Mum!" She stands up and throws her arms around me once more.

"Rachel, this is an awfully big step, have you thought this through?" Mum walks over to me, her voice laced with concern.

"Mum, I am so happy. I wasted so many years of my life just settling, and not being happy. Tad loves me, and Ami. He wants to look after us both, and I want to move on with my life. Obviously if Ami had said she wasn't comfortable with it, then I wouldn't have questioned it and we'd have stayed here. But as long as she is okay with it..." Ami pulls away and smiles at me.

"Definitely okay with it." She beams.

Mum doesn't look convinced at all, but Ami is happy and so am I, and that's all that matters right now.

Tad

The thought of having to tell Rachel everything that has happened this weekend is filling me with dread. She is going to be so upset that I kept it all from her. I'm aimlessly flicking through the channels on the TV to try to find something to distract me, when I hear the distinct rattle of keys, and the grinding sound of the lock being opened. I stand up, confused, Rachel has a key, but she never uses it?

The door swings open. "Honey, I'm home!" Rachel calls through the open door.

"You used your key?" I question as I walk over to her.

"I also said I was home." She says with a smile on her face.

"You mean"–

"Yep." She beams before I can even ask the question. "You're moving in? Both of you?" I can't help myself, I have to know we are talking about the same thing.

"Yes!" My heart feels like it's about to beat out of my chest and I just want to kiss this woman until I have to come up for air.

She wraps her arms around my neck and I pull her in close to me.

"I swear Rach, I'm going to look after you and Ami until I take my last breath. I love you so much."

She leans in and her lips gently brush against mine. I can't help myself. I lift my hands into her hair and push her back towards me, my lips desperately searching for hers. All the stress of this weekend just melts away as she kisses me, her tongue slips into my mouth and every single thing in my life just fades away, the only thing left is Rachel and I. Well, and the swelling coming from in between my legs. She pushes herself against me, and I want to lift her up and fuck her right here.

"Let's make the most of having the house to ourselves." She whispers in between kisses.

As much as I want to say yes, and my God do I want to say yes; I know that I need to talk to her about everything that happened this weekend.

I lean my forehead into hers. "Let's talk first." I say as I try to get my breath back.

"Oh." She mumbles and takes a step back. "What's wrong?"

"Nothing, well not exactly nothing." I scratch my head, unsure how to tell her what I've kept from her. "Come, sit down." She looks worried, so I hold both of her hands in mine when we sit down. Although that does nothing to help the concerned look on her face, if anything, it makes it worse. "So, while you were away, there were a couple of, uh, issues."

"Issues?" She questions. "Kevin issues?"

"Well, yes." Her face drops. The smile from a few minutes ago has vanished.

"What happened?"

"I don't actually know where to start."

"The beginning is usually a good place." She half smiles at me.

"Well, I woke up early Saturday morning and saw someone outside, under my car. He ran off and the police didn't get here in time. When they did get here, Robins was right behind them as he had already been called out. To your work." I risk a glance at Rachel's face, and wish I hadn't. "For some reason, Kevin decided to vandalise your office. Don't worry, everything is sorted already, nothing was stolen, and when you go to work tomorrow everything will look the same, well maybe newer, or cleaner at least." She is just staring at me, and I can't make out what she is feeling at all.

"Why was he under your car?" She asks matter of factly.

I exhale loudly. "Look, don't freak out, but he planted some kind of small homemade explosive under the car." Rachel's eyes widen and her mouth drops. Her hand slowly travels to cover her mouth and I decide I need to just get everything out now. "Before he came here, he was spotted outside your parents' house, trying to get to your dad's car in the garage."

She is silent for a long time.

"Rachel?"

"Yeah." She answers, without moving her eyes from the spot she has found on the wall.

"Are you ok?"

"No." She says bluntly. "What if he got his car? What if Ami was in the car? Why would he want to hurt, to *kill* his own child?" Her eyes start to fill up, and I pull her into my arms.

"Robins says that it wasn't particularly well made, and it was placed somewhere that wouldn't have caused a great deal of damage. I don't think he wanted to kill anyone, just scare us. We can't let him win Rach."

"How has he not won already Tad? I'm terrified wherever I go, we all have to be looked after by guards twenty four hours a day. Nothing will be normal again."

"He will be caught. If I had been ten seconds faster, I would have caught the fucker myself." She shoots back and glares at me.

"And then what Tad? What if he had a weapon on him? He might have killed you."

"Or I might have killed him..." I mutter under my breath.

"I don't want you to kill him. I want the police to do their jobs and catch him. I want him to rot in prison for the rest of his life. But until then Tad, he has won."

"Rachel, I swear, no more fuck ups. Yes we will have to be *looked after* for a bit longer, but he's doing such stupid things now, someone will catch him sooner or later. I promise." She smiles weakly at me and leans her head on to my shoulder.

"Coffee?" She asks after a little while.

"You sit there, I'll get it."

I'm just getting two mugs from the cupboard, when I hear footsteps behind me.

"I've changed my mind, I think I want a real drink." I laugh and put the mugs back in the cupboard and I replace them with wine glasses. I turn to go to the fridge but stop dead in my tracks. Rachel is standing in the doorway, completely naked. She is just stunning, her beautiful body curves in the sexiest ways. Her long hair flows down past her shoulders in waves, covering her breasts so that just her rosy nipples are peeking out.

"They offered waxing in the spa." She grins at me.

My eyes trail down her stomach. "So I see. Come here." I command.

She slowly walks over to me, flicking her hair behind her back as she walks so that I get a full view of her incredible chest. It feels like I haven't fucked her in an eternity, and I am absolutely desperate to sink myself into her. She reaches me and goes to kiss me, but I pull away.

"Turn around."

"Yes Sir." She turns and I take a step back to admire her perfect arse.

"Oh I've missed this." I say as I grab a handful of her beautiful soft cheek. Her hushed moan tells me she has too. "Would you like me to spank you Rachel?"

"Yes please, Sir." Her voice is quiet and breathy.

"Would you like me to use my hand, or something more exciting?"

"Whatever Sir would like."

"Good girl." I pull my hand back and slap her backside quickly, before I walk over to one of my drawers. I open it and look for something firm, but flexible. Something that's going to be more intense than my hand, but won't hurt too much.

Bingo.

I pull out a silicone spatula and test it on my hand by hitting my palm firmly. The resulting sound makes Rachel quickly turn to look at me. My eyes meet hers and I can't help but grin at her.

This is going to be fun.

I slowly walk over to her, and gently stroke the soft material over her skin. She visibly trembles and my cock twitches in excitement.

"I am going to spank you with this Rachel." I walk around in front of her, stroking her breasts with the spatula. "When the pain gets to a point where any more would be uncomfortable, you say *amber.*"

"Tad, I"– She interrupts. I swat her nipple quickly.

"No, Rachel, this is important. There might be times when you instinctively say stop, but you won't really want me to. So I need to know exactly what's going on in your head. So *amber* when you are at your limit, and I can continue, but no harder. When you need me to stop, say *red*, and whatever I am doing I will immediately stop. Do you understand Rachel?"

"Yes Sir."

"What are your safewords?"

"Amber and red."

"Good girl."

Rachel

I can feel my pulse speeding up as it throbs through every part of my body. Every time Tad even moves near me, my breath hitches, my entire body is excited for what's coming. He is circling me, the way a predator does when it is sizing up its prey. Occasionally touching me, nowhere particularly sensual, just my back, my stomach or my arm. But every time his skin connects with mine, I feel myself getting wetter and wetter.

He stops moving for a moment, and the only sound I can hear is my heavy breathing. Without warning, he slaps the spatula on my back of my thigh. It stings, but it feels so good. He hits me again, slightly further up, the sound of the soft silicon hitting my skin echoes around the kitchen. He keeps hitting me, higher and higher, and I can feel all of my blood rushing down to every spot he has touched. Just when he reaches my arse, he switches legs, and starts to spank my other thigh. I'm practically panting by the time he reaches the top this time. I feel the soft tip brush against my skin, and I prepare myself for the next slap. But it doesn't come. I strain my ears to see if I can hear anything, but the only noise is my blood thundering through my ears. Suddenly, I hear the fridge door open, and I can't help but turn to look at Tad. He is pulling a bottle of wine from the fridge.

My face must be a picture, because I see the briefest of smiles on his face before he composes himself.

"Eyes front Rachel."

I do as I am told, the warm, tingling from the top of my thighs feels like it is spreading upwards and I just want him to come and fuck me. I start slightly circling my hips to try to get some relief, but all it does is intensify the throbbing between my legs. I hear the sound of a cork popping out of a bottle, and then wine being poured into a glass. He walks back around to me, and takes a sip of the solitary glass of wine he has poured himself.

Takes a break to get wine, and doesn't even get me one.

"Open your mouth." Instantly and without question, I open my mouth. He brings the glass to my lips and tips it slightly, so the cold liquid spills into my mouth. Before I have even finished swallowing, he is walking back behind me, trailing the smooth makeshift paddle across my skin. He immediately spanks me, harder than on my thighs, and it makes me gasp and I instinctively go to move my hands to cover my behind. But I steady myself as the sting turns into a warm tingle. Then he spanks me again, and again, alternating between cheeks, and delivering the blows with varying force. My knees start to buckle with each hit, and it feels as though I am on fire. Both the skin on what I can only imagine are extremely red cheeks, and deep inside of me. I yelp with the last few strokes, and start to grit my teeth.

"Amber." I say in a strangled voice. He slows, and his swats become gentler.

"Good girl." He whispers in my ear. The spatula drops somewhere near my feet, and then I feel his teeth nibbling on my ear lobe. His fingers start to slowly move down from the top of my spine, all the way down until they reach my scorching hot skin. The contrast of his gentle touch, compared to the hard spanks of before is insane, and I can't help but wriggle away from his hands.

"Still."

"Sorry Sir."

"Open your legs." I quickly move one of my legs to the side, and see Tad grin.

"Look at how wet you are."

He walks back behind me, and I feel his hand one my arse again. He moves his hand, so slowly down through my legs and onto my sex. I can hear his breathing start to speed up next to my ear. His expert fingers find my swollen clit, and I can't help but close my eyes and throw my head back. I quickly manage to compose myself, as he starts to move his magic fingers.

"I don't want you to come yet." He whispers in my ear. I bite my lip and try to steady my breathing. A second later, I feel another finger, he pushes it inside of me and a loud moan escapes. I can't help but start panting, as he slowly moves his finger in and out of me.

"Not yet baby." He says once more, and I am trying, I really am trying. I taste blood from my lip from where I am chewing on it so fiercely. His finger suddenly moves from inside of my sex, and teases at the one place he has never touched before. I stop breathing as his finger begins to probe.

"Breathe baby." I do as I am told, and feel the tip of his finger enter me from behind. It hurts a little, but the intense pleasure coming from him working my clit is about to send me over the edge. His finger is well lubed with my own juices and he starts to push in further.

Fuck!

I've never felt anything like this before in my life. He is slowly, gently working my arse, at the same time as he is rubbing my clit in just the right way. I start panting again, and I can't hold it in much longer.

"Come baby." And I do. And I keep coming, and coming, and everything tightens around his finger, and I swear I start to see stars. He removes his finger, and my breathing begins to slow.

"Well done, baby. Now bend over."

CHAPTER TWENTY FIVE

My car is parked up outside of the office, but I am terrified to go in. Tad told me he had already spoken to Chris and James, and they were completely understanding about the whole situation. But how can they be. Their office was just broken into a vandalised all because of me. I couldn't even manage a coffee this morning as I felt utterly sick with nerves. If I sit here any longer I am going to be late, and that's going to look even worse.

The walk to my office feels a bit like walking the green mile. I'm sure they are going to let me go. Maybe I should just resign when I get in. Better to jump than be pushed, right?

I open the door to an empty office, but I can hear Elaine talking to Chris somewhere in the back.

Deep breaths.

Everything looks the same, if Tad hadn't told me what happened I would have no idea about any of it. As I am walking over to my desk Elaine emerges holding two steaming mugs.

"Hey you." She calls over to me.

"Hi." I say meekly. "How was your weekend?" Maybe if I just pretend like nothing happened then nobody will bring it up.

"It was good thanks. How was your hen do?" Either she knows nothing about what happened, or she is doing a really good job of trying to take my mind off of it.

"It was good thanks, far too much to drink, but we had a laugh." I thank her as she hands me a mug of coffee.

"Listen," her voice turns to almost a whisper and my stomach knots, "don't worry about what happened okay?"

I just nod as I take a sip of my coffee and start to switch on my computer.

"Oh Rachel, you're in." Chris calls from his office. "Come in here for a moment will you?"

Shit. Oh shit shit shit.

Elaine smiles kindly at me as I walk toward Chris' office.

I walk in and close the door behind me before I take a seat in front of the desk.

"Now listen, there is no point in me beating around the bush, so I'm just going to get straight into it."

Oh God, this is it. Bye bye job.

"What happened was shitty." He continues. "Really shitty, but it was not your fault Rachel. And no major damage was done, so let's just forget about it. Your boyfriend did a wonderful job of having everything sorted out quickly, so I don't want this to affect your job here, okay?"

"You mean- wait, you're not going to fire me?" I ask, genuinely surprised.

"Fire you? No! Of course I'm not." He half laughs. "Listen, I met your husband, sorry, ex-husband a few times, and the more I spoke to him, the more I thought he was an arrogant twat. I mean, I've no idea what on earth an intelligent, attractive lady like yourself was doing with him, but that is none of my business. All I know is he is a criminal, and you are a good employee. That's it. Now, Elaine is going to talk you through how to update our website this morning, so I will need you to keep on top of that for me."

I'm so happy that half of me wants to lunge over the desk to hug him. But I have a feeling that's not going to go down well. So I thank him and head back to my desk, feeling much better.

Tad

I've finally managed to get through the pile of work that needed doing from the weekend and I can smell something amazing coming from the kitchen.

Rach and I decided that we would wait until after Celine's wedding for her and Ami to officially move in. Which is good, as it gives me enough time to make sure the house is ready, and to put a lock on the basement door!

I lock my computer and head to the kitchen.

"I have no idea what you are cooking, but it smells almost as good as you." I wrap my arms around Rachel from behind as she is stirring something in a saucepan.

"It's just risotto."

"Well it smells amazing." I kiss her softly on the neck and she giggles, whilst trying to use her backside to push me away.

"Can you make yourself useful and pass me the parmesan from the fridge please?" I head to the fridge while she starts plating up. She finely grates some cheese on top and takes the plates over to the island. There is already a bottle of wine in the cooler, and two glasses waiting there for us.

"Honestly Rach, you're the perfect woman. Beautiful, perfect body. Amazing in the kitchen, amazing in bed! Is there anything you aren't good at?"

"Jogging. Or any form of exercise really. Other than that I guess I am perfect." She smirks.

When we have finished eating I clear away the plates and Rachel comes to stand next to me.

"He hasn't actually won." She says out of the blue.

"Who hasn't?" I ask confused.

"You know. Him. I said he had won until the police caught him. But he hasn't. Not even close. I have never been happier in my life, and as long as I am happy, he has lost." I smile and kiss her softly on the forehead.

CHAPTER TWENTY SIX

Rachel

We are already about fifteen minutes late for the ceremony, and Celine is still running around panicking.

"Where's my fucking veil gone?"

"Ami, just go and watch the TV for a minute, Aunty Celine is having a little breakdown." Ami skips off in her beautiful pink dress, and sits on the bed. I retrieve Celine's veil from the bathroom where I hung it up to steam the creases out.

"Here babe. Now calm down. Today is supposed to be the happiest day of your life." I walk behind her and push the comb of the veil into the bun in her hair. "There. Ready and perfect." Her face softens.

"Do I look okay? I don't think I like the dress anymore." She starts patting down the sides of her stunning dress and I take her hands in mine.

"Cel, you look like a princess. Now let's go before Dan gets cold feet." I joke.

"I got him a pair of really thick socks to wear, so no chance of that!" She laughs.

"Right, flowers? Ready?" She nods and we head for the door. Ami hops along after us and we meet Alice, the registrar at the top of the stairs.

Alice and Celine go into a little room for a quick chat, and Ami and I position ourselves by the doors leading into the ceremony room.

"Mummy," Ami whispers, "can I be a bridesmaid at yours and Tad's wedding?"

I look over at her and smile.

"Would you like it if Tad and I got married then?"

"Yes!" She squeals. "And then I want a brother and a sister!" I can't help but burst out laughing and Ami's face drops a little.

"Let's take things one step at a time okay baby?" She nods. "But of course you can be a bridesmaid!" Her little face lights up again.

A door opens from behind us and we both turn to see Celine and her dad walking out of the room.

"Ready?" I ask her.

"Ready." She beams.

The registrar walks into the room and we hear the guests fall silent, and then a beautiful piece of music starts up.

"See you inside." I squeeze her arm gently and then get ready to walk in with Ami.

As we are walking down the aisle, I see Tad out of the corner of my eye. He is smiling from ear to ear.

"Love you." He mouths at me, and I just blush and smile back at him.

"You may now kiss your bride." Alice says. Dan leans in and kisses Celine, and the room erupts in applause and cheers. I am crying like a baby, and no amount of self-control is helping. Celine turns to me and gives me the biggest smile I have ever seen. She and Dan start to walk back up the aisle under a shower of confetti. I don't think I have ever seen two people look so happy, or so in love.

I see Tad walk over to us.

"You two look absolutely beautiful." He leans down and gives Ami a kiss on the cheek, and then gives me a long kiss.

"Yuck, get a room you two!" Ami laughs from somewhere next to us.

We follow the crowd out and are handed drinks by a server at the door. Champagne for Tad and I and orange juice for Ami. Tad grabs hold of my hand as we are walking.

It's incredible just how much my life has changed in the last couple of months. I look from Ami to Tad, and I could cry again I am so happy.

Our stuff is mostly all packed up back at Mum and Dad's, and we will be moving it all into Tad's tomorrow. He even arranged to collect a load of things from our old house, to help us feel more at home. All of Ami's toys, games and books are all waiting for her in her new room.

We have finished a wonderful meal and I notice Dan stand up next to Celine at their table. He lifts his wine glass and taps it gently with a knife. The guests chatter turns to silence, and they all turn to watch him make his speech.

"Thank you all so much for coming, and sharing our special day with us. And I would like to say a big thank you, to my wife, the stunning Mrs. Jenson, for agreeing to put up with me for the rest of her life." Everyone starts laughing and Dan turns to Celine. "Now, as you all know, Celine and I had what I guess most would call a whirlwind romance. The second she got on that train, I knew I wanted to see her again, and by the end of that journey, I knew I didn't want a day to go by where I didn't see her. Now, my friends will all tell you that out of all of us, I was the one who never wanted to settle down. I wanted to stay single, and just enjoy my life, because the thought of being tied down to someone, quite frankly, scared the shit out of me! But the second this beautiful creature started talking to me, I realised the real reason I had never even considered settling down. It was because I was waiting for her. I always thought love was such a complicated emotion, and it scared me. But honestly, nothing has ever been easier than loving this woman." Tears are streaming down Celine's face and it is taking a lot for me not to sob with her. "So please, if you would all raise your glasses, and wish Celine a lifetime of luck, because I am never letting her go!"

Once the speeches finish, the evening guests arrive. Including Mum and Dad.

"Oh my goodness, you two look beautiful!" Mum walks over to us and gives Ami and I a huge hug. "And Tad, you're looking very handsome too." She says as she leans in and kisses him on the cheek.

"Thank you Mary, you look amazing." Mum blushes and Ami and I laugh. Dad walks over and shakes Tad's hand before giving Ami and I a kiss.

"Mum, wine?" I ask.

"Red please darling. Your Dad will have one too, better for his heart." I catch Dad rolling his eyes next to her.

"Tad and I will go if you want to find somewhere to sit."

Mum, Dad and Ami head off towards the few tables that have been left out, while Tad and I head to the bar.

Celine is sitting at the bar talking to a few of the girls from the hen do.

"Well hello Mrs. Jenson." I say as I wrap an arm around her. "How are you?"

"Oh I'm amazing, and a little bit drunk! You okay?" She slurs slightly.

"I'm good." I smile as I lean into Tad.

"What are you drinking?" Tad asks her.

"Wine currently, these bitches all got me shots earlier, but no more. I still have a marriage to consummate!"

Tad orders our drinks, plus a glass of wine for Celine. As he is paying, he leans in to the barman. "Can you put all of the bride and groom's drinks on my room tonight please?" He hands over his credit card and room key and the barman shuffles off. He turns to look at me and I just smile at him.

"What?" He laughs at me, and I just shake my head and lean in for a kiss.

The party is in full swing, and Tad and I are dancing to "All of me." Ami is curled up asleep on one of the chairs in a corner, and I can see Mum and Dad dancing at the other side of the room. Celine and Dan are sitting, deep in conversation with each other, and the rest of the guests are either drinking or dancing. It's a far cry from my wedding, where I was in bed feeling ill at about nine.

I quickly shake that thought from my head and look at Tad, who is staring at me.

"What?" I ask.

"Nothing. You're just so beautiful." I jokingly slap him on the chest and then lean into his shoulder.

I glance back over to check on Ami, but I can't see her.

"Ami's up, I'm going to go and find her." I say as I pull myself away.

I can't see her in the crowd of people, so I head for the bathroom. When I get there, all, of the stalls are empty. I can feel the panic rising in my chest, but I try my best to keep calm. She has probably walked back up to our room wanting to go to bed. I head towards the stairs and run up them, but when I reach our corridor, I can't see her. I race to our room and almost snap my key card in half trying to force it into the door so fast, but when I get in the room, the lights are all off, and the room is empty.

I can't help it now, I'm hyperventilating, and on the verge of a massive panic attack. I race out of the room without even bothering to shut the door and head back for the stairs. My heels are slowing me down so I take them off mid run and sprint down the stairs. Tad is waiting at the bottom and his face falls when he sees me.

"What's wrong?"

"I can't find Ami." I cry, I'm desperately trying to catch my breath, but the fear is taking over.

"Relax, she can't have gone far, go and get your mum and dad and I will look for her too."

Tad runs off back in the direction of the dancefloor and I head to the bar. Mum stands as soon as she sees me. "Rachel, what's wrong?"

"Ami, I can't find her." I don't even recognise the voice coming from my mouth. I have never been this terrified in all my life.

"It's ok, you two go and look for her and I will get someone to turn the lights on." Dad says before he sprints to reception.

I turn around and Celine and Dan are walking over to me.

"Rachel, what"-

"Ami is missing." I sob. Celine cups my face in her hands.

"Hey, breathe. Try to calm down, we'll find her. Come on." She turns to Dan. "Babe, go and tell the DJ to shut off the music and use the microphone to tell Ami to come find Rach please." She turns back to me and pulls me over to the doors. "She is probably hiding under a table or something babe." She flicks some light switches on the wall, and the room is suddenly bright, and quiet. Dan's voice suddenly booms from the speakers.

"Ami, your Mum is looking for you, can you come back into the room so we can stop her worrying. Ladies and gents, if any of you see a young girl, blonde hair, in a pink dress, can you please bring her to Celine or myself. Thanks." There is a loud whistling noise as the microphone is turned off, and all the guests start talking amongst themselves, and a few of them start looking around for Ami.

"Cel, he got her. Oh my God he got her." I fall to a heap in the floor and start sobbing. She sits on the floor next to me and wipes the tears from my face.

"Babe, how can he have got her? Tad's guards are everywhere, they would have seen something. She's probably wandered off and got lost somewhere. Everyone is looking for her now, we will find her, I promise.

Hours pass, maybe minutes, I have no idea. One by one people keep coming over and saying they have searched everywhere and can't find her.

The room is spinning, and I can't focus on anything, but the need to find my daughter.

How could I be so stupid? How could I let this happen?

The next thing I know I am being helped to my feet by Mum and Dad, and they walk me over to a chair. I notice there are at least half a dozen police officers dotted around the room, talking to people.

I can't believe this. This can't be real.

I look up and see DCI Robins talking to Tad and Celine. They turn to look at me, both of them have red, puffy eyes, and look exhausted. They walk over to me and Tad kneels next to my chair. He grabs my hands, and I go numb.

"Rachel, the police have been looking over the CCTV footage, and it shows someone carrying Ami out of the kitchen door." His eyes are filling up, and Celine is sobbing next to me. I look up and see Mum sitting in a chair on the other side of a room, with my Dad trying to calm her down. I can't feel anything. Nothing at all.

"Rachel?" Tad whispers. "Did you hear what I said?"

I nod and slowly stand up.

"Where are you going?" Celine asks.

"I just need the toilet." I answer.

"I'll come"– She starts.

"NO!" I shout. "No thank you." I suppose I must be walking, as I am moving closer to the toilets, but I'm not even sure that my feet are moving. I feel like I am watching myself on a TV screen. Nothing feels real.

I walk into the bathroom and towards the mirror. I have no idea who the person staring back at me is. Bloodshot, swollen eyes. Make up smeared all over almost grey looking cheeks. As I look at myself, a wave of nausea flows through me and I have to run into the cubicle. I barely make it before I am throwing up loudly into the toilet.

When it feels like the entire contents of my stomach has been emptied, I stand and lean against the wall to try to catch my breath. Suddenly, the realization of what has happened hits me like a ton of bricks right in the chest and I can't breathe. I desperately try to suck in air, but my lungs feel like they are on fire. Tears are streaming down my face, and the thought that I may never see my baby girl again is just too much for me. I open my mouth, and scream. It's a sound like I have never heard before, a mix or utter terror and desperation. Once I start, I just can't stop, and

I slide down the wall of the cubicle onto the floor. Images are flashing through my head of all the terrible, unthinkable things Kevin might do to my beautiful girl.

I hear a banging from somewhere and realise that someone is trying to break down the cubicle door. Mum's face is poking under the door and her hand is reaching for me.

"Rachel, darling, please open the door." Mum sobs.

If feels like I am moving in slow motion, but I manage to stand up and open the door. Mum, Dad, Celine and Dan are all standing, looking utterly broken.

"Where's Tad?" I whisper.

"He has gone out to look for Ami."

I close my eyes and hear his voice from a few nights ago.

"Or maybe I'd kill him..."

If Tad finds Kevin and Ami, there is a good chance of only two of them getting out alive, and Kevin is so unhinged right now, I can only imagine the things he would do to Tad if he got him alone.

"I had everything. This morning, when I woke up, I had everything. And now I'm going to lose it all." I cry as I crumble into Dad's arms.

CHAPTER TWENTY SEVEN

Tad

The weather has taken a turn, the snow is falling thick and fast and the strong winds are absolutely freezing. I go to pull my phone from my pocket, but I can barely feel my fingers anymore.

"Boss, we aren't going to be able to see anything now it's snowing again. Any footprints or tyre tracks are going to get covered." Tommo calls to me from somewhere in the distance.

"No, I have to find her." I shout back at him. This is all my fault. I promised them they would be safe. I can't believe I have done this. "I can't go back and face Rachel without her daughter."

"Tad," Tommo's hand grabs the top of my arm. "It's more than likely they got into a vehicle and drove off. The police and the rest of the guys are already out looking for the van like the one Rachel told them about. Why don't we go and check any petrol or service stations?" His normally stern expression is softer, showing a side of him I have never seen before. I nod and turn to head back to the hotel.

The sun is rising by the time we make it back. I have no idea how long it's been since this all started. The reception is still buzzing when we walk through the doors, and immediately Celine runs up to me, but seeing my expression she stops dead.

"Where's Rachel?" I ask her.

"Over there." She points to a sofa in the seating area. I can see Rachel asleep on the sofa, laying with her head in Leo's lap. "She's exhausted. She fell asleep a couple of hours ago. We weren't sure what to do."

"Why don't I arrange for you all to go back to my house? I'm going back out to search any local petrol stations, and garages. But I will give you my keys and you can make yourselves at home." I start patting down my pockets trying to feel for my keys.

"Tad, you're exhausted too. There's nothing more you can do. Go home, get some rest and start back out in a few hours. Her photo has already been shared online almost ten thousand times. Someone will find her." Celine smiles kindly at me, and while the thought of sleeping until this nightmare has ended is tempting, I have to find Ami.

"I can't. I let them both down. I have to find her." I quickly turn before she has the chance to say anything else, and I head over to reception. A middle aged man with unnaturally dark hair greets me with a sympathetic smile when I get to the desk.

"How can I help you Sir?"

"Could you please arrange a cab, it will need to be for five people? And please, try to get it here soon." I hand over a handful of fifty pound notes to the confused looking man. "For the fare, plus something to make sure they get back quickly."

"Understood Sir." He nods, immediately picks up the phone and starts dialing.

I walk over to the seating area. Leo is a million miles away and doesn't even turn to acknowledge me. Mary sees me coming and her lips curve into some sort of a smile.

"She is still sleeping." She whispers to me. Rachel looks so peaceful, if it weren't for the mascara stained cheeks and her red puffy eyes, it would look like she was just exhausted after a night out.

"I have ordered a cab for you, Celine and Dan. I thought you could take Rachel back to my place and wait it out there?"

"What about you?" Leo says without moving.

"I'm going to go and ask around at the local garages and service stations, to see if anyone has seen anything." I say weakly. Leo just continues staring off into the distance. "I'm so sorry. I can't even begin to explain how guilty I feel." I'm trying to keep it together, but I hear my voice start to break as the guilt hits me.

"Tad, this is not your fault, at all." Leo finally turns to look at me. "In fact, this probably would have happened much sooner if my girls hadn't had you looking out for them."

"I swear, if the police don't find him, I will." I regain my composure, and talk in a voice so convincing I even believe myself.

The roads are so busy. Everyone is out doing their last minute Christmas shopping, or they are on their way to spend the day with their families. My mind wanders back to a few days back, when Rach, Ami and I went to pick out a huge Christmas tree, and we spent an evening decorating it, laughing and singing along to cheesy Christmas songs.

The image calms me for a second, until a pang of sadness takes its place. What if that is the only memory of Christmas I ever get with Ami? Tears sting at my eyes, and I quickly shake that thought from my head. Thinking like that is not going to help right now.

Tommo and I decided the best course of action would be to leave the hotel and head onto the biggest roads we found, but ones that didn't go anywhere near London, as we didn't think he would want to risk being spotted by congestion charge cameras or the like. We started on the M27, then made our way along the busier A roads and motorways that would avoid any big cities. We have stopped at every petrol station along the way, but nobody has seen anything of any help. We are currently on the M1 somewhere near Nottingham and we have been driving for almost nine hours straight. My eyes are closing and I am completely drained, but I have to keep searching.

Tommo pulls into another petrol station and I jump out of the car before he has even turned the engine off. My eyes search every car, every person I see, even though I know deep down, that even if they had been here, they will be long gone by now.

The lady behind the counter is wearing a fluffy red Santa hat, and flashing Christmas tree earrings.

"Happy Christmas eve!" She almost sings at me. "Which pump?"

"I'm not getting petrol. I pull my phone from my pocket and unlock it immediately on to a photo of that scum bags face. The anger that surges through me, just seeing him makes me want to scream. "I was just wondering if this man has passed through here any time today? He will have looked a lot scruffier than this, a beard perhaps. He would have paid in cash. Possibly driving a white transit van?" The woman's eyes narrow and something flashes across her face.

"I only started my shift a couple of hours ago. But the lady who was in before me said there was a bit of an incident with a man who sort of fits your description."

My stomach lurches and a wave of hope washes over me.

"An incident? What time was this? Do you have any CCTV that I could look at?" I blurt out.

She looks me up and down before speaking. "We do have CCTV, but I can't just show it to anyone. Can I ask what this is about?"

I swipe across on my phone to a photo of Ami I took at the wedding.

"That man has abducted this little girl. It's all over the news if you don't believe me, and I can contact the investigator dealing with the case. But please, I'm begging you, can you show me the footage?"

"Let me go and get my manager." She says as she walks through a doorway behind the counter.

He was here, call Robins.

I quickly send a message to Tommo while I am waiting.

A few minutes later an older man comes through and unlocks a gate at the counter so I can follow him through. As I turn to close the gate Tommo walks up behind me, with his phone to his ear.

"Is that Robins?" I ask and he nods whilst listening to whatever he is saying. I let him through and we follow the man through to a back room. In the corner is a TV screen, split with four different CCTV images, and they flicker between other cameras every few seconds.

"I saw on the news this morning about that poor girl, but there was no real mention of who to look out for, otherwise I would have put two and two together sooner. Sorry my name is Simon, please sit." He gestures towards one of two chairs in front of the screens.

"I'm Thaddeus, and this is Tommo, my security."

"Boss," Tommo says from behind me, "Robins is on his way."

Simon is looking between me and Tommo.

"DCI Robins is the detective in charge of the case. He will be here as soon as he can." Simon nods and starts tapping away on a computer next to the TV screen.

"When I got in earlier, one of my staff members told me that she'd had a *dodgy looking bloke* in earlier in her shift. He was driving a white van, and the number plates were completely covered over with mud. He had an issue with one of his tyres, and while he was outside trying to sort it, a customer went over and asked if he could be of assistance. The man started to get very agitated and started shouted and swearing at the customer, so he left. This guy then filled up with a small amount of petrol, paid in cash and left. He was wearing a cap and a hood, and the staff were quite intimidated so didn't say anything to him, but they thought I should know."

"What time was this?" Tommo takes the lead while I try to take in all the details.

"This was almost five hours ago, so about half ten this morning."

Fuck. He will be hours away by now.

"Here." Simon brings a video up on the computer screen. It shows a disheveled looking man pulling up at a pump, walking round to the passenger side and looking at the tyre. He gets up and runs his fingers through his hair, as if he is stressed out, and then he kicks the wheel. A man walks up behind him and starts talking, and the guy starts flipping out, throwing his arms all over the place and kicking the van. The other man backs slowly away and gets into a car. The man suddenly looks around, looks straight at the camera, and pulls a cap from his jacket, which he puts on, and then pulls his hood up too. He fills up with petrol and then walks in to pay. Simon brings up another video which shows the back of the counter. The man walks over, looks up, and Simon pauses, and there is Kevin.

"Shit." Tommo mumbles from behind me.

His face is covered with a scruffy beard, and his nose is bent like it has been recently broken, but there is no denying it is him.

"What do we do?" I ask Tommo. "We have no idea where he was headed, or what his plans are. We could drive for hundreds of miles in the wrong direction, and then what?"

"I can get onto our main office, and have them send this photo round to all of our garages, so if he goes into one of them someone will notice him." Simon says and I could honestly kiss him. "If he only put a small amount of petrol in then he would have had to fill up again soon after, at least then you may get some sort of idea where he is headed."

"Brilliant idea. I know it's going to take time, but Tommo, can you get a list of all the local garages in a ten mile radius of here. Find out the number of their main offices and call with the information. It's probably also worth calling all the local garages, if he has a problem with the tyre, he might go somewhere to get it fixed."

"I'm on it boss."

"You can both stay here and I will help if you want." Simon says and my eyes start to burn at the sheer amount of kindness radiating from this perfect stranger.

"Thank you so much." I manage to get out.

He opens the computer on to the internet and Tommo sits and immediately starts typing. Simon is already on the phone. My heart lifts ever so slightly. We might get him. I stare into his eyes on the paused image and I feel rage like I've never felt before. I am going to make the rest of this man's days on this planet a living hell, in whatever way I can.

Rachel

My hands are outstretched in front of me, and I am trying to feel my way around. The room I am in is pitch black and I have no idea how I got here.

"Hello?" I whisper.

"Mummy?" A quiet voice calls from a distance away.

"Ami! Ami, where are you?"

"I'm here Mummy, but you can't see me anymore."

"Why baby?" I am frantically searching the room for something, anything. My hands connect with a wall, and I start to feel my way along it for a door, or a light switch.

"Because I'm not really here anymore."

"What- What do you mean baby?" I strain my ears to try to hear where she is coming from, but I can't hear anything. *"Ami?"*

My hand connects with a switch on the wall, and when I flick it I am blinded by the bright light.

My eyes open and my confusion doesn't end. I am laying in Tad's front room, on his sofa.

How the hell did I get here? Was this all just a bad dream?

I slowly sit up and see Celine asleep on the armchair in the corner of the room.

Not a dream then.

I stand and make my way towards the kitchen, where I can hear hushed voices.

"Just let her sleep, I don't want to tell her anything until we have something concrete to say." Mum says.

"What time is it?" I say as I walk in and everyone turns to look at me.

"Rachel, darling, go back and sit down. I'll make you a coffee." Mum walks over to me and tries to lead me back into the front room.

"I don't need coffee. I need Ami back. What time is it?" I snap.

"It's half four." Dad says.

"In the afternoon? I've been asleep for hours? Why didn't you wake me up?" I shout.

"You needed your rest"-

"No Mum, what I needed was to be out looking for Ami." I turn around and head for the front door, grabbing my bag as I go.

"Rach, where are you going? There's nothing you can do except wait here for her to come home." Celine walks out from the front room and stands in front of me to block my way.

"No! I can't just stay here and do nothing. I have to go and find her!"

"Half the police force are out looking for her, and so are Tad and his guards. We put Ami's photo up on social media this morning and our posts have had over a million shares and comments. The best thing you can do right now, is wait here for any updates." I try to push past her but she grabs my shoulders. "Where would you even go? Just get in your car and drive for hours on end, with absolutely no idea where you are going?" Tears start streaming down my face and Celine pulls my head into her chest and wraps her arms around me. "I know babe. I know." Her own tears fall onto my face and I drop my bag at our feet, admitting defeat.

She is right. I don't know where they are headed. I could end up driving hundreds of miles in totally the wrong direction.

"We have had an update, but we weren't sure whether to tell you or not." Mum says softly from behind me. I turn around so fast I almost send Celine flying. "Tad is at a petrol station somewhere near Nottingham. There is CCTV footage of Kevin at the garage, and Tad and Robins are currently contacting every petrol station, and garage in the area with the CCTV image of Kevin."

Everyone is staring at me, as if they are waiting for me to say something. But I just don't know what to say. I don't know what to feel. I still don't feel like any of this is real.

A buzzing sounds starts coming from my bag on the floor and it takes me a moment to realise it must be my phone.

I grab my bag and pull my phone from it to see Tad's name on the screen.

"Tad!"

"We've found her Rachel! We've got her. And that fucking slime bag." My legs just stop working and I collapse in a heap on the floor. Everyone around me stats talking all at once and asking me questions.

"SHUT UP!" I shout at them. "Is she okay?" I ask down the phone to Tad.

"She is absolutely fine. I mean, she is shaken up, but he didn't touch her. His car only made it as far as Sheffield before the tyre blew. He had to push the van to a garage and it's one that we had called earlier. So when he turned up they called the police straight away. He's been arrested Rach, it's over." The relief in Tad's voice makes me start to bawl my eyes out.

"She's ok." I manage to blurt out in between sobs to Celine who is sitting next to me.

"They're taking her to Sheffield children's hospital, purely to check her over. Robins and I are on our way there as we speak."

"Well, what should I do, should I come to you?" I stand and start pacing.

"Let me get there first and see what they say, they might let her come home straight away and then I can bring her back with Robins. We will be there in about half an hour. I'll call you the second I see her."

"Oh my God, Tad I love you so much."

"I love you too. I'm going to bring her home to you."

I hang up the phone and Mum throws her arms around me, Dad joins her and we just stand holding each other.

"She's ok?" Dad asks after a while.

"She's ok." I answer. "And he has been arrested."

"Oh thank God!" Mum squeezes me tightly.

"What happened?" Celine asks.

"I'm not sure. Something about a tyre blowing and Kevin went to a garage to get it fixed. It was one of the places Tad had already called, so they called the police as soon as he walked in. I can't believe it."

"I told you Tad was perfect." Celine smiles at me and I can't help but smile back.

CHAPTER TWENTY EIGHT

Tad

Rachel and her Mum are singing along to "Last Christmas" in my kitchen while they are cooking what looks like it is going to be a spectacular Christmas dinner. My offers for help have been rejected, and instead I have been sent back to the front room to watch yet another Christmas film.

I pass a glass of red wine to Leo and sit next to Ami, who is laying on the sofa in her new unicorn pyjamas that I got her.

"What are we watching now then?" I ask her.

"A Muppet Christmas carol. It's great!"

"Oh not again Amelia!" Leo groans. "Every Christmas Tad!"

I take a sip of wine and relax back into the sofa.

This time twenty four hours ago I was wondering if I would ever see Ami again. And now here we are, enjoying Christmas together. This will be the first family Christmas I have had in, well, ever.

"While I have the two of you alone, I was wondering if I could ask you both a question." I quickly pause the film, and they both turn to look at me. I suddenly feel hot, and start to doubt if this is a good idea. "Well, uh, I know this is all a bit premature, and there is still lots to sort out. But, well, I was wondering if I could have your blessing to ask Rachel to marry me?" I'm staring at the floor because I am simply too scared that they are going to say no. But within seconds I hear a squeal and feel two tiny arms wrapped around my neck.

"Yes, yes yes! Definitely!" Ami screeches in my ear. I laugh and cuddle her back and then turn to Leo who is smiling from ear to ear.

"Of course you have my blessing. You're a good man Tad, a very good man."

"Do you have a ring yet?" Ami asks excitedly.

"Not yet, no. Maybe you could help me to choose one?"

"Ooh yes, that's a good idea. She will need a big diamond!" Leo and I laugh.

"A big diamond was already on my list."

"Good. When are you going to propose?"

"Well, I was wondering about New Year's eve. But now, I'm- Well, I'm not sure Rachel will want to be away from Ami, so I might wait a while until things have calmed down."

"Don't be silly, we can have Ami over for New Year's." Leo says. "You take Rachel somewhere nice and make it's a special night."

"Are you sure?"

"Of course- Ssh! I hear footsteps!" He quickly lifts his newspaper back up and pretends to be deeply interested in whatever is on the page. Ami shoots back to her spot on the sofa and I quickly press play just as Rachel walks into the room.

She walks straight over to Ami and wraps her arms around her from behind. She has hardly left Ami alone since we got back last night, and I don't blame her in the slightest. They fell asleep in each other's arms and stayed that way until the morning.

"How you doing baby?" She asks as she kisses Ami's head.

"I'm good Mummy." Rachel lets go of Ami, walks behind me and puts her arms around my shoulders.

"And how is my hero?"

I laugh. "I'm good thank you babe, are you sure you don't want me to help with anything?"

"You are helping, by staying out of the way!" She giggles, and it is so amazing to hear her laugh again. "I think we may have a slight problem though."

"What?" I ask.

"Well Mum has fallen in love with your kitchen, and I'm worried she will want to come round all the time!"

Rachel

We are all sitting on the sofa, our stomachs full to the brim with roast turkey and all the trimmings, plus copious amounts of Christmas pudding and extra thick cream. Love actually has just started, and Ami is sandwiched between Tad and I as we settle down to watch the movie.

Tad's fingers wrap around mine behind Ami's back, and I smile. I feel on top of the world right now. I thought the absolute worst yesterday, I thought my life was over. But here I am now, sitting with my amazing daughter, and the love of my life. My parents are cuddled up on the sofa opposite us, and there is just a feeling of contentment.

The intense relief that Kevin is locked away and unable to hurt us anymore feels like a drug. I don't think I have ever felt like this in my life.

EPILOGUE

"Can you please, *please* take the blindfold off now?" I beg Tad for the tenth time.

"Oh go on then!" He laughs. My hands quickly pull the soft material from in front of my eyes and I turn to look out of the car window. I can see lots of cars, and shops and an insane amount of people. And just in front of us is a red bus.

"Are we in London?!" I squeal like a school girl.

"We are. I thought it would be nice to watch the best display in the country while seeing the New Year in." I throw my arms around Tad and breathe in his beautiful smell.

"Thank you." I say as I pull my head back and kiss him softly on the lips.

The car pulls up, and through the swarm of people outside, I realise we are on the Southbank. Freddie walks around and opens the door for me. I step out into the freezing cold air and wish that I had worn a more sensible outfit.

"I wish you had told me that we would be outside, so I could have worm thermals and a scarf rather than heels and a dress!" I laugh at Tad as he walks around and grabs my hand.

"Who said anything about staying outside?" He winks at me.

He starts pulling me along with him as we walk through the crowds, and I realise we are heading right towards the London Eye. I turn to look at Tad and he just grins at me.

"Hang on, the London Eye is closed? Or it's supposed to be! We can't be going there?" I question, knowing full well that the last entrance is 3pm on New Year's Eve as I was thinking of taking Ami one year.

"Rach. Come on!" Tad rolls his eyes at me and I suppose this has something to do with the obscene amount of money he has, so I won't bother pressing the subject!

We get to the barriers at the entrance, and Tad tells me to wait with Freddie. He goes to speak to one of the members of staff and then they shake hands. He motions for me to come over, so I walk over, grateful for the chance to move as I feel like I am slowly turning into an ice cube. We are lead to the platform to wait for a pod, a few go by without us getting on and it becomes clear that Tad has planned something seriously special.

"Okay, the next pod is yours, just hop straight on and enjoy!"

The pod arrives, and before I have even got on, I can see it has been decorated in hundreds of sunflowers. I walk inside and there is a bottle of champagne in a bucket of ice, and a platter of chocolate covered strawberries in the middle of the pod.

"Tad, I" – But I don't know what to say. I'm completely overwhelmed. My life has turned into a fairy tale.

I feel his arms snake around my waist from behind, and he softly kisses my neck. He lets go and walks over to the middle of the pod. A few seconds later he has handed me a glass of champagne.

"To the rest of our lives together." He says as he lifts his glass to mine. I gently tap my glass against his and take a sip.

The countdown has started and our pod has stopped at the top of the wheel to give us the best view of the fireworks. I feel like a kid waiting for it all to start!

Five!

Four!

"Tad you're going to miss it!"

Two!

One!

Big Ben starts to ring out and the first fireworks shoot into the sky.

"Tad!" I turn around, and have to look down as Tad is bent down behind me. It takes a second until I notice he is down on one knee, and is holding out a ring. My hands fly in front of my mouth as I realise what is happening.

"Rachel Lily Bennet, I didn't think this through and didn't realise how loud it would be in here, so I am sorry for shouting. But will you do me the absolute honour, of becoming my wife, as soon as we can get you divorced?"

I'm so shocked I can't even speak. I can see flashes and hear the bangs from the fireworks, Big Ben is ringing, and the crowd has burst into "Auld Lang Syne".

"Rachel?" Tad is still waiting for me to answer.

"Oh, God, yes! Yes, of course I will marry you!" I throw myself on to him and he falls backwards. My mouth rushes to his, and I kiss him with everything I have.

I come up for air and Tad sits us both up. He then takes my hand, and slides on the most beautiful ring I have ever seen. I can see the reflection of the fireworks sparkling on an enormous diamond in the middle of the ring.

"As soon as these fireworks have finished, we are going home, and making the most of Ami staying at my parents."

"Talking of Ami, there's one more thing I wanted to ask you." I climb off of Tad and we sit together. "I want to adopt her. Obviously only if she wants me to, and I won't even bring it up if you don't think it's a good idea. But, well, I love her. And I want to be a real family."

"Oh Tad." I feel a tear slip down my cheek as I stare at this amazing, beautiful man in front of me. "I think you should ask her." He wipes the tear from my cheek and leans in to kiss me. Then we sit and watch the rest of the fireworks in each other's arms.

Tad

Rachel is sleeping peacefully tucked up under my arm as the car pulls into the driveway. I stroke the hair out of her face and try to wake her.

"Rach baby, we're home." She doesn't open her eyes, just moans and scrunches her eyes even tighter. I open the door and climb out of the car. The cold air hits her and she suddenly opens her eyes.

"Okay, okay, I'm coming. You don't need to try to give my hypothermia!" She says sleepily.

We walk into the house, she kicks off her heels and then sits on the bottom step.

"My feet are killing me." She complains as she rubs the balls of her feet.

"Here, let me help." In one swift move I pick her up and carry her up the stairs. She wraps her legs around my hips and leans her head into my shoulder. I kick open our bedroom door and lay her as gently as I can on the bed.

"I'm just going to get some water baby."

"Okay." She yawns and closes her eyes.

I head into the kitchen and over to the fridge, when all the hairs on the back of my neck prick. Somewhere behind me, I hear a loud clicking sound and I spin around to see someone standing in the kitchen door way, arms outstretched, holding a gun.

I fly backwards into the fridge, causing the door to slam shut with a loud bang.

Fear courses through me, but I can't show weakness. "What do you want?" I say as calmly as I can possibly manage.

"Well, what I want is upstairs. I'll just head up and grab her, shall I?" I recognise that voice. He walks forwards into the light, and standing in front of me is Ted Castle.

"Castle? What the" –

"Shut the fuck up Turner." He screams like a maniac. "You have ruined my fucking life. I lost everything because of you."

"I already told you, I had nothing to do with what happened to you. I just tried to help you out of the hole you dug yourself." He starts to walk towards me and I instinctively move sideways, trying to put as much distance between myself and that gun as I can.

"You made me believe my company was about to go bust. You told me there was no way out of it with me involved. But look how successful it is now. All it needed was time for everyone to forget what happened."

"It hasn't just fixed itself, it took a lot of time and effort, and lots of money to get it to where it is now. If you wanted to discuss the possibility of buying part of"-

"Will you just shut the fuck up!" He shouts. "Fuck the company. I've lost my wife, my home, my money. I have nothing left. Yet you have all the money, nice cars, beautiful house and get to fuck that gorgeous woman every night. How is that fair?"

"Look, put the gun down and let's discuss this properly."

He just laughs at me. And I instantly recognise that laugh. It's the same, spine chilling sound that the person made on the beach that night. The person that I thought was Kevin.

"It was you. On the beach."

"Oh, lots has been me. I guess I just got extremely lucky that I'm not the only person that wants to see you suffer, so the poor husband got the blame! But at least I was never a suspect. It's just a pity my explosive making skills aren't as good as they could be. *Boom!*" His deranged laugh echoes around the room.

I spot movement from the corner of my eye, and see Rachel standing at the doorway with her mouth open.

"Rachel, no!" I call out, but she is already walking into the kitchen.

"Theo?" She asks.

Theo? Who the fuck is Theo.

"Hi Rachel. I'm so sorry it's come to this." He turns and aims the gun at Rachel. Her eyes widen in fear, and I go to move in front of her.

"I wouldn't move if I was you." I stop in my tracks and look at Rachel.

"I don't understand, what are you doing here?" She asks, surprisingly calmly.

"Well, you know that house I am being forced to sell? You can thank your boyfriend for that. He practically stole my company from me, and because of him I have lost everything. My plan at first was just to sleep with you, maybe make you fall in love with me and leave him all alone. But it became clear that wasn't going to happen, so it has come to plan B I'm afraid."

As if in slow motion, I see his finger move towards the trigger. Instinctively, I lunge sideways to throw myself in front of Rachel.

BANG!

OUR LIFE

Keep up to date with all of my latest news and updates, including information about the final part of Tad and Rachel's story. Like my page on Facebook
www.facebook.com/d.gourlay.writer

Previous titles:
Another Life

Printed in Great Britain
by Amazon